Morton Bain

# Psychopath!

Published by Rosden 2012

Rosden
372 Old Street
London, EC1V 9LT
info@rosdenpublishing.co.uk


A CIP catalogue record for this book
is available from the British Library


ISBN 9780955888229

For Dr P., whose inability to treat me
I have to thank for the publication of this book.

# Chapter One

Most people would describe me as normal. Not everyone, but a good proportion of the people I spend time with think I'm a regular guy. That's not altogether surprising, I suppose. I don't look odd. I don't have a strange speech impediment; in fact, I've got a warm voice that pronounces 'thank you' quite acceptably. I suppose it helps that I keep things superficial with most people. The weather, a bit of politics, football results – that's about as far as I generally take conversation. I have an attractive wife, which helps as well. We don't have much of a relationship, but people guess that we do, and see that as a sign of my regularity. My wife is a fucking moron, by the way, whose only goal in life was to get married. She would be happy married to a lamppost if it meant she could circle 'Mrs' when she's filling out forms.

My name is Adam Cuthbert, and though I fool most people, I don't fool myself. I know I've got a heart of blackness and a corrupted mind. My heart is so black and my mind so corrupted, I really don't give a shit about the fact. In fact, I like being me. It's incredibly liberating not giving a shit about anything. Nothing can really hurt me. I'm not scared of loss, I'm not fearful about my prospects, and I don't care what people think about me. When I see the amount of effort people put into worrying about tiny slights, panicking over what their boss thinks about them and generally wasting energy on bullshit, it makes me laugh. They should take themselves off to the Natural History Museum, and look at some of the fossils they have on display there. One day that could be them, an outline of a human preserved in rock, contorted into a weird shape that demonstrates the random nature of death. *Seething, spitting, I crunch, crunch, on words and feelings that are too much, much. I'll kill, I will, that's what I'll do. I slit your throat and stab you too.*

It's ten thirty-eight in the morning, and I'm currently preparing my sermon for tomorrow. Yep, you didn't misread that last line. I'm preparing a sermon for tomorrow because I'm a vicar. Little do my parishioners know that when I teach them about Hell, it's as someone who's bound for the fiery pit, if not already there. The working title I have for tomorrow's address is 'Joyful Living' and I plan to spout an obscene amount of bullshit for twenty minutes on this subject. My father was a vicar, and I have the notes he took in preparation for over two thousand sermons. I will use one of these, from August 1974, to create the skeleton of my sermon, then embellish it with all sorts of crap. I like to slip the titles of films into my sermons, along with dialogue wherever possible. In the eight years I've been a serving minister no-one has picked up on this game of mine, which shows how inattentive my congregation is – either that or they are ignoramuses when it comes to popular culture.

Given the aid my late father is providing me from beyond the grave, I would normally be able to polish off my sermon preparation in an hour or so. I'm distracted today, however. For the last few weeks an idea has been brewing in my mind, and I just can't get rid of it. I don't know whether I really want to get rid of it – I think that's the problem. You see, I've decided that there is a particular parishioner of mine that really needs to die, and I'm tempted to become the chief instrument in making this happen. The person in question, a Mrs Whittaker, is an elderly whinge-bag, who has been driving me crazy for as long as I've known her – about five years – and has become worse since her husband passed away six months ago. She keeps pawing me and whimpering after services, banging on about how she wishes she had gone first, and I really think I'd be doing her a favour by despatching her. Of course, that's not why I would do it – if I send her on her way it'll be because I think I'd derive much pleasure from the act. And therein lies my dilemma. I know if I kill Mrs Whittaker, I'll probably find a whole bunch of other people I'd like to eliminate. Do I want to become a serial killer? I know I don't want to spend time in jail, so if I become one I'll have to ensure I'm never caught. Perhaps that wouldn't be that hard. Policemen are pretty stupid, and if I'm careful I think I can avoid detection. It will help me no end that I'm a vicar.

My mind's running away with me. I haven't so much as laid a hand on someone in over twenty years, and already I'm fantasising about having TV specials devoted to me after my crimes are revealed (after I'm dead, preferably). The Klerical Killer, they might call me. Or Reverend Death. I certainly wouldn't mind any murders I commit coming to light after I'm gone. I think this ties in with my fascination with fossils, and wanting to leave more behind than an assortment of bones.

I suddenly decide I'm going to do this. I'm going to become a killer.

I'm interrupted by my wife, who pops her head into my study and says, 'Darling, can you pick Ben up from Charlie's?'

'Can't you do it?' I counter. 'I'm busy with sermon preparation.'

Lucy walks into the room. She's wearing an apron and has flour on her hands. She waves her hands at me, and says, 'Not if you want freshly baked bread tonight.'

'Oh, alright then.'

Lucy smiles at me, then leaves.

As I pull up at Ben's friend's house I remember that I'm at least going to see Charlie's mum, Victoria. She's a filthy whore from what I can gather, constantly with a new man, and has an absolutely stunning body, with gigantic tits that always seem to be trying to escape from her top. Being a vicar she obviously sees me as forbidden territory, which no doubt makes me even more irresistible than I would normally be as a breathing male.

'Would you like a coffee?' Victoria asks as I stand in the living room, waiting for Ben and Charlie to finish up on the XBox.

I would normally decline, but my decision to become a killer has put me in a good mood. 'Go on, then,' I reply. 'Milk no sugar.'

After the drinks have been poured and stirred we sit on the sofa, watching aliens being splatted by our offspring. Victoria takes a sip from her drink, then announces: 'I'm thinking of coming along to church soon. Myself and Charlie.'

I'm busy trying to imagine what Victoria would look like in the nude, so it takes me a couple of seconds to register this comment. When I do I almost choke on my coffee. Is she looking for more victims? is my first thought. I control my urge to laugh, and putting on my church face, reply, 'Well, we'd be glad to see you.' *Especially out of hours, you filthy slapper.*

'What time do services start on a Sunday?'

'Eleven am,' I reply. *But yours start at an hour earlier. Just me and you, baby.*

'Charlie's never been christened,' Victoria continues. 'It's something I've always felt bad about. Is there any sort of christening or baptism that can be done at his age?' She crosses her legs, giving me a good view of supple thighs.

'Never too late to be baptised,' I say.' Come along to church for a couple of weeks, and we can talk about the next steps.' I'm thinking about the possible need for several intimate one-to-ones with this sleazy bitch as a prelude to splashing some water on Charlie's forehead.

Victoria leans over and squeezes my hand. 'Thankyou. You'll see us next Sunday.'

This brief encounter gets me all horny, and on the way home I can't resist making a brief visit to my favourite whorehouse. 'Whorehouse' makes me think of Mexican bordellos, and my destination is actually a suburban semi; but it's certainly a house, and it certainly has whores in it. I park about a hundred yards from the brothel. 'I'm just going to see a Mrs Simpson,' I tell Ben. 'She's very unwell with an itch between her legs. You'll be okay waiting here for twenty minutes?'

Ben looks uncertain.

'I'll put the radio on,' I say, punching buttons.

Without waiting for his response, I get out of the car and walk away.

I press the house's doorbell and wait for the door to open. Seconds later Sharon, the maid, appears. 'Hello, dear,' she says. 'Come in.'

I follow her into the living room, which serves as the viewing and waiting area. With sofas and a television it looks just like any living room, the only items that betray the dwelling's purpose being a laminated price list hanging on the wall, and a pile of wank mags on the coffee table.

After I've taken a seat Sharon launches into her spiel. 'Well, honey, we've got two lovely girls today. I'll send them in in a second. Can I get you a tea or coffee?'

'No thanks. Thanks anyway.'

'Okay, well let me get the girls to come and say hello.'

Sharon waddles off. I've never asked her, but I'm guessing she used to be a tart herself, back before she lost her looks and figure. I've never accepted hot drinks in a massage parlour. There always seems to be an aura of filth hanging over such places, tentacles of miasmic ectoplasm that swirl around, on the verge of being fully visible. I'd half expect to get a glob of cum in my tea if I accepted refreshments.

My thoughts have turned to Ben, when the door opens

and a leggy brunette with sharp and pleasing features walks in. She walks over to where I'm sitting, offers me her hand – which I accept – and says, 'My name is Bella.' The accent is Eastern European.

'Hi Bella.'

She leaves the room, and seconds later the other girl walks in.

'Hi, babe,' the hooker says by way of greeting. She leans over and plants a kiss on my cheek. 'I'm Kathy.' This one's from London, no mistaking, and probably grew up a stone's throw from Bethnal Green – or Befnall Gween, as it's known locally.

Kathy withdraws, and then the maid returns. 'I think I'll go for Bella,' I tell her. 'I can't stay long, so I'll take the minimum period – twenty minutes?'

'That's fine, honey. Forty pounds that will be.'

I hand over two crinkled notes, after which the maid says, 'Through to the second room on the left, darling. Bella will be with you in a jiffy.'

I start undressing as soon as I enter the room. I'm careful to place my wallet in my trouser pocket, and then plonk shirt, underwear and shoes on top of the trousers. I don't want to leave anything other than a cumstain in the room, and don't trust the girls not to have a little rummage when I'm looking the other way.

When Bella walks in I'm lying on my back on the bed, naked as the day I was born, with my hands behind my head. The hooker gives me a sassy grin, and walks over to me. Kicking her shoes off, she crawls onto the bed. After removing her bra she starts to move her tits over my dick. It's a great sensation, I have to tell you.

'So, where are you from?' I ask her. I've decided to have a bit of fun.

'Madrid,' she lies

'Madrid, Romania?' I ask with a straight face. 'I didn't know there's a town of that name there.'

'I'm Spanish!' she says in her Romanian accent. 'You don't believe?'

I'm just about to launch into my own near-fluent Spanish, but I resist. I don't want her to bite my prick when she's going down on me. Why do these girls lie? I'm just hiring a pussy for twenty minutes. Why should I care if it's a Spanish or a Romanian pussy?

A few minutes later I remember Ben. I don't want him to start wandering the neighbourhood. 'Ready to go?' I ask Bella. 'I'm in a bit of a hurry …'

The whore applies a smear of vaginal lubricant to her snatch, and off we go. Ten minutes later I leave. Not a moment too soon. Ben has been blubbing, and an elderly couple are standing next to the car, staring in at him with concern. I grin at them as I open the car door. 'Just dropping off something to my mother! She's such a talker!'

Once inside my car I do my best to calm my son down. 'Sorry, Ben. Daddy got held up helping a lady. She had a problem I needed to fix with my tool.'

Ben rubs tears from his eyes. 'You were so long. I thought you weren't coming back.'

I start the car. 'Of course not, son. You know Daddy's job means he has to help people? That's what I was doing. Let's get you home.'

Pulling up at traffic lights a few minutes later, I rub an itchy nose. I can smell the pussy juice on my fingers, and resolve to have a shower as soon as I get home. I'm paranoid about getting HIV from touching a scratch with fingers that have been smeared with sexual secretions. I'm not sure it's even possible, but it would be a dreadful way to contract the disease. If I get AIDS I want to at least get it in the course of boning some chick.

I was going to tell Ben not to mention my little detour to Lucy, but I know that doing so will pretty much guarantee he says something, so I keep silent. Little bugger. First thing he does when we get home is open his mouth. 'Daddy had to use his tool, and he kept me in the car for ages,' he announces as soon as we got through the front door.

Lucy raises her eyebrows.

'Yes, I'm sorry Ben. I had to call in on Mrs Parker. She had a problem with her cat flap. It jammed shut, and she hadn't seen her pussy for two days. I thought I could fix it in a matter of seconds, but it took much longer.'

'Who's Mrs Parker?'

'Mrs Grey's friend. She doesn't come to church very often, but you *have* met her.'

'Mrs Grey doesn't come to church much, either. I thought she'd passed away?'

'No, no,' I say. 'Still very much alive, as is Mrs Parker.'

Mrs Grey is dead, and Mrs Parker is fictitious. I decide to avoid further questions by retiring to my study. 'Better finish this sermon,' I announce. 'I'm just going to grab a quick shower.'

# Chapter Two

*Trouble and strife, that's the wife. Boil her, bash her, take a club and smash her. Kill, kill, drink my fill, of blood and guts. Fingers like nails, arms thrash and flail, you'll die before I'm finished with you.*

I wake up in the middle of the night muttering to myself. I try to go back to sleep, but there are dark thoughts in my mind. I feel like I've already got blood on my hands, without even deciding who my first victim is to be. I know it will happen; maybe that's what it is. I haven't murdered, but I definitely will, and so I guess in some sense the most important part of the crime – the decision to commit it – has already occurred.

My mind has obviously been processing my criminal intentions, because as I lie in bed it becomes apparent that some part of me has decided I won't kill any of my congregation. As much as I'd love to despatch several of them, it would be rash to do so. No sooner do I have this realisation then the means by which I will select my first victim comes to me. There is a Lloyds bank branch on Bethnal Green Road; I decide to keep it under surveillance one morning, with the fourth person that comes along to use it being targeted. In theory there should be no link between myself and anyone I select in this manner – and this should go some way to frustrating a police enquiry.

I think there's something quite apt about the concept of the 'fatal use of a cashpoint machine'. You're playing with the devil whenever you have anything to do with a financial institution, and this way, someone will actually get to meet him through a bank transaction. The randomness of my victim selection also appeals to me. We end up on this earth through a gigantic sperm-lottery, and someone will be checking-out because they chose the wrong morning to use the wrong cashpoint machine. I'm reminded of a woman I read about recently, who was brained by a falling flowerpot that was hanging outside a pub she was drinking at. There she was, standing on the pavement one summer's evening, undoubtedly enjoying some downtime with friends, and the next second she's killed by a basket containing four kilos of soil and a flowering plant. I start thinking about the plant the basket contained. It, no doubt, was discarded after falling, probably swept aside dismissively by pub staff the following morning. So it was a double tragedy, really.

It occurs to me that I'm going to have to develop my tailing skills in order to kill my cashpoint victim. I might be able to murder my target in close proximity to the bank, but quite possibly I'll have to follow them to their home or workplace and stick a knife in them later. I'll also need somewhere to keep watch on the hole-in-the-wall. I remember that there's a cafe almost opposite the branch I have in mind: that could be a good spot to watch from.

Thinking like this has got me all excited. I'm tempted to get up and start doing some Internet research into knives and killing methods. I would, too, if I was totally stupid. I know that computers are the first place the police look if you're suspected of committing crimes. Apparently the only way to make sure the police can't extract information from your computer – apart from totally extreme measures like throwing it into a volcano – is to drill through the hard drive. I used to think submerging your computer in a bath would fuck it up, but apparently that isn't the case.

I really should get some sleep. I could have a wank as

a way of inducing tiredness, but the thought of waking Lucy up and forcing myself on her appeals to me more. We haven't had sex in about a year. If I don't stick something up her cunt soon it will probably heal over.

I start shaking her shoulder. She grunts. I shake her more violently. An arm swings out and catches me in the face. 'Oi, you bitch,' I mutter. She still isn't properly awake. There's a glass of water on my bedside table, so I slosh its contents over her.

'Whaaaat?' she moans, hoisting herself up onto an elbow.

'Sorry, darling,' I say. 'I was having a sip of water, and had a little accident.'

Lucy turns her bedside lamp on and stares at me through half-closed eyes. 'What time is it?'

'No idea.'

She switches the lamp off and puts her head back on the pillow. I snuggle into her and put a hand down her pyjama bottoms. Her arse is so hot you could boil an egg on it.

'Not now, sweetie. I need to sleep.'

'We haven't made love for ages,' I whisper. 'I hope our relationship isn't being damaged by our lack of closeness.'

Lucy snuggles into me. I've just pressed a BUTTON. A big button, one that always jolts her. She turns over and puts an arm around me. I've just been flashed a green light, but now I've lost interest. She should have put up a bit more of a fight, pleaded tiredness for longer. I've got her to agree to fuck me, and now I'm going to pour a bucket of water on her misguided passion.

'I don't want to force you,' I whisper.

'No,' she says with pussy-warmth. 'You're not forcing me. I want sex.'

'I feel bad. I'm going to let you sleep.'

Lucy puts her hand on my cock. 'You can't sleep yet.'

'Goodnight,' I say, before turning over.

Lucy paws at me for a few minutes, but I remain motionless, and after a while she turns away from me. I hear a whimper and a strangled sob, but a few minutes later her breathing regulates to that of a sleeper.

I give it another couple of minutes, then pull my boxers down and grab my cock. I prefer to masturbate to pornography, but I can't be arsed to get up and switch my laptop on. The bed starts to squeak and rock as I get going. I find the thought of Lucy waking up and finding me pleasuring myself a turn-on, and consequently the rocking soon stops. I wipe a smear of cum on Lucy's pyjamas, then turn over to rub the rest onto the sheet. I would get up and grab a shower but I can't be arsed. I'm now feeling like I can probably get some sleep.

The next morning I decide to check out the cashpoint and make sure it really is going to be a suitable means of victim selection. Walking down a dusty Bethnal Green Road, I become aware for the first time of the huge number of CCTV cameras trained on shoppers. There seems to be a camera every twenty yards, and I'm sure there are plenty of concealed ones that I don't spot. Watching crime documentaries and reading the paper are enough to have taught me that when I start murdering CCTV will be crucial to the cops in trying to collar me. I have to neutralise this threat. I'm well enough known in the community to be recognisable to a significant proportion of local residents. Just as I'm having this thought a woman in a niqab walks past, and I have a light bulb moment. What a perfect disguise. Could I ...? I'm five ten – taller than most Muslim women, but not so tall I would look ridiculous. I don't have womanly proportions, but some padding around the backside and a pair of those fake tits would probably do the trick.

I go into the cafe opposite the Lloyds branch and order a coffee, taking a stool at a counter that runs the length of the window, and which gives me a perfect view of the bank. It's just after eleven o'clock, and I observe that the machine is in steady use. Never a queue, but someone seems to come along every couple of minutes or so. Most people withdrawing cash seem to be over fifty, which I guess makes sense given that most people under that age are at work, school or in nappies.

I'm so busy with my thoughts I don't notice the figure looming over me at first. I turn, and with a start see that Malcolm is waiting to join me. Malcolm is a member of my congregation who I've socialised with on a number of occasions since joining my church. We have a relationship of mutual tolerance, which sometimes tips into full-blown liking. Malcolm works as a social worker.

'Malcolm!' I say. 'Not at work?'

'Day off. Haven't taken enough time off this year and was in danger of losing some paid leave.' The man scratches his beard, an annoying habit that leaves me feeling I've got an itchy face if I spend too long in his company.

'Well, we can't have that. You need to be properly rested to look after your caseload.'

'Most of my caseload are beyond helping, but that's another story.' Malcolm plonks himself onto a stool. 'I was going to ask you, where's that Julia Walker been recently? Haven't seen her at church in about a month.'

Malcolm's primary reason for regular church attendance is to prey on single middle aged women that attend – a reason that I applaud because when he's sticking his dick into a given member of my congregation she'll likely be making fewer demands on me – and Julia Walker *is* an attractive forty-four year old divorcee. She's also recently become a Buddhist and ceased attending church. I break the news as gently as I can.

'Buddhism?'

'Yeah, apparently. I heard through Jackie Smarteens.'

Malcolm pauses to allow this news to sink in, then has another beard scratch, before saying, 'What a shame.'

'You're referring to her spiritual wellbeing, no doubt?'

'Yes. Yes, of course. A real shame.'

'There are other waverers you could be reaching out to,' I comment.

'Mary Chambers, I suppose. She used to be a Page 3 Girl. Did you know that?'

'No, but it's not altogether surprising.'

'What are you doing here, anyway?' Malcolm asks. 'Unlike you to be whiling away the morning over a cappuccino.'

I stir my coffee. 'Just pausing for thought. Watching the world go by.'

'A question for you,' Malcolm says. 'Do you think Hell really exists?'

'I hope not,' I reply, a little too quickly.

'You mean that?'

'Well, not exactly. It would put us vicars out of business if there weren't a Hell or a Devil. Why do you ask?'

'I dunno. Had a dream last night. Can't remember all the details, but I think it involved me being in Hell.'

'Hasn't regular attendance at church for the last twenty years convinced you that Hell exists, but that you're not going there?' I ask.

'Not really.'

I have to admire Malcolm's honesty. 'Well, I wouldn't worry about it too much. If you're going there, so are most people.'

Malcolm opens his mouth to say something, and I fear it will be more Hell waffle, but I distract him by saying, 'Hey, look. Isn't that your brother?' I point to an untidy looking man in a grey suit who is walking on the side of the pavement farthest from us.

'Yes, that's Graham. Must have popped out for an early lunch.'

I only know Graham through having married him. He got hitched to his third wife the year before. He is a fairly unremarkable person from what I can gather, and I would normally have no interest in talking about him. He is, however, a policeman, and in light of my recent plans I now have a few questions. 'How long has your brother been a copper?' I ask Malcolm.

'He went into the force straight from school. Had his heart set on wearing the uniform from the age of about eight.'

'What does he do in the force?'

'He's a detective. I'm not sure which area he's working in at the moment, but he's done vice, murder – robbery as well.'

'He must have a few interesting stories to tell.'

'Yeah, but he only talks about the really juicy cases he's worked on if he's had a few drinks. Otherwise he's really hush-hush about it all.'

'I remember someone telling me that the psychological make-up of detectives is often very similar to that of criminals. I wonder if there's anything to that?'

'I wouldn't know. Saying that, I know a lot of cops are a bit crazy. They sleep around a lot, and loads of them have a drinking problem.'

After we've finished our coffees we leave and go our separate ways. I'm in a state of excitement as I drift down the road, as if I'm just about to slit a throat, not several weeks away from my first kill, as is probably the case. As I stare through the window of a stationery shop I suddenly remember the recurring dream that has haunted me since my youth. In it I have killed someone – sometimes recently, sometimes many years before – and I am now confronted by the risk of the body being found. Normally I'm aware of some digging going on in the vicinity of the buried body, and am convinced the corpse is on the verge of being discovered. I wonder idly whether these dreams were foretelling my new ambition, or whether they are just symbolic of a subconscious urge. I can't say I really care either way.

Approaching my car, parked on a residential road that runs at right angles to the main shopping drag, I notice a shadow over my left shoulder. I turn, expecting to see a tall man about to overtake me, but there's no-one there. The shadow reappears as I'm walking up to the front door of my house. Again I turn, and again there's no-one there. I begin to wonder whether there's something wrong with my eyesight. The dark blur is not totally unlike the halo effect I used to get when I suffered from migraines during my teens – just that it's darker, and affects my peripheral vision.

The memory of my teenage affliction brings back all sorts of stuff. I remember my first girlfriend, a fatty called Polly Anderson. I went out with her for two weeks, just long enough to lose my virginity, after which I dumped her. At about the same time that I was going out with Polly I killed a cat. A neighbour had a fat tabby, which I befriended over a number of weeks by leaving saucers of milk and pieces of fish for it in the back garden. Eventually, when it was used to me, I grabbed it. Feeling the warmth of the cat's body through its fur, I struggled with the animal for a few minutes as it struggled to get away. The cat clawed and struggled like crazy; I think it sensed that my intentions were not good. Eventually I managed to get it into a sports bag, which I zipped up with some difficulty; the cat kept sticking its paws in the way of the zipper, clawing at my fingers as I tried to get the bag closed. The cat became so frantic after it had been contained that the bag began to move as it lay on the grass of our back garden. My mother came out of the house at this point to hang up some laundry, and I had to quickly move the bag to the little alley at the side of our house. The cat stayed there for about half an hour while I waited for my mother to finish outside. I was dying to get on with my fun, but having this stay of execution forced me to put some thought into the disposal process. When my mother went back inside the house I was ready. It was summer, and we had a paddling pool in the back yard. My younger sister Clare had been using it the day before, so it still had six inches of water in it. I grabbed the bag and tossed it into the pool. I could see straight away that the depth of water would do no more than soak the pussy, so I got the garden hose and started to fill the pool up. The cat really started going for it as the water got deeper, limbs pummelling the bag as water rose around it. I actually almost dragged the cat out at this point. I felt what must be a feeling akin to sympathy, just for the briefest of moments. I didn't though. I let the water rise until the bag was fully submerged, and the cat's struggles had pretty much ceased, then turned the hose off. I waited about thirty seconds, then pulled the bag out of the pool.

At this point Mrs Jackson from next door stuck her head over the fence and asked me what I was doing. She said is with a smile on her face, so I knew she didn't have a clue what I was up to. It was her cat I was torturing. Just mucking around, I told her. She raised a hand in acknowledgement, then disappeared, as if a detached head had just fallen off the fence. Turning my attention to the bag, a total lack of movement from within made me think I'd gone and drowned the cat. I was just about to give up and throw the bag in the rubbish, when a barely detectable bulging of the carrier showed that the cat still had one of its lives left. The next step was daring, even by my standards. I attached a long section of cord to the bag's handle, then took the bag out to the front of the house, crossed the road with it, and dumped it on the footpath. Walking back to our front garden, I took up a position by the hedge that separated the small square of grass from the pavement. I wasn't ready when the first car passed, and missed my opportunity to pull the cord. There followed a wait of about ten minutes, until finally a yellow Volkswagen van came into sight. When it was about twenty yards from the bag, I gave the rope an almighty tug, and the bag lurched onto the road. I had applied just the right amount of force, as the front left wheel of the vehicle passed over the centre of the bag. Even from where I was crouching, I could hear the crack of bones as the cat was run over.

This reverie has so totally consumed me that I suddenly find myself in the kitchen with a knife in my hand, no memory of having walked into this room or picking up this implement. I realise I am hungry, and guess that I must have been planning on making a sandwich. I get on with this, grabbing a loaf and starting to saw off a couple of thick slices. As I cut the bread I revel in the feel of the knife's handle. It fits my hand perfectly. I imagine that instead of cutting bread I'm taking off someone's limb. I know an arm could never be chopped off as easily, but it's fun to imagine.

I hear footsteps and whirl around, knife brandished offensively. It's only Lucy, and she looks at me with alarm as I hold the knife between us, point aimed at her.

'Put that thing down,' she says. 'You look like you're about to attack me.'

The thought occurs to me that I could do just that. Lunge at her, stab her four or five times, then stand back and watch as she bleeds out on the floor. This healthy woman of thirty-eight could be stiff and cold in a matter of minutes. The instinct is getting stronger all the time. I *could* kill Lucy very easily this afternoon, but by tomorrow morning I'd be in a prison cell. No, killing will not be done at the expense of my liberty.

'Sorry, darling,' I say, putting the knife down. 'You gave me a fright.'

Lucy pokes her tongue out at me.

'You look tired,' I say. 'Is there anything I can do for you?' I love this sort of thing, having evil thoughts, but masking them so completely with my well-rehearsed nice act. No-one does it better than me.

Lucy smiles. 'You could wash up, I guess. And think about getting someone out to fix the dishwasher. It's only since it broke that I've come to realise how much I rely on it.'

'Leave it to me,' I reply, reaching for the kitchen gloves.

'Don't you want to finish making your sandwich?' Lucy asks.

'No, let me get this out of the way first.'

As I wash up, Lucy humming in the background, my thoughts return to the question of exercising self-control and taking precautions when I commence my killing. I'm going to have to do some research, I realise, on things like forensic science, police investigative methods, and clear-up rates for murder. I know that detection rates for murders involving people who know each other are very high – probably over ninety-five percent – but I'll be interested to see what they are for stranger killings. My experience of the police up to this point has led me to have a very low opinion of them. I've only really encountered them following a couple of burglaries, and they've always come across as being quite thick – certainly not the sort of people I'd have much faith in to solve a crime committed by a clever and careful person. Detective shows and the media give the impression that the police are pro-active and successful crime-fighters, but I suspect this flatters them. What sort of person becomes a policeman? Someone who isn't smart enough to become a lawyer or doctor, who likes bossing people around (due to low self-esteem most of the time), and who has a calcified sense of right and wrong. The very last person I'd want to spend any time with, in other words. Nevertheless, amongst proper detectives there are bound to be a few smart cookies, so I'm going to need to be careful. Even if I don't come up against sharp cops, the police have man-hours, CCTV and the media on their side.

I eat my sandwich in the living room with the news on the television. The second item in the broadcast is a report on the arrest of a man for the murder of his ex-partner. An unflattering photograph of a bald fatty flashes up on the screen. Talk about the very stupid making the police's job easy for them. You have a bust up with your old lady, who kicks you out of the house. What do you *not* do? What you do *not* do is go around there and stab her. The guy was probably better off without her, anyhow, something he would have realised after the shock of being dumped had passed, and now, because of this idiot's rashness, he has to spend the next twenty years behind bars, watching his back lest he get bummed. Actually, this particular man is unlikely to get bummed. Even the most short-sighted gay would think twice about anally violating him. I'm really getting quite impatient to start killing, so I can show the rest of the country's murderers how it's done.

I remember reading the novel 'American Psycho' about ten years earlier. Now that's a book that definitely wasn't written by a real psycho. 'American Poof' would have been a better title for it. My memory of the storyline is hazy, but the fact that a scene involving business cards is foremost in my mind says it all. The novel's main character is obsessed with material objects and looking good, presumably because the author read somewhere that narcissism is on the same psychological spectrum as psychopathy. What he fails to realise, because he isn't a proper psycho, is that the sort of narcissism that overlaps with psychopathy is the type that transcends physical objects. It is my spiritual destiny to kill, I'm coming to realise, a birthright that I inherited on account of my innate ability to see society's rules for what they are – bullshit. Any muppet can wear an Armani suit. Only I and a select group of others view the world in the way I do.

The next few days go by as a blur of automatic actions, carried out while my mind is focused on my forthcoming Kill Day, which I've decided will be a Tuesday morning in two weeks' time. I preach a sermon, visit a number of elderly parishioners, ferry my kids to and from school, and screw one of my casual lovers. The weather stays good, a little blowy, but bright and free of rain. We eat paella on Saturday night, a meal Lucy has really mastered. She makes it properly salty, necessitating several large glasses of white wine to quench my thirst. On Sunday afternoon I take my daughter of six, Chloe, to the local park. I watch her as she clambers over the climbing frame, paying particularly close attention to the way her limbs, hands and feet co-operate. The human body truly is remarkable, but how remarkable that one human body can cause another's to become still through the act of murder. I have no desire to kill Chloe. I wouldn't say that I love my children, but I tolerate them in the way that cows tolerate birds that share the field they are grazing in.

On the walk back home from the park, the visual distortion I'd experienced earlier reappears. I keep swinging around to see if I can catch sight of something fluttering above my left shoulder, but of course I don't succeed. Is this my personal devil trying to alight on my shoulder, in preparation for the forthcoming gorefest? I remember watching a ludicrous TV programme called 'Dexter', where the hero is a psychopath with a heart. Caring psychopaths just do not exist, and my inability to see past this largely spoiled my enjoyment of the programme. It did introduce one concept I'm finding myself resonating with, however, and that's that of the 'dark passenger', conceived of as the psychopathic tendencies of Dexter embodied in a person that 'rides' with the killer in his car. Where the dark passenger is when Dexter isn't in his car isn't made clear, but I guess there's something about the stillness a solo motorist experiences on a long night drive that might encourage the appearance of one's shadow side. Is this blur I keep seeing my very own dark passenger?

Around about the time the blur first appeared I also noticed a tightness in my abdomen and difficulty breathing easily and rhythmically. It's as if there's a tension building up inside me, and I've got a strong suspicion I know what's going to relieve it. The other day just before my Sunday morning service this tension became so strong I had to help myself to some Communion wine in the church vestry. I felt a bit like a rock-star in his dressing room, dosing myself up before coming on stage. I think I overdid my medicinal gulp, because I felt quite giggly during the first half of the service. I was beaming and emanating uncustomary warmth, and could see from faces in the congregation that my flock simply thought I was filled with the love of Our Lord and Saviour. Fools.

There's a person that has been on my mind quite a bit recently, and that is a man who is incarcerated because of me. He's also someone who is due for release from prison soon, and I can't help wondering if my murderous desires have been stirred by this knowledge. At university my best friend – if friend is a word that can ever be used to describe someone I'm in a relationship with – was a fellow student called Jake Forte. We were in the same hall of residence in our first year, on the same course – Economics – and shared an appetite for mayhem. When I say we shared an appetite for mayhem I don't mean the hooligan variety. Psychological mayhem would maybe be a better description of what we got up to. We would choose a woman at random from our year, then subject her to the most cruel and unusual mental tortures. There was Jane Gonzalez, for example. Jake got to know her, bedded her, and then saw her regularly for about three weeks, during which time she fell for him. He then suddenly dropped her, claiming he'd been told something about her from an unnamed person that had totally changed his opinion of her. She was devastated, even going home for a week to try and get over Jake. On her return I moved in, taking advantage of her wounded pride and raw emotional state to quickly seduce her. I spent a month in a relationship with her, before suddenly declaring that I had come to the realisation that I was gay, and wanted to start seeing Jake romantically. A few days after I dropped this bombshell Jake paid her a late night visit, quickly leading her to the bedroom. A few minutes after they started making out, Jake stopped suddenly, and said the information he'd been given about her – which remained unspecified – was still bothering him, and that he wanted to see me straight away. With that he left her.

Soon after this, Jane started drinking heavily and taking lots of drugs. She flunked her first year and dropped out. Someone I bumped into about five years after graduating said that she had become a prostitute. I've often wished that I'd bump into her on one of my whore-visits, but it hasn't happened yet. I sometimes wonder whether I'd have to pay if I ever did. I think I'd either pay her nothing or twice the going rate.

Jake and I had several 'Janes' during our first two years at university. It got so bad – or good – that the Women's Union organised a petition to get us kicked out. Of course, that had the opposite effect to the one intended; we weren't kicked out, and the curiosity of several women who would otherwise have been unaware of our existence was piqued, with predictable consequences. We ended up dubbing our project 'Girl Snooker'. Jane Gonzalez, our first victim, had red hair, and we likened her demise to 'sinking red' in a game of snooker. The challenge, then, was for us to move through the rest of the colours – yellow, green, brown, blue and pink – before culminating with black. A girl could be linked with one of the colours by virtue of her appearance (green eyes, for example) or name or circumstance (one of the girls we fucked over was a Sarah Brown).

Girl Snooker only ended when Jake met Charlotte Greening. You could say she well and truly snapped Jake's cue. I knew from the moment I met Charlotte that with her arrival on the scene everything was going to change. She looked like Jake's twin sister; both had small, button noses, cleft chins and deep-set eyes. When they were together a calm descended on them that they never seemed to achieve in anyone else's company. From pretty much the moment they met they were finishing each other's sentences and generally behaving as if they had known each other from birth.

Needless to say, I was not pleased by Charlotte's arrival. Jake was my plaything as far as I was concerned, and the fact that his happiness increased immeasurably after meeting his soul mate was of no interest to me. After my preliminary tactics of talking Charlotte down and trying to distract him with other women failed, I resolved to take things to a new, more intense level. My plan was to convince my friend that Charlotte had been cheating on him. Knowing Jake as I did, I knew that he wouldn't be capable of dealing with this. I began by one day asking Jake who Charlotte's new friend was, then going on to describe a tall guy I had allegedly seen her with on a couple of occasions. Jake wasn't alarmed by this question – though he couldn't say who this fictitious person might have been – but this served to plant a seed. The crucial step in my plan followed about a week later. Knowing that Jake stayed over at Charlotte's flat from Wednesday evening to Sunday morning, I broke into the latter's home on the Wednesday morning by jimmying a living room window. I snuck up to Charlotte's bedroom and deposited a condom full of semen in the woman's bed.

As I walked away from the flat I considered the chances of success in my relationship-wrecking attempt. I realised there was a possibility that Charlotte would change her sheets prior to crawling into bed with Jake, but also knew that they would be getting home together quite late that evening, and probably wouldn't bother. I knew that Charlotte was on the pill and didn't use any other contraception with Jake. If Jake found the condom he would know that it hadn't been used by him, and there would be absolutely no way Charlotte would be able to explain away the presence of the rubber in a manner that allowed her to retain her innocence. All said, it was a devilishly good plan, and the only shame was that I wasn't going to be on hand to witness the fireworks if the johnny was found.

My plan worked. Oh, it worked. Thursday morning I got a phone call from Amber, Charlotte's flat mate. The former was hysterical as she tried to relate to me the events of the previous night. It took me a couple of minutes to calm her down sufficiently to be able to understand what she was saying, but eventually the tale emerged. Jake and Charlotte had returned to the flat just before midnight. They had been in the Student's Union bar since about seven, and were both very drunk. They went straight to bed, and it seems Jake almost immediately found the condom. His reaction hadn't been to storm out, vowing never to see Charlotte again. Instead he'd gone into the kitchen, picked up the biggest blade he could find, and stabbed his girlfriend to death. Amber and Charlotte's flat was now a crime scene. Amber had gone home. Jake was in custody, having been charged with the murder of Charlotte.

This happened some twenty years ago, and now Jake was very nearly a free man. I don't know for a fact that he's going to try anything stupid when he gets out, but it wouldn't surprise me. It's my own fault if he does. If I'd just kept my mouth shut he would just have hated Charlotte eternally, remaining convinced that she had been putting it about. My mistake was going to visit him in prison about three years after he was locked up, and letting my mouth run away with me. I'd been out the night before, and turned up at HMP Chelmsford hung-over. Jake and I had gotten into a stupid row over British foreign policy of all things, and in the heat of our argument I'd told him the truth about how the condom had ended up in Charlotte's bed. Jake's initial reaction had been to lunge at me, prison wardens having to intervene to keep us apart. That was the last time I'd seen Jake. About ten days after my prison visit I was interviewed by the police, Jake having passed on the infor-mation I had given him. I, of course, denied everything. I claimed I'd refused to lend him money, and that he was just making up these allegations as a way of getting back at me. With years having elapsed since the killing, and Jake's assertion not changing the fact that he had killed Charlotte, that's as far as the police's involvement went. Jake hasn't threatened me since, but I imagine he's going to come out of prison a very angry man – an angry man who probably won't feel he has much to lose.

The next day I go over to see my friend Joey LaMotta, the priest at St Joseph's, which is about half a mile from my church. Joey is something of a curiosity, being an ex-Mafia street soldier from Atlantic City. His cover story is that he found God and decided to dedicate his life to the Church – a marvellous example of redemption, blah, blah, blah. He *is* ex-Mafia, and he is a bona fide priest, but his reasons for entering the service of God are not quite what they seem. He fled New Jersey after falling in love with a fellow wiseguy's wife (crucially, before anything happened). On arriving in England – he had a cousin living here whom he initially stayed with – he considered his career options and quickly realised there were only two things he knew from his former life – the Church and crime. Having become dis-illusioned with the life of a gangster he decided to become a priest. Five years' formation at a seminary in a Durham not only opened the way to ordination, but also meant that by the time he had completed his studies he was eligible to apply for permanent residency.

Recent developments that make Joey's life even more bizarre are a resumption of his former Mafia ties. The wise-guy whose wife he fell for was killed some time back after being suspected of snitching, and Joey has recently reached out to his former boss, who has responded positively. Money motivates Mafiosi above all else, and if Joey can start a crew in England that will kick up to his old chief, this is consid-ered a good outcome. Globalisation, it seems, evens applies to the Mafia. Staying in the Church is deemed crucial to this plan, providing the ideal cover for illegal activities.

I met Joey through our mutual attendance at a swinger's club.

'Joey!' I give my friend a bear hug after he opens the door to me. Joey's is the kind of guy who likes to be greeted enthusiastically.

'Adam! Good to see you. Come in, come in. You must be psychic coming over this morning. I was going to ring you.' I'm lead into a large living room. 'Adam, this is Tony.' Tony, fortysomething, short and stocky, stands up and extends a hand. 'Adam here is an old friend of mine.'

'Good to meet you,' Tony says, displaying his strong New Jersey accent.

We all sit down, before Joey abruptly stands up and says, 'I'm forgetting my fucking manners. What can I get you guys? Coffee, whiskey?'

'Coffee,' I say.

'Whiskey,' Tony says.

'You a relative of Joey's?' I ask when I'm alone with Tony.

'Not blood family,' he says. 'We used to run together back in the day. I'm over from the States for a couple of days. On my way to Italy.'

I nod sagely. I'm being told that Tony is Mafia.

'How do you know Joey?' Tony wants to know.

'Both men of the cloth. Men of the cloth that don't always behave like men of the cloth.'

Tony laughs. 'As long as you don't mess around with kids that's fine by me.'

'We were just talking about a little business opportunity,' Joey says after presenting us with our drinks. 'We've been talking to a couple of Albanians Tony knows who say they can provide us with top-grade ass for a good price.'

'You're going to run a brothel?' I ask.

'Nah. More like act as a wholesaler. Buy maybe fifty women at a time, then farm them out to different pimps and madams at a big mark-up. I don't really want to be dealing with Johns myself.'

'Who would?' Tony mutters

'Where are you going to keep fifty women at a time?' I want to know.

'That's where being in the Church could really pay off. Our parish has strong links with a convent in Surrey. It's a huge old place, with hardly any nuns living there. In the past St Joseph's has sent small groups of women there for a week or so on retreat. Well, I'm thinking, let's start sending a whole bunch more people there. We can tell the nuns that these are disadvantaged girls from Romania or wherever. The girls won't know what's just around the corner for them, so there's no chance of them spilling the beans.'

I laugh. 'A brilliant idea.'

'I think this could be great for you guys,' Tony comments. 'Demand for pussy will never die. The lady trade. Perfect.'

'Yeah, I think so. I can even take a confession from any of the girls that are feeling bad about what they're being made to do!'

'And Adam here can take your confession if you ain't feeling too happy about *your* sins.'

'I'm Church of England,' I point out. 'We don't do confession like you Catholics.'

'Oh,' Tony says. 'Well I guess he'll just have to find another priest.'

We all laugh.

'Say, guys,' Joey says. 'All this talk of broads is making me horny. Why don't we all go and check out a massage parlour somewhere? We can think of it as research.'

I look at Tony, who looks at me. We both shrug. 'Why not?' I say. 'You'd better bring me a whiskey though, Joey.'

'You nervous?' Joey asks, grinning.

'Not at all. I just have to shift into clocked-off mode. Whiskey will trick me into thinking it's after sundown.'

'I'm going to grab a shower,' Joey says. He takes a few steps towards the door, before stopping and turning to face us. 'Hey, why are we bothering to leave the house when we can get a couple of girls to come here? We've got booze, coke. Why move?'

'Don't you want to keep the action away from here?' Tony asks.

'My ass, I do. If a couple of hookers try and blackmail me over this I'll slit their throats. Who'd believe them, anyway? You know what? I'm going to be wearing my robes when they turn up.'

'Way to go, Joey,' Tony says. 'You'd think you'd never been outta the game.'

Half an hour later we've each had a couple of whiskeys and a couple of lines of coke, and we're all feeling ready for some action. I ring a hospital I'm due to visit that day and cancel. I say I'm with a dying parishioner, and really can't get away. My contact at the hospital says she totally understands, that we can reschedule for another time.

Joey walks into room having changed into his clerical robes. Instead of wearing normal shoes he has flip-flops on. 'When did those hoowahs say they were turning up?' he asks. His face is red from the booze and snuff.

'Should be here any moment,' Tony says. He had made the call.

Ten minutes later the doorbell rings. I open the door to two busty Brazilians who giggle and wave. Without waiting for me to say anything they walk past me into the hallway. I see a car parked directly outside the house with a big-looking guy at the wheel. He's obviously the girls' ride. I hope he's got a book, because he's going to sitting outside for a long time.

When I return to the living room I see that Tony has wasted no time in grabbing one of the girls. He has one hand on her arse and the other between her legs. Joey meanwhile has lifted up his robe to allow the other girl to start giving him head. I notice she's not bothering to use a condom. I feel a bit stupid just gawking at the two couples, and am about to head for the kitchen to pour myself another drink, when a hand reaches out and grabs me by the belt. It's the girl giving head, and while continuing to do fellatio on Joey she fumbles with my zipper with one hand. I help her out, then move in to share her mouth.

'If only my parishioners could see me now.' That's the thought I have as the orgy moves into full swing. There follows about an hour of multi-position and partner humping, interrupted by brief breaks to top up on booze and coke. Finally Tony brings a halt to the proceedings by flopping on a sofa and announcing, 'I'm done.'

'Thanks girls,' Joey says, his face glistening with sweat,

'You're welcome,' the taller of the two hookers says. 'Can we use shower?'

'Sure, sure,' Joey replies. 'Come on, I'll show you where it is.'

'How much did you pay them?' I ask Tony when the girls have followed Joey upstairs.

'Two hundred.'

'Worth every penny.' Reaching for my wallet, I say, 'I'm going to give them another hundred as a tip.'

Later, as I'm driving back home it occurs to me that killing a prostitute might be a good place to start. Not one as good as the two I've just shared. I could pick up a rough old street walker and start there. I'm reminded that lots of serial killers seem to target prossies. A lot of them seem to have an issue with women, which certainly isn't the case with me. I've got a problem with humans of either sex. No, I just think stabbing some old junkie slag that is known to virtually no-one might be a low stress way of getting my first blood. I could take her out to the countryside and take it nice and slow. Maybe even fuck her first if she isn't too minging. Fuck it, I think. I'll stick to the original plan.

Joey rings me a week later. He's taken a first delivery of five future whores, and wants to know if I want to help him break them in.

'What do you mean break them in?' I ask.

'Well, they still think they're in England to work in hotels. And I guess some of them *will* work in hotels.' He laughs. 'But you know what I mean. We need to slap them round a bit and generally lower their expectations. This bunch are staying with me until I can move them on. The convent will be able to help out for the next batch.'

'I should bring my wife along. She needs a bit of that treatment.'

'So are you coming?'

'Okay. When?'

Two mornings later I'm sitting with Joey in his living room. I have a whiskey, which I am more gulping that sipping. 'You ever done anything like this before?' I ask.

'Once. In Brooklyn. This was before I was made. I was young.'

'So we just go in and start getting fresh with them? What do we do when they tell us to get lost?'

'Give 'em a slap. They have to know who's boss.'

'And you want me to fuck a couple of them?'

'No. Just one. And you can take your girl upstairs. I do the same with one. Those two will tell the others, and they'll start getting the message.'

Joey takes my silence as agreement, and says, 'Okay, let go to it.' He leads me to a heavy door in the hallway that has numerous bolts on it. Tapping the door he comments, 'An elephant couldn't knock this down.' Unsliding bolts he goes on, 'We'd better be careful now. Just in case they've heard us and try to barge out.' He opens the door. 'Get that switch over there.' As I flick the switch a bulb on a short length of flex illuminates, revealing wooden steps leading down to the basement. I follow Joey down, smelling damp brick. Turning left at the bottom I see two mattresses, on which five young women are sprawled. They lift their heads, looking at us through squinted eyes; they've obviously been dozing. I quickly take in suitcases stacked to one side of the space, a few half-empty bottles of mineral water and a bucket.

'Joey, you've got all the makings of a fine hotelier.'

Joey grunts. 'Which one do you want?'

There's a blonde with really long legs to the right. 'Her,' I say, pointing.

'Good choice. Take her up to the bedroom next to mine.'

I walk over and pull the girl up by the hand. She looks confused, but doesn't struggle. 'You speak English?' I ask as I lead her towards the stairs. She shakes her head then nods. Whatever that means. 'Come on, let's get you out of this vampire lair'. She's in front of me as we take the stairs, and I give her butt an encouraging push. 'This way,' I say when we're out of the basement. Up to the beddy bed.'

As we climb yet more stairs I find myself considering the similarity between vampires as they are typically portrayed in popular culture and real life psychopaths. I know quite a bit about psychopathy – for a layman – having decided that the maxim 'Know Thyself' is of utmost importance. A psychologist by the name of Hare devised a 'Psychopathy Checklist', which has become the most commonly used diagnostic tool when assessing this condition. Traits and behavioural characteristics that feature in the checklist include glibness and superficial charm, parasitic lifestyle, grandiosity, lack of remorse and lack of guilt, all of which would seem to apply to your common or garden variety vampire. Has the mythological figure of the fanged bloodsucker evolved to make sense of a class of individual that has been wreaking havoc from time immemorial, a class of individual that includes me? I think I might give this woman I'm following upstairs a bite on the bum in a second. See how it feels.

I push my girl into the designated room. She's still looking at my blankly, like she doesn't know what's coming next. How stupid can someone be? Does she think I've brought her up here to read her a story?

'Take off your clothes,' I say.

More blank staring.

'Clothes – off.' I try to mime the act of disrobing. 'It's okay – I'm a priest. We'll say a little prayer after we're finished.'

Still nothing. I start to undress. There seems to be some

comprehension dawning, as the girl puts a hand to her mouth in alarm. 'That's it. Take your clothes off.'

When I'm down to my boxers I decide to give my companion a hand. I place my hands on her waist, then start to lift her top up. She pulls away from me, shouting something in her language. I can see now that this isn't going to be a walkover. A scream from the room Joey is in confirms that he's having a similar experience. Deciding it's better to go in hard rather than pussy-foot round for half an hour I grab the girl by her wrist, twist her arm behind her back, and force her over to the bed. 'Now, let's get one thing straight ...' I say.

I suppose you could say I raped her. I wouldn't say I enjoyed it that much. I might be sick in the head, but I don't think I'm a natural born rapist. Sex is always enjoyable I guess – that nice wet and warm feeling on your cock – but the fact that I was having to use my body weight to constrain the girl, along with the fact that I had to hold her wrists for fear of being scratched in the eyes, combined to distract. I certainly didn't have any desire to go at it for ages, and squirted pretty quickly. After finishing I shout out to Joey to see what he wants me to do with her. 'Hold her in the room until I come in!' he shouts back.

Joey finishes up about ten minutes later, and we take the girls back downstairs. They kick and fight when they see we're returning them to the basement, but we manage to push them down the stairs and lock the door behind them.

'What did you think?' Joey asks me.

'Different. If you're taking twenty or thirty at a time you'll have a job breaking them all in.'

'Like I said, you give a couple the treatment, and they tell the rest. '

'You won't be able to do this when your girls are staying at the convent,' I say.

'I know. That'll just be a place for them to stay at the beginning. We'll move some of them straight on to customers and some will probably spend a bit of time here after they've had their two weeks with the nuns.'

I hang around with Joey for a while, talking crap. At one point we hear a commotion from the basement. To hear it from the living room the girls really have to be making a racket.

'What's going on?' I ask.

'I think a couple of those girls hate each other. I've seen scratches on one's face, and bruises on the neck of the other. They tried to go for each other when I was taking their bucket out once. Must be the worst thing imaginable, being held hostage, and with someone who hates your guts.' Joey snorts a laugh.

'When you going to move the girls on?'

'Two are leaving in a couple of days. I'm going to make sure one of the fighters goes.'

'What's to stop them just disappearing when their working from a flat? You can't watch them 24/7.'

'That won't be my problem. Once they're sold, they're sold. New owner's responsibility. Apparently they don't normally run away, though. Their boss will hold their passports, tell them he's saving a bunch of money for them from their earnings, and that they can have it and go in three months or something. Of course, three months becomes six, which becomes twelve. By the time they've been doing it a while they're used to it.'

On the way home I think about women as a commodity. How they can be so easily bought and sold, and then rented for a while to strangers in return for money. I wonder if at some point in the future, when society has well and truly gone to hell, you'll be able to get a mortgage on a working girl. Buy-to-let babes. I think deep down women want to be possessed, and in a fucked-up way that's what happens when they are trafficked and bought and sold. They might belong to cunts, but at least they belong to someone.

Thinking along these lines gets me onto the whole Internet dating thing. When I feel like something a bit more classy than a whorefuck I sometimes use a well known Internet site. Throughout the day I get emails telling me that so-and-so has 'winked' at me, or that such-and-such a person has sent me an email. Most are from women in their mid-thirties or early forties, second-time-arounders who, having fucked up one long-term relationship, are looking to start and then fuck another one up. It's quite amazing how similar most profiles are. I would almost suggest women read a few of their sisters' profiles in order to be able to distinguish themselves in some way. They all love travel. They all like fun nights out, but also enjoy cosy evenings in in front of the fire. Without exception, they're keen for a bit of cock. Of course, what women write is less important than the photo they post, but here I would like to point out that displaying a photo that is ten years old is cheating, and likely if you meet me to result in an unfavourable outcome. I've just walked out of a bar on a couple of occasions when the reality did not meet my expectations.

I normally opt for the approach of not telling my dates that I'm married. I guess that goes without saying. To get around the fact I can rarely see them in the evening or stay over at their place I say that I'm a doctor who is currently working nights. Weekends are out because I'm generally looking after my son. Poor things lives with his mother, I explain, and really cherishes quality time with me on Saturdays and Sundays. Of course, unless the woman is really stupid – which *is* sometimes the case – this arrangement tends to come with a built-in life-expectancy of about a month. After this time the excuses start to run dry and become shaky. It suits me in a way, because after a month I'm ready for some fresh blood.

So normally the woman will start to smell a rat, and that will precipitate our separation. I find if I start behaving a bit oddly this helps to encourage her withdrawal from the scene. If the woman isn't becoming suspicious, and is happy to carry on seeing me, then I generally terminate things myself. Normally I just stop returning phone calls or replying to emails. They generally get the message. Other times I've feigned a change of sexual preference, or a sudden decision to migrate to some far-flung corner of the world.

There has only been one woman who has reacted badly to my decision to withdraw from the field of play. Sally was her name. She was desperate to get married, and within about five minutes of meeting me had, I think, decided that I would be the man to make an honest woman of her. To be fair, she wouldn't have made a bad wife. Good in the sack, well-paid job, could scrub up quite well. But of course, I wasn't interested in a wife, and when this became apparent to Sally she sort of flipped. It was as if she thought by dropping her pants we had entered into an unspoken and unwritten agreement to eventually tie the knot. It all culminated in her setting up a bogus profile on the site we both subscribed to, posting a photo of some knock-out babe and writing a witty personal summary. Then she sent me a warm message from this 'member'. Of course, I took the bait, and after swapping several messages with 'Samantha', agreed to meet her in a pub. Well, it wasn't Samantha waiting for me in the pub, but rather Sam, Sally's brother. Sally had told him I'd been knocking her around, and he was consequently set on knocking *me* around. Which he did. I came away from the pub with a black eye and a chipped tooth.

Of course, this sort of behaviour wasn't going to go unavenged. If this happened now I would probably murder Sally, but I was still warming up back then. Blood was shed, however. Sally had an elderly cat called Twinkles, which she doted on. Personally I found Twinkles to be a smelly, hair-shedding nuisance, so it was with some pleasure that I decided to despatch her. I wanted it to be very clear that I was behind Twinkles' demise, without it ever being provable. I knew that when the weather was fine the cat often spent mornings basking in the sunshine in Sally's back garden, so one sunny day when I knew Sally would be at work I jumped a gate and put my plan into operation. Butterflies hovered over grass that was growing longer than a conscientious gardener should allow, and there, lying on a wooden deck was Twinkles, now minutes away from its final tail shake. The stupid moggie knew me well enough, so didn't react as I approached it. It realised something was up as I lurched at it when I was near enough, but age had obviously slowed its reactions, because I grabbed the cat before it could flee.

My kill method was basic. I simply placed a plastic bag around the cat's head, which I secured with a cable tie. I released the animal after doing this, and it staggered around the garden for a while, it's vision totally obscured. I could see the bag expanding and deflating as the cat tried to draw breath. It took about three minutes before the cat died. It began to slow down during the last minute of its life, then just keeled over on the grass. I waited a couple of minutes before I approached the cat. Just to be doubly sure. As I waited I listened to the sound of the next-door neighbour crank up his lawnmower.

When I took the bag off there was cat vomit smeared over the animal's head. Cat sick. Cat so sick it dead. The next step was the bit I was really looking forward to, though also the most dangerous stage of the operation. Luckily Sally's front door is shrouded by a large hedge, so I wasn't as exposed as I might have been as I stood in front of it with cat in one hand, hammer in the other, and several nails protruding from my lips. I placed the cat's head against the door at chest level, and whacked a nail into the door through the cat's right ear. The nail went in firmly enough to hold the cat, allowing me two hands to drive a nail into the door through the cat's left ear. I stood back to survey my work. What can I say? It definitely didn't look like an accident. Sally would get the message.

I took a few moments to wipe any part of the door I might have touched. I didn't think prints would show up so easily on varnished wood, but I didn't want to take any chances. As I drove away it occurred to me that it was quite apt that as a vicar I should have chosen this way to display the cat. I had nailed it to wood just as Our Lord was nailed to wood all those years ago.

# Chapter Three

I'm driving to see an elderly parishioner who has just had an unfortunate medical diagnosis. Under normal circumstances I would dodge such a commitment – I find the elderly pretty tedious and a reminder of how I will one day be. Nevertheless, Mrs Parsons is wealthy and now an Alzheimer's patient. Joey has suggested that I should be ripping off members of my congregation – he's been doing it for years – and I think it's a good idea. My salary as a vicar is pretty miserable, and I spend a lot of money on whores and blow. I don't really have an idea how I should play it with Parsons – whether to distract her and try and swipe something from the house, or maybe sweet-talk her into putting me in her will. I'll just have to see how it goes.

I have to drive through one of the rougher parts of Clapton to get to her house. I see the normal signs of deprivation – graffiti, abandoned cars, litter – but what really gets me is how many young women are out pushing prams. It makes me mad that the modest amounts of tax I pay are going to subsidise these good-for-nothing benefit junkies. Righteous anger is something I can never fully embrace given my non-existent moral code, but I'm filled by the closest thing I can get to it. It makes me feel even more warmly towards whores than I normally do. At least hookers fucking work!

I'm reminded of an article I read recently which argued that psychopaths have an evolutionary advantage over normal people, and that's why so many of us exist. The idea is that psychopaths, through their aggressive acquisition of goods and money, are able to attract plenty of mates, thereby ensuring the survival of their nasty genes. This makes sense to me. Nature doesn't care about the birth of nice people – just people who can procreate. The shame with these benefit junkies is that the government is basically subsidising the expansion of an underclass, ensuring the survival of genes that I'm not sure we really want.

Mrs Parsons greets me cheerily after opening the door. What's she so fucking happy about? I wonder. I wouldn't be happy if I'd just been diagnosed with Alzheimer's. I wouldn't even be answering the door. 'Come through dear,' she says. 'I've just put the kettle on.'

I sit on a floral-patterned armchair, and await the arrival of tea and biscuits. I'm going to have to try and gauge the degree to which Mrs Parsons' mental faculties have declined in order to see what – if any – conning activities I can attempt. I last spoke to her properly about a year ago. Her diagnosis was about two months after that conversation. I scan the room for signs of wealth. I can't see any antiques or works of art that look like they might be valuable, but then I'm no expert. I know her late husband did something in property, and the size of her house is proof she has a few quid salted away.

'Here we go, dear,' Mrs Parsons announces, walking into the room with a tray that is shaking alarmingly. I thought it was Parkinson's that gave you the shakes. Maybe she's got a touch of that. It's impossible to keep up with all the ailments that beset the elderly.

'How is your wife?' Mrs Parsons asks after we're both holding a teacup. 'Such a lovely woman. Always has a smile on her face.'

'She's well. She's taken up sky-diving as a hobby recently. Gets a kick out of falling from high places.'

This is rubbish, of course. I'm just testing the old lady.

'Well that's lovely,' Parsons responds. 'Falling is one of the things that comes most naturally to humans.'

Inconclusive. Not a totally barmy answer.

We talk about how my children are for a few minutes, before I broach the subject of the woman's illness. 'So, Mrs Parsons,' I say. 'How are you bearing up since your diagnosis? Are you finding you can cope?'

'So far I haven't noticed too much change. We all get a little forgetful as we get older, and it's hard to know how much my lapses of memory are due to age, and how much they are due to the Alzheimer's. I know it will get a lot worse. Strangely enough, the one comfort I have is that when it's really affecting me badly I won't be in a position to realise how far gone I am. The illness will stop me from grasping how bad the illness is.'

'That's one way of looking at it.' I take a sip of tea. 'Have you got someone you can trust to help you when things get worse? Someone who can look after your financial affairs?'

'I'm selling the house. It's going on the market next month. I'll be going into a home, and my sister who lives in Basingstoke will have power of attorney to use funds as she sees fit.'

I can't resist. 'Mrs Parsons, If you feel that your sister is too busy or too far away to oversee your condition and needs, feel free to talk to me about any help that I might be able to provide. My primary responsibility is to the spiritual needs of my flock, but we can't totally forget about the mundane aspects of existence.' I reach over and place a hand on Mrs Parsons' arm. *Is this going too far?* 'I'm here for you.'

I make strong eye contact with the old lady as I say this, and it's immediately obvious that my words are hitting home. She looks like she's about to start crying.

'Well, thankyou. I'll … I'll see. I think my sister should be able to manage, but if she can't … I suppose she's getting on herself.'

'I'm here to help. Just remember that.'

'Actually, there is something you could do for me …'

I look alert. 'Yes …?'

'Well, there have been quite a few burglaries on this road recently, and I'm a bit worried that I might be targeted. I have some jewellery that is quite valuable and I'd be so upset if it was taken. Would you … would you be able to look after it for me for a little while? My sister's coming over in a couple of weeks and I'm going to give it to her then for safekeeping – but until then …'

'I'd be honoured to be entrusted with your jewellery. Are you sure you need me to take it, though? I mean, of course I'd be happy to do so.'

'I suppose the risk is small, but if you've got them it's one less thing for me to worry about.' Mrs Parsons purses her lips as if she's trying to keep an assortment of jewels contained within her mouth.

We talk for another twenty minutes – my mind wandering to how I can keep the precious items I'm about to be given – before Mrs Parsons announces, 'My television programme is on shortly, and I'd like to watch it if you don't mind.'

I nod.

'Let me get those things for you.'

The old lady rises unsteadily to her feet, then goes upstairs. Ten minutes later she returns with a black shoebox. Lifting the lid she shows me the contents: watches, bracelets, necklaces, brooches, most displaying silver, gold or precious stones. It looks like a robber's haul from an upmarket jeweller.

'Are they insured?' I ask.

'They are, but insurance can't compensate for sentimental value. Most of these are gifts from my late husband and mother.'

'I understand. Well, they'll be safe with me. In fact, they'll be in a safe. We have one at the church. That's where I'll keep them.'

'Oh, that's wonderful.'

At the door I say, 'Just call me a call a couple of days before your sister arrives. I'll drop them back to you.'

On the drive back I wonder about killing Mrs Parsons. If I do it before she tells anyone she's entrusted her jewels to me, I'd be able to keep her stash. I am a predator, and I need to predate. Let me predate soon, God, and I promise I'll pray to you for forgiveness as soon as I've killed or robbed. This gets me to thinking about the ludicrousness of Christian theology. God made me, so we are taught. In which case God made me a psychopath. How can I then be considered to be evil, or anything other than an integral part of Creation? All living things behave according to their instincts. The dung beetle is drawn to animal excrement, the lion pursues and kills gazelle, and I will soon be murdering other humans. How am I any different to the dung beetle or lion? I have self-awareness, something the dung beetle probably doesn't possess in any meaningful sense, but my psychopathy hinges on self-awareness. I have to have a sense of self to want to gratify that self's need for blood and personal enrichment.

That week in church I'm really on fire. I take as the theme of my sermon 'The Blood of Atonement'. I know from listening back to a recording of the address that it made no sense. I jump from subject to subject with abandonment. Arguments are begun but not made. Such is the passion with which I speak, however, that my congregation is enraptured. Blood is everywhere in my talk. The blood of Christ, the blood of the Saints, the gallons of spilt Philistine blood after the Israelites had smitten them in a fictitious battle I invent. I try and I think succeed in inducing a mild hypnotic trance in my audience by varying my speed of delivery, using lots of sex/death imagery, and incorporating much alliteration.

I can see the appeal of being on stage performing a concert or stand-up act. Having the attention of so many people, and being able to influence their mood and mind.

Hitler got it. He understood the power of oratory combined with setting to do amazing things. I remember once delivering a sermon during a massive thunderstorm. It was a storm of tropical intensity – not the sort of thing you commonly experience in the British Isles. My sermon was on forgiveness, but as the winds rattled slates on the roof, and thunder crashed like an artillery bombardment, I found myself focusing on the importance of valour and courage in life. My congregation were swept along like wind-torn clouds. I could see them sitting up straighter, fidgeting less, and hanging on every word I spoke as my sermon was accompanied by an awesome display of Nature's power.

After church that week I decide to play a little game with my wife. She's obsessed about smells – both emitting them and having to endure unpleasant ones. On the drive back from St. Michael's I say, 'Hey, can anyone smell that pong?'

'What does it smell like?' Lucy says, quick as a shot. It's as if she's been waiting all her life for me to ask this question.

'I don't know …' I sniff a couple of times. 'A bit … fishy.' This I know is guaranteed to panic Lucy. She's paranoid about female hygiene.

'Fishy?' We haven't eaten fish for days.'

'I hate fish!' Chloe announces.

'Have we all been bathing?' I ask the car. 'Changing our underduddies every day?'

'Well of course,' Lucy snaps. She puts her window down a couple of inches and crosses her arms.

'Smells,' I say. 'You haven't experienced smells until you've been to India. Woah. Nice smells, bad smells, but smells. My nose was worn out after I got back from my trip there.'

Talking of smells other than those currently wafting seems to relax my wife. It sends me on a daydream to my time in the Subcontinent. I went to India for six months in my mid-twenties, largely to get away from some bother regarding an ex-girlfriend whose brains I'd mashed up. She had some large, aggressive brothers, and making myself scarce for a while had seemed like a good idea. I've always sensed there might be something wrong with me, and while I was in India I figured it might be a good idea to check out some guru guys – see if they couldn't diagnose and fix me. The Indians seemed to have invented spirituality, and aren't burdened with all the Western bullshit of dog-collars and church fetes. If a guy is so devoted to his beliefs that he is willing to wander the country naked and dusty, it seems likely that he might actually have glimpsed something.

In Bendares I spent a few weeks in an ashram. I enjoyed the simplicity of my life there. Simple food, few distractions, meditation. I didn't find God during my meditations, but meditation did have a profoundly relaxing effect on my body and mind. After a couple of weeks I felt so much lighter it was as if the Earth had lost some of its gravity. Towards the end of my stay at the ashram I met Jagdish. He worked part-time as a handyman at the ashram; the rest of his week was spent working as a consulting astrologer. As my time at the commune neared its end Jagdish suggested I come and stay with him and his family. He explained that I would never truly understand India until I'd spent some time living with the locals. There were no better offers forthcoming, so I agreed.

I spent the first few days of my stay with Jagdish trying to seduce his younger sister, but when it became apparent that she wasn't having any of it I just hung around in the courtyard, watching people make food, sweep and do their normal household chores. One morning Jagdish pulled me aside and explained that he wanted to do my horoscope. At the time I rated astrology along with flying saucers in the credibility stakes, but heck, I was his guest and felt I should humour him. 'No problem,' I said. 'You need my date of birth?'

'That and the timing of your birth. And the where.'

'The where was London. 1971. July the 10th.'

'I need exact timing.'

'Actually, you're in luck. My mother remembered the exact moment I popped out because it was quite memorable – eleven eleven in the morning.'

'Very good,' Jagdish said with a grin. 'Most peoples just know morning, afternoon – not exact like you. I make you chart today, then talk to you tomorrow.'

Jagdish didn't wait until the following day. Later that afternoon he came into the room where I was dozing and said, 'I must talk to you now. Your chart is showing very strange things.'

I'd been having a very pleasant erotic dream, and wasn't overly happy at the intrusion. Sitting up, I said, 'Okay. If you must.'

'Did your mother die when you were twenty two?' Jagdish wanted to know.

'She did, as a matter of fact.' I immediately began racking my brains for a time when I might have let this fact slip to Jagdish or anyone else at the ashram. I couldn't think of such an occasion.

'I knew it! I knew it!'

'That is pretty impressive,' I conceded. 'What else can you tell me?'

'Well, I can see that you will have many relations with women.' The Indian gave me a sly grin. 'But not always happy ones.

I nodded. That was on the money.

'And when you were ten you might have broken your leg.'

That really got my attention. 'How the hell could astrology have told you that?' I asked, alarmed.

Jagdish wobbled his head and smiled. 'Many things astrology can tell you. And one more thing for you, something that is not so good.'

'What's that? I'm not going to be trampled by elephants, am I?'

'No. You have Gohanta Yoga.'

'I certainly haven't. I've never done yoga in my life.'

'No, no. It's not a body yoga. Yoga means 'joined'. You can have planet yoga, where planets be in a pattern. Gohanta Yoga is Jupiter in eighth house, and bad planet in an angular house with no good aspect.'

'What does it mean?'

'It means you will be butcher. Could be normal butcher, could be bad one. Someone who kills people with a knife.'

'I've never done that,' I said.

'And I hope you never do. I'm sure you never will. I only really see this strongly because my uncle had same yoga. And he did kill some peoples.'

This conversation with Jagdish was to have a profound effect on me. It got me to thinking about whether astrology *could* actually work, which in turn led me to invest in a couple of books and computer programmes, which enabled me to prove to my own satisfaction that the stuff *did* work. How it works I have absolutely no idea, and nor do I really care. What I do care about is having a tool that enables me to get the jump on other people and forewarning of occurrences that Life throws at me. Astrology allowed me to seduce my wife easily, firstly by giving her the impression I was a spiritual kind of guy, in touch with finer realms, and, more importantly, by revealing her trigger points. Astrology has also given me the insight that Lucy will probably die young; a relief to know, as it will save me the expense of divorcing her after she has done her child-rearing duties.

We arrive back home and evacuate the car. Lucy gets on with Sunday lunch. I go upstairs to my study and have a wank.

# Chapter Four

Later that week I'm hanging out with Joey again at his place. No whores or Charlie this time, something I'm actually quite pleased about. It took me a good few days to get over our recent crazy one. Joey's banging on about a journalist he's recently started seeing.

'I really like her. I just can't shake this suspicion that she's setting me up for a story.'

'You'll know soon enough,' I say. 'If you're just a story then she's unlikely to spend more than a month or so on you.'

'I met her through a friend,' Joey explains.

'How long has she known your friend? If it's forever then that makes it less likely that she's up to something.'

'A couple of years, I think. But that got me to thinking that she might have heard about my background through this friend – Janet knows my past. So maybe the fact that she's come via her makes it more likely she just wants to write a piece on me.'

'Ask her. Tell her you'll break her legs if she does the dirty on you. If she knows about your past she'll bloody well believe you.'

Joey grunts. 'Yeah, maybe I should.'

'Who does she write for?'

'The Guardian.'

'What does she look like?'

'She's hot. Long blonde hair. Big brown eyes. Good figure. Apart from her ass. Her ass it a teeny bit too big. But I forgive her that. If bitches are a hundred percent perfect they don't seem real, if you know what I mean.'

'Tasty. Tell me, is it such a big problem if she *is* writing a story about you? I mean, the Church knows about your past – that's your USP. Who cares if she writes a piece on you? Your congregation will probably just get bigger.'

'Yeah, but with the plans we've got at the moment, I want to keep a low profile. It would be a disaster if she prints a story linking me to the Mafia.'

'I guess …'

'Her ex is that writer Julian Felton.'

'Fucking wanker,' I say, spittle flying.

'Yeah?'

'He's part of the Arts-Media Club that dominates bestseller lists, gossip columns and award events. A plague on them, and their ditsy little fucking Camden lives. Talentless idiots, by and large, but as the only people allowed to comment on them are other talentless idiots they get away with it.'

'Jeez, you've been wanting to let that out for a while …'

'It's what I appreciate about the Internet,' I continue. 'At least other people have a voice now. It's one way in which the moronic gasbags are being diluted.' I *am* fucking mad. Madder than I should really be. I feel like grabbing a knife and rampaging through a Primrose Hill cafe. 'You have to understand the role of the media in our society. They've created something akin to a huge room full of distorting mirrors, but with ideas not images being reflected, bounced around and altered. They voice an opinion, then comment on it, and the response to the comment on it. They're like a huge schizophrenic head that spends all day arguing with itself. I find the bestseller lists in the papers very useful, you know. I make a careful study of them, and ensure I never buy a book that appears in them.'

'I go one better,' Joey says. 'I don't read at all!'

'No, it really makes me mad. If you talk to Joe Average, be he upper, middle or lower class, you'll find he has a totally different opinion on most things in life to those writing for papers. And yet he buys the papers, just the same.'

Joey starts blinking quickly whilst appearing to swallow something large and uncomfortable. He does this every so often. I've always put it down to him having consumed too many drugs. 'Most people are stupid, man,' he says. 'But don't worry about it. If you don't like the media, throw out your television and stop buying papers. Problem solved.'

'Yes, I'm able to exercise that sort of control. But most people are not able to. All newspapers should be banned, with a single media outlet replacing it controlled by a committee of a hundred responsible people. They'd have a website, and every day at six pm ten pertinent news items would be displayed, five good and five bad. No commentary, no analysis, just factual information. "The war in Sudan has ended." "A new treatment for malaria has been developed." People can then analyse the implications of these pieces of information for themselves. Teach them to use their brains for a change.'

'Well, that's not going to happen.' Joey says.

'I know.'

'The only people that could make something like that happen are politicians, and they rely on the newspapers to spread their bullshit.'

*Strike bolts of steel into the necks of journalists. Crush their fingers – their smelly, sweaty, typing fingers – in a vice. Slice their throats, their bullshit-spouting, cum-swallowing throats.* The more I think, the more targets I find for my first murder. I could kill a thousand people and still just be warming up. Control. Patience.

'Are those bitches still here?' I ask, changing the subject.

'No. Last one went two days ago. I'm not keeping women here anymore. Too much hassle.'

'The nunnery?'

'They're taking the first lot next week. It's going to be interesting to see if we can get away with it. You can imagine the newspaper headlines if what we're up to gets out.'

I nod my agreement.

I stay with Joey for a couple of hours, then drive over to see my drug dealer friend, Carson. Carson's almost forty, but has lived the same dossy student lifestyle since – since he *was* actually a student. He lives in a shitty terraced house with Emma, his twenty-three year old girlfriend. Emma's got lots of freckles and huge thighs. I fancy her for some fucked up reason.

'Come in, man,' Carson says after opening the door.

The flat smells like stale socks and pizza as I walk through to the living room.

'What can I do you for?' Carson asks when we're seated.

'I'm after some hash oil.'

'Hash oil?' Carson's tone suggests I might as well have been after ostrich claws. 'Yeah. I've got some. But that's so weird. I haven't had any for years.'

'Lucky me.'

'You've got to be careful with it. Blow your head off if you're not careful.'

'Blowing heads off is just what I had in mind. Other people's heads. How long does it take to work if you swallow hash oil?'

'Most people smear it on a cigarette and smoke it. Swallow it? I dunno. Maybe half an hour?'

Half an hour … that should just about work I decide as I pull away from Carson's, narrowly avoiding a cat that darts out in front of my car. My plan is to put some of the hash oil in selected communion glasses the following Sunday. I want to see the spirit move amongst my congregation in a way it never has before. Luckily my church uses small individual glasses rather than a large chalice. I can't have everyone have the special communion wine …

My drive home takes me past a car boot sale. The decision to stop is made a few seconds too late, and I brake hard. Watching cop shows has convinced me that murderers often fuck up by using murder weapons that can be traced back to them, and I'm determined not to make this error. No-one will be finding my blades, but even if they do it won't lead them to a store and CCTV footage. Mid-week car boot sales are pretty depressing affairs, with nothing like the crowds those at the weekend attract. The one I have stopped to visit is being held on waste ground between a laminate factory and a car lot. Two rows of sellers face each other, cars and vans parked behind their wares. Up the corridor thus created drift a handful of buyers. I walk past the guy selling second-hand fishing equipment, the guy flogging cheap batteries and electrical items, and the woman selling piles of children's clothes. Just when I think I'm out of luck I see an old man who is surrounded by piles of tools. In a bucket he has an impressive selection of knives. I pull a bayonet out of the bucket, marvelling at the weight of the blade.

'That's taken care of a Jerry,' the stall owner says. 'So my father claimed. He was in the War. North Africa.'

'They were still using bayonets in the Second World War?'

'Oh, yes. Soldiers preferred to kill with bullets, but if you ran out of ammo and someone was almost on top of you ... My father reckons he got a German in the neck with that. He might have been pulling my leg, but I wouldn't be surprised if it was a true story.'

'How much do you want for it?'

'I don't know whether to charge more or less for it as it's claimed a life. How about a tenner?'

'Done,' I say, pulling a note from my pocket.

As I walk back to the car I stab the air a couple of times with the bayonet. It needs sharpening, but otherwise I think I've got myself a good blade. Good for slicing and running a victim through. I'm aware that killing people isn't like it's portrayed in the movies. You don't just stick someone and they fall down in front of you. Like strangulation. It takes a long time to choke a person, and apparently unless you're strong your fingers are likely to cramp up before you've seen someone off. A big, strong blade should make despatching victims easier.

That night Lucy is bitching on about wanting to move to a bigger house.

'Darling, that's not the way it works. I'm the vicar of St. Michael's, and as part of the package we live in this house. Do you have any idea how much it would cost to rent or buy a property the same size as this one, let alone a bigger one?'

'But it's not big enough! I had more room when I was a student.'

I never get this kind of talk. 'What do you mean not big enough? You can only occupy the space your body takes up. If we lived in Hong Kong we'd probably have a third of the space we've got here.'

'If we lived in Hong Kong I'd be called Yip Dip Lip and know how to use chopsticks. But I don't live in Hong Kong. I live here.'

This is quite a good retort for my wife. 'Listen darling,' I reply. 'It would be unthinkable for us to move from here. If you like we can have a clear out of junk at the weekend. If we get rid of unused stuff it might feel as if we've got more room.'

'I'll help!' Ben exclaims. He's been listening nervously to our conversation, expecting a full-blown argument to develop I imagine. He'll do anything to soothe tension between his parents, and I'm guessing that urge is behind his eagerness to help.

'That's a deal,' I say.

Later as I'm in the living room watching some rubbish on television I think about my comment to Lucy about only being able to occupy the space our body takes up. A very basic way of looking at the murders I'm going to commit is to see them as the act of depriving people of the ability to take up space on this planet. This is obvious, and yet quite profound, I find. I won't be able to deprive my victims of the ability to live on in people's memories, I won't be destroying letters they might have sent, or works of art they might have created, but they won't be taking up anymore space on this planet. Once their bodies have rotted away, at any rate.

I decided about three weeks ago that I wasn't getting enough sex. I'm now forty-three, and am aware that in ten years or so I'm probably going to start getting visits from Mr Floppy. My looks are also on a slow but inexorable downward arc. I remember some old codger saying near the end of his life that his only real regret was not having more sex, and that there wasn't any sex he'd had that he wished he hadn't, including paid-for (hurrah!) and adulterous sex. In a bid not to have the regret of insufficient sex in later years – especially as there is a small but appreciable chance that I may at some point get locked up for the rest of my natural life – I have set myself the goal of having sex with a new partner every week, with only half of these shags being paid for. Some people resolve to lose weight; some people promise themselves they'll ring their parents at least once a week. I prefer the goal I have set myself.

I have managed to meet my challenge for each of the last three weeks, but with only two days to go, and unable to go the paid-for route this week, things are looking a little grim. I have a free afternoon, so jump in my car and let the vehicle take me where it will. When I was a student I got laid by walking up to an attractive girl at a bus stop and asking her if she wanted to join me for a meal at the restaurant directly behind the bus stop. Fifteen minutes after approaching her we were eating, and half an hour after that I was eating her pussy. We screwed for an hour or so and then I dropped her off at the home of the family she worked for – she was an au pair from Turkey. I remember driving home, wondering if I'd just dreamed the whole episode. It happened so quickly, and with a girl from a really conservative country.

Could I try something similar this afternoon? I'm not quite as hot as I was twenty years ago, but I'm still not bad looking. Maybe if I target someone who's just average-looking that will boost my chances. A slightly overweight single mum would be ideal. I head the car towards some shitty estates in Haggerston. I'm bound to see some losers pushing prams, I figure. If the bambino is young enough I can get it on with the mother without the baby knowing what the hell is going on.

I can't remember exactly what I said to the Turkish girl all those years ago. I think it was something like 'Would you like to join me for a meal?' It helped that it was early evening when I approached her – suggesting supper wasn't totally ludicrous, I guess. 'Can I have a chat with your twat?' I don't think that would have worked.

A later model of car parked on the street and more rubbish on the pavement signals my arrival at the estate that is my destination. I slow down, scanning each side of the road for someone that might make a suitable target. All I see are a few old people, stooped with age, and a couple of hoodies, walking along with sticks in their hands. Fucking hoodies. Someone's bound to show soon, I'm guessing; a woman's going to need to go to the Post Office to collect her social, or the newsagent to pick up twenty Benson.

It takes longer than I expected, but eventually I see a woman in her early thirties walking in my direction. She's alluringly dressed in tracksuit bottom and trainers, with a leather jacket over a pink t-shirt. She's plain, but not ugly. Bit heavy around the legs and arse. When she's only a few feet from my car I get out and approach her. I still haven't got a clue what I'm going to say.

'Hi there,' I begin. The woman looks at me as if I've got shit smeared on my face. 'Is there a Post Office around here?'

'Yeah. Down this road. First left.'

'Thanks.' It's now or never. 'You know, you look just like an old girlfriend of mine. You're not Laura Cassidy's sister by any chance?'

'Who?'

'Laura Cassidy. An old girlfriend of mine. You look just like her.'

'Never heard of her.'

The woman tries to push past me, but I block her way. 'Maybe you're not Laura Cassidy's sister, but can I buy you a coffee?'

'Piss off!' the woman says, stepping away from me.

'Steady on! I've only asked you to join me for a coffee.'

The woman looks behind her as if hoping to see someone she recognises. She turns back to face me and says, 'Not interested. Now leave me alone.'

I suddenly find my hand moving upwards, then down, hard, contacting the woman on the face. I can feel her cheekbones as the palm of my hand connects with her face. There's a loud thwacking sound accompanying my blow.

We both stare at each other, seemingly equally stunned at what has just happened. Then, as if a spell has been broken, the woman starts screaming at the top of her voice. Her shouts snap me out of my trance. I look around to see if anyone has observed me. I can't see anyone. The woman has run off down the road, still hollering. I get into my car and start the engine. My car is facing the fleeing woman, and for a second I think about running her down. I see the folly of such an action – luckily – and instead drive away, past the woman, and away from the estate.

When I'm a mile away from the scene of my attack I pull over and stop the car. What the fuck just happened there? I ask myself. Impetuous, amateurish behaviour, and not the sort of thing I can ever do again if I want to be a successful murderer. I doubt the woman would have had the presence of mind to memorise my registration number, but I can't rule this out, and there's always CCTV. I fervently hope that slapping strangers is a way of life for people living on the estate, and that my attack isn't reported. For this week's shag I think I'll get back onto the dating websites.

The following Sunday I put the hash oil I've bought to use during the Sunday morning service. In order to be able to witness the effects of my poisoning I announce after initial hymns and prayers that we will be moving straight to communion. 'Let us let the blessing of this Holy Sacrament wash over us from the outset of today's service,' I tell my congregation.

Before the service I beat Trevor, a church deacon, to pouring the wine into forty small communion glasses. To five of these I added what I consider to be a hefty amount of hash oil. Who will end up drinking these cups I have no way of knowing. It's even possible Lucy will end up getting high, something I could do without, as I'll have to babysit her all afternoon.

'Draw near with faith. Receive the body of our Lord Jesus Christ ...' In ones, twos and threes, members of the congregation that are eligible and willing come up to the altar to drink wine and eat a small crouton (a little touch I added some years before). By this stage I have totally forgotten which glasses contain the hash oil. I try to judge by the appearance of a grimace on swallowing which people are getting the special doses, but everyone who drinks displays the same serene facial expression.

In order to give the poison time to work I have prepared a real belter of a sermon, one that I'm going to drag on for an extra twenty minutes. A few roasts might get burned today, but no-one is leaving until I have seen the results of my narcotic lacing. The theme of my sermon is 'The Salvation of Animals', in which I argue for the possibility of animals going to heaven. This is controversial, but I know my church has many animal lovers among its members, so I'm prepared to take the risk.

'... I draw your attention to Isaiah Chapter Sixty Five, Verse Five: "The wolf and the lamb will feed together, and the lion will eat straw like the ox, but dust will be the serpent's food. They will neither harm nor destroy on all my holy mountain". Here we clearly see that lions will be in Heaven, along with other animals, but that they will eschew meat, opting instead for a vegetarian diet. This is a clear indication that animals will be more evolved in Heaven, suggesting also that it may be more evolved pets and other animals that go to Heaven. If humans can go to either Heaven or Hell, it stands to reason that if some animals go to Heaven, some may also go to Hell. For this reason I would suggest basic morality lessons for your pets. Perhaps you could get them to watch children's cartoons that contain simple messages about good citizenship. In addition to the commands "Sit" and "Stay" you should also add "Love" and "Respect".

'... I want you also to consider the following verse, from Ecclesiastes, Chapter Three: "For that which befalleth the sons of men befalleth beasts; even one thing befalleth them: as the one dieth, so dieth the other; yea, they have all one breath; so that a man hath no pre-eminence above a beast: for all is vanity. All go unto one place; all are of the dust, and all turn to dust again." Here we see animals being treated as the same class of being as humans, suggesting strongly that Heaven or Hell could be their final destination. If a man has 'no pre-eminence above a beast' why would our Heavenly Father have eternal life as a possible outcome for one and not the other?

'... the question then becomes, which beast from the animal kingdom is the most holy, the most deserving of a place in paradise. Well, we've all used the expression "Holy Cow", and the Hindus as you all know venerate this animal ...'

A sudden snort of laughter from a member of my congregation interrupts my sermon. Looking into my audience I see that it is Mr Cross who has caught a dose of the giggles. Ah, good old Mr Cross. A widower in his mid-fifties, he's needed cheering up for some time. I quickly scan faces to see if I can spot my other victims, but without immediate success.

'... so as I was saying, I feel it would be appropriate to consider the cow to be the holiest beast. Which then is the most accursed, the creature we are least likely to see in Heaven? I think the answer is obvious – the serpent. As the creature that stays closest to the ground - and hence farthest from the heavens – and as the beast that most resembles a fanged male member, it is surely deserving of this status ...'

A scream from Mrs Jennings alerts me to the fact that someone else has succumbed to my poison. I'm surprised that we're getting a strong reaction from *this* member of the congregation, though, as rumour has it that the forty-something has quite a wild background, with drugs a lot stronger than cannabis being consumed in huge quantities. Maybe it's the shock of being reminded of her past life in a place which has come to symbolise her escape from it.

Ten minutes later and four of the cannabis imbibers have revealed themselves through behaviour I know is atypical of them – and certainly atypical of them in a church. The fifth person remains a mystery. Perhaps he or she just feels a bit closer to God during this particular service.

Later that afternoon, after Sunday lunch, I'm sitting comfortably in the living room, watching footage of a civil war in some despotic North African state. Reporters seemed to be getting braver all the time, because they're right there on the front line, bullets whizzing all around them. I see a ferocious barricade of AK-47 fire being directed into a building. You can really see the punch those guns pack by the way they kick around. It looks like attempting to wrestle an angry polecat trying to fire one of those things.

My curiosity piqued, I check out YouTube to see if I can see any uncut footage of the same conflict. Sure enough, there's plenty of it. I don't have the patience for the grainy, shaky footage on offer, but after a few false starts I see some pretty gruesome stuff that's been well shot – a bit like their subjects. In one a couple of men are hauling the corpse of a dead fighter into view. The guy's obviously been dead for more than three hours but less than a day, as his limbs are frozen in rigor mortis. It's as if he's been in a freezer for a couple of days. I'm intrigued as to the details of his last seconds. It's obvious that he's been killed by gunfire, and he seems to have been in the middle of doing something just before he breathed his last, as one arm is outstretched and bent at the elbow, as if in his final moments he was trying to signal, or reach for something. The corpse drips blood onto dry sand. The men carrying it drop the body, and then begin to inspect it, using a stick to probe. They open the man's tunic, revealing a blood-soaked torso. There is a large bullet wound to the man's cheek, and when the camera moves around to the other side the exit wound is apparent, at the top and rear of the man's skull. The back of his head is blood-matted and muddy, but I can see what looks like brain tissue beginning to ooze out. The man's eyes are somewhere between open and closed – it looks like he's squinting – but the pupils aren't visible due to a build-up of blood. The camera moves around to focus on the hand that's pointing skywards. Just to add insult to injury it looks like a bullet caught the top of his index and middle finger. The top of the middle finger is missing, and the top of the index finger is crooked with a section of bone visible. It strikes me that this injury alone would be agony – if the man was alive to feel pain. Instead he's got this gormless 'I'm fucking dead, mate' look on his face. His mouth is open, as if his last act was to try and curse his killers. Death really doesn't do much for your image. You just become an immobile piece of meat.

This is the reality of war. One man surviving and another dying, with nothing but dumb luck separating one from the other. The mortar is fired, and because it was angled just so, and because the wind struck the projectile just so, and because of the slight manufacturing imperfection that weighted it to veer in just such a direction, Bob got killed instead of Bill. And Bill and Bob had swapped positions a second before the missile landed.

It occurs to me that if I'd fought in a war, perhaps that would have suppressed my homicidal urges. Perhaps if I'd killed a dozen men, and seen a dozen of my fellows-in-arms slaughtered, I wouldn't be so intent on murdering. There's an interesting statistic – I'm not sure how true it is – that in most armed conflicts only a minority of soldiers actually shoot at the enemy. Two-thirds of troops will shoot high or low, left or right, anything to avoid actually killing or injuring the other side. What does that say about the third that shoot to hit? Are they, like me, psychopaths? Are they more patriotic than the others? More obedient to orders? Fuck knows. All I know is that I would have shot to kill, and I doubt I'd have come back from war minus my bloodlust. If anything I think it would make me worse.

When I was in my early twenties I had been eager to see combat. I couldn't be bothered to go through a formal military training, then wait around for a war that might never happen – one in which I'd have to worry about rules of engagement and all that jazz. No, I wanted a couple of days learning to use my weapon, then the opportunity to get stuck in. No binding contracts or enlistment formalities, so I could cut and run if I didn't like being shot at. I considered most of the world's trouble spots – Afghanistan, Iraq, Lebanon, Sierra Leone. My idea was to just show up and offer my services to whoever was most eager to use them. Cause wasn't really something I was worried about. A week fighting with whichever bunch I chose and I figured I'd be able to see some validity in their call-to-arms. I think I would have gone with this urge, coming down with glandular fever just about the time I was preparing to book a flight in the end scuppering my plans. Maybe I should put this plan into action now. I feel like I'm straining against a leash I can't see. I'd get to kill people without risk of being arrested.

As quickly as I have this idea, I give up on it. It's just too much trouble to start shopping for trouble spots. I'm in my forties now; I want to be able to kill without getting vaccines. My victims will have to live in this country.

My reverie is interrupted by a call from Joey. 'You busy this afternoon?' he wants to know. 'Someone you have to meet is back in town.'

'Who's that?'

'A special guy. Someone everyone could do with knowing.'

'I don't know …'

'Don't argue,' Joey butts in. 'Just come over. I'll see you in an hour.'

I open my mouth to protest, but the phone goes dead. I get up and tell Lucy I'm going on a house call.

'On a Sunday?'

'The Lord's work doesn't run according to human calendars,' I say, before walking out.

'Come in, come in,' Joey booms after answering the door to me fifteen minutes later. 'Come and meet Courtney.'

I follow Joey into the living room. As soon as I walk in an incredibly fat black man with dreadlocks stands up. His huge grin reveals sparkling white teeth, with a prominent gap between the front teeth. Courtney starts chuckling as soon as we make eye contact, as if the very act of breathing is humourous to him.

'Adam – Courtney. Courtney – Adam.' Joey never uses twenty words when he can get by with four.

The next few hours whizz past in a crazy blur. Drinks come out, then coke, then weed. Music is played, eventually so loudly that my teeth start to vibrate. At one point I look up to see Joey and Courtney ballroom dancing to some

Rare Grooves tune. Then suddenly I'm dancing to a similar track.

After a while it's impossible to tell which particular substance is having the bigger effect on me. You'd think it would be the coke, but the weed seems pretty mind-blowingly strong. I go to the toilet at one point, and when I return I'm confronted with the sight of Courtney waving a handgun around. For a second I think he's gone crazy and is about to shoot Joey, but a huge smile reveals he's just having fun. I join the other two in dancing around the room. Suddenly something black flies in my direction. Only after catching it do I realise it's Courtney's gun. I appreciate its weight for a moment, before holding it aloft in one hand. I'm totally fucked, but not so fucked I don't forget to keep my finger away from the trigger. After a few minutes I hand the gun back to Courtney. He takes it with a grin, strokes the barrel with one hand, then aims and fires it at the television. I look at Joey to see what his reaction will be, but he just smiles and gives a thumbs-up sign. My ears ring from the loudness of the report for several minutes. I can see that the bullet fired went straight through the television, lodging in the wall behind.

The craziness carries on until eventually I go into a state of blackout. The next thing I know, I'm coming to my senses on the carpet of Joey's living room. A weak light indicates it's either very early the next morning or almost nightfall on the following day. I lift my head from the floor and immediately see Courtney lying a couple of feet from me, on his back. He even grins when he's asleep, I discover. I can't see Joey. I get up and head for the kitchen. I need to drink something cold and non-alcoholic. Joey collides with me in the kitchen doorway. 'Whoa,' he says. 'Back from the dead?'

'I'm not sure about that. I need water.'

'We can do better than that,' Joey replies, waving a bottle of Jack Daniels in front of my face.

'You must be joking.'

'I'm deadly serious. Come on. A big shot of this and a line of coke and you'll be fine.'

Joey's recipe for revival works in my case, but Courtney needs about half a bottle of bourbon and three lines before he's fully awake. 'Jesus motherfucking Christ,' he says after his third line. He sniffs and rubs his nose vigorously. 'That's fixed me up just fine. I remember who I am now.'

'Back on planet earth, eh?' Joey asks. 'That's good. We've had our party. Now it's time to talk.'

'Talk?' I say. 'I need to talk to my wife. She's probably called the police by now.'

'Forget your wife. If she hasn't figured out you're a cunt by now, it's time she did. Courtney's back from Jamaica, and he's got a very interesting business proposal for us. Courtney?'

Courtney rubs his face with both hands, then says, 'Well, yeah. I think there's some business we can do together that could make us all a lot of money. Get you back in the mob's good books.' He looks at Joey. 'Get you with some serious cash in your pocket.' He looks at me.

Why are they including me in all this? I ask myself. I'm an aspiring killer, not gangster. Sharing other men in your criminal plans seems to be a form of male bonding, like going to a strip-joint together.

'What's the plan?' I ask, without much enthusiasm.

'This is the great bit,' Joey says giggling. 'Being in the Church is about to pay off in a big way.'

Courtney smiles and takes another sip of Jack Daniels. 'Well ... I grew up in Jamaica, but my family are originally from Haiti. I still have some family living there, including a cousin who works for a charity.'

'She must be busy,' I observe.

'Very busy. There was plenty to do before the earthquake, but now it's just crazy. She works with orphans for a charity that is basically managed by the Catholic Church. Since the earthquake they have been sending ten orphans over to the UK once a month. The idea is get them away from the chaos of Haiti for a while. Get them eating proper and away from all the death and disaster.'

'Very noble,' I say. 'But what's the angle here?'

'Be patient,' Joey tells me. 'He's just getting to that.'

'Well, the orphans are coming over to stay with Catholic families. Any church can put forward people to take in a kid. So, now we get to the good bit. I've got some great coke contacts, and they can dump as much of the stuff as they want in Haiti without any fear of getting caught. What's left of the police force just couldn't give a fuck about dope smuggling, and even if they did you could bribe them with a couple of loaves of bread.'

'Where did you say the coke would come from?' Joey asks.

'Venezuela. Originally Peru, but it would be shipped from Venezuela.'

'I still don't get it,' I say.

'Come on man,' Courtney says, lightly punching me on the upper arm. 'We've got an easy supply of coke to Haiti, and ten kids a month coming from there to the UK. Do I have to spell it out?'

'So the kids are going to carry the coke?'

'Correct,' Courtney says.

'They swallow it or something?'

'No, no, no. They'll each have a little suitcase. And each suitcase will be carrying more than clothes and a teddy bear.'

'And your cousin. Is she involved in this as well?'

'You bet. She'll get her cut, and she hasn't got a problem using drugs money to help fund the charity.'

'So where do we come in?' I ask. 'I haven't got time to go traipsing off to Haiti.'

'Nothing as demanding as that,' Joey says.

'Course not,' Courtney confirms. 'We'd just need you to

enrol your church in the scheme. Get some church people to take a few kids in.'

'And the coke? I don't have to handle it?'

'Not at all,' Courtney replies. 'You just need to be around when the kids arrive. Before dropping them off with their families we switch their cases or just get the stuff out of them.'

'And listen to how much you'll get for every kid you handle,' Joey says, chuckling.

'Well, that depends on how much we get for the coke,' Courtney says. 'What you reckon Joey? Not sure if your guys or mine will pay better money. Adam's end's gotta be at least five per kid.'

'Five only?' Joey says. 'Each case is going to have a kilo of the white stuff. I reckon more like ten.'

'It'll depend how much we get for it.'

'Five is too low.'

'Okay, okay. Figure on seven then.'

Joey looks at me. 'Tempted?'

A big wad of cash might pay for a good defence lawyer if I get caught for murder, I think to myself. 'I could be,' I concede. 'When would this all start?'

'A month or so's time,' Courtney says. 'You could start sounding out a few people in your church straightaway.'

Joey slaps me on the back. 'We'll make a proper gangster out of you yet. Next thing you know you'll be packing heat.'

Courtney laughs. 'Sure. I can get you a piece, man. No problem.'

'What, to coerce churchgoers with?' I say.

'A gun is like a cell phone,' Joey says. 'Once you've have had one for a while you wonder how you ever lived without it.'

'Did you ever do hits when you were in the Mafia?' I ask.

Joey and Courtney laugh loudly. Courtney's laugh sounds a bit like a chicken being strangled. 'You don't join the

Mafia *without* doing a hit,' Joey informs me. 'Ever since that guy Donnie Brasco infiltrated the New York Mafia they won't make you unless you've done an execution. No Federal agent would go that far, so it's a fool-proof way of making sure they never get taken seriously by the mob.'

'Makes sense,' I observe. 'Then again, if the Feds know this, couldn't they legitimately arrest every member of the Mafia on the basis that they must all have committed a murder?'

'A bit more complicated than that.' Joey pauses before continuing, 'If you want to know about killing, then Court-ney here's your man. Popped a lot more people than me ...'

I look at Courtney, trying to figure out how this laugh-ing teddy bear could have killed several people. Maybe he hugged them to death.

'Yeah, man,' Courtney says. 'Your first killing mashes you up some. It's on your mind for a couple of weeks after you done it. You know, what's the guy's soul doing right now? Is he looking down at me from the sky? But after a while you forget about him. You know, we all have to go. I just brought that time forward for him. I lost count now how many people I killed. Gotta be more than ten.'

'Shit,' is the best I can manage. I look at Courtney through slightly different eyes from this point onwards.

'So you're in?' Joey asks. 'You wanna play the game?'

'Count me in,' I reply emphatically.

# Chapter Five

The big day arrives. I'm sitting in the coffee shop, watching the cashpoint machine. The café has just opened, and I'm the second customer of the day. As previously decided, the fourth person to use the hole-in-the-wall will be my target. So far two people have withdrawn money, so I shouldn't have long to wait. I'm wearing a bunch of clothes that I took from outside a charity shop – clothes I've never worn before and which cannot be traced to me except through my theft of them. I have my bayonet, which I'm carrying in a Monsoon bag. An unfortunate incident a couple of years back involving a bottle of whiskey, a car and a breathalyser means I have a criminal record, and as a result there's a database somewhere which holds a sample of my DNA. I'm thus paranoid about leaving any genetic evidence behind at a crime scene. The clothes I am wearing are long-sleeved. I exfoliated and shaved my hands and face before leaving this morning, and I have with me a builder's face-mask, which I'll don just before killing, along with surgical gloves. Apparently tiny particles of saliva and phlegm can be exhaled during the normal breathing process, and I don't want these ending up on my victim's body. Shoes seem to be a common way of getting caught – footprints, traces of blood left on footwear, etc. – so I'm wearing a pair of shoes that my brother left at our house a couple of years ago. I've burnt the soles to corrupt any print that might enable identification of the make by frying the base of the shoes lightly for ten minutes at a medium heat with a couple of tablespoons of olive oil.

The third person to use the cashpoint approaches the machine. He looks like a stupid hoodie, and I'm actually sad that he won't be my target. *You don't know how lucky you are, you little shit.* My body tenses up. I could be just minutes from committing my first killing. I've promised myself that I'll only slice and dice if the circumstances favour me. I'll have to be able to follow my target to a spot that will enable me to kill without being caught. If this can't be done I'll try and follow him or her to a place of work or home. I'll then stalk them for as long as it takes for the right moment to arise.

I've got my nose in a cup of cappuccino when the fourth person to use the cashpoint rocks up. It's a young woman with shoulder-length blonde hair. I'm somewhat surprised, even though it's obvious that young, blonde women use cashpoints just like everyone else. I put the rubber gloves on and stuff the mask in my packet. I wait until she's finished taking cash out before leaving the coffee shop.

The girl walks away from the cashpoint, down the High Street. I follow, keeping as big a distance as I dare without risking losing her. After she's walked for a couple of hundred yards she takes a right onto a side road. I pick up my pace, almost tripping over a cardboard box that has been dropped on the pavement. When I turn onto the side road I'm alarmed to see that the woman has disappeared. I break into a jog, but she's nowhere to be seen. Fuck, fuck, fuck. Having waited this long to kill I can't accept the loss of my quarry. I walk back down the street towards the High Street. Just before I reach it I see the girl – she's coming out of the front door of one of the first houses on the road. This time she's carrying a bag. I put the mask on.

I glance around quickly to see if anyone's in sight, before rushing the girl, pushing her into the house and onto her back. She screams loudly, and kneeling on her chest I put a hand to her mouth. 'Scream again, and I'll kill you,' I say, waving my bayonet in her face. Her eyes widen in terror. 'Is there anyone else in the house?' I ask. The girl shakes her head. I pause for a moment to listen, but can hear no sounds. If anyone else had been in the dwelling the commotion would surely have summoned them.

Now or never, I think to myself. Raising the knife as high as I can, I bring it down on the woman's chest. I must have glanced a bone, as the blade doesn't sink into her flesh as smoothly as I had expected. The woman continues to struggle, but she's light, and by pressing more firmly on her mouth, my knees on either side of her torso, I manage to keep her in place. I strike downwards again with the knife. The girl moves just at the last moment, and instead of hitting her heart area the knife sinks into her neck. Though accidental, this blow proves very effective. I figure I must have hit a major artery, as blood gushes upwards like a geyser. I don't think she needs another stab, but I give her a couple anyway, focusing on the heart area. Soon her body becomes still, her only movement a rhythmic opening and closing of her mouth, like a fish out of water.

I stand up and survey the scene. One very dead woman in a large pool of blood; me, covered in blood as well, particularly my hands and chest. Though I don't want to tarry longer than I need to, I've watched enough TV and read enough books to know that there's a certain protocol that needs to be followed as a serial killer. My killings have to have a signature, and I need to keep some sort of souvenir. I'm not particularly bothered by either custom, but feel I should enter into the spirit of things. By way of signature I place a red snooker ball in my victim's mouth. This is a nod to the game of Girl Snooker that Jake and I used to play, and I feel guaranteed to get detectives scratching their heads and keeping local pool halls under surveillance. As for the souvenir, I decide to go for a post-modernistic approach to the whole tradition. Instead of chopping of an ear or stealing jewellery, I'm going to take a toothbrush. Much less incriminating than a bloody ear, and an ironic comment on the whole keepsake phenomenon.

I run upstairs and grab both toothbrushes standing in a glass by the bathroom sink, before rummaging in one of the bedroom cupboards until I find a denim jacket that just about fits me. The jacket will cover my bloody torso. I run back downstairs and head straight for the kitchen, where I wash all traces of blood from my face and hands. I return to the hallway where the body lies and look for anything that might give me away. I've left bloody footprints on the wooden flooring, but I'm pleased to see the sole pattern is indistinct. I left everything but knife, keys, snooker ball and a ten pound note at home, so there aren't any receipts or personal items that could have fallen from my pockets.

Leaving the house is going to present one of the greatest dangers. I've covered my bloody shirt, but it occurs to me that covering my head might be a good idea as well. I rush back upstairs and hunt around until I find a black baseball cap that bears the word 'Mobil' on the front. Donning this, I head back down to the front door. Looking through the peephole, I can't see anyone outside. My view is restricted to quite a narrow angle, however, so I walk through to the living room and peer out from its large bay windows. Being mid-morning it's fairly quiet, but I can see an old man walking his dog on the other side of the road.

I decide I need to take further measures to protect my identity. I return to the kitchen, and remove a large black bin bag from the rubbish bin. It's pretty much full, and if I walk out of the house holding it directly in front of me I should be able to shield my face from any passers-by. I go back to the living room and wait until I can't see anyone in the vicinity of the house, then quickly rush out the front door, hat on head, bag in hands. As soon as I turn onto the pavement – heading away from the High Road – I see a woman with a small child bearing down on me. Luckily the child is kicking off about something and the woman too harried to pay me much attention. I raise the bin bag to obscure my face nonetheless. I keep the bag up to my face even after they have passed me, almost colliding with a dustbin as a result. When I'm a good twenty houses from the scene of my crime I dump the bag at the base of a plane tree. I take a quick look around – there's no-one in sight. I head straight for my car.

When I get into my vehicle I take a deep breath and start to relax. Not too much, though; I still need to get rid of some of my kill garb. I drive to a row of recycling banks outside a nearby supermarket. Pulling on the spare set of shoes that have lain in the foot well of the front passenger's seat, I stuff gloves, shoes, cap, knife, face mask and jacket into a plastic bag and get out of the car. I almost make the elementary mistake of shoving the bag in the clothes recycling unit. I don't want a charity shop worker examining my bloody discards. Coming to my senses in time, I shove the bag in the dark glass recycling bin. I'm guessing everything it contains will be melted.

It's only when I've arrived home, burnt the remainder of the clothes I've been wearing, and put the kettle on that I can finally savour my first kill. Like losing your virginity, where the novelty of the experience gets in the way of a full appreciation of the pleasure of the sex act, I can see that future murders will be more enjoyable; nevertheless, I still relish the memory of this first offing. The primal fear of the victim, the finality of the act that I committed. I mean, how can any sport compare to it? I can see now why people go parachuting, or climb mountains, but neither can be a patch on killing.

I talk a big sip of Earl Grey – milk, one sugar – and wonder what my victim's soul or ghost is up to. Is she wafting over the scene of her death, desperately trying to communicate with police officers, trying to give them a description of me? Is she in Heaven, her earthly life totally forgotten as she finds herself reunited with long-lost loved ones? Or, as I think most likely, is she simply no more, an absence of thought and emotion? Who knows? Who, frankly, cares?

My thoughts turn to how long it will take for the woman's murder to hit the news. Unless she lives alone – unlikely given her attractiveness and the fact that there were two toothbrushes in the bathroom – I'm guessing first reports will be tonight. It'll be fascinating to listen to all the speculation as to the identity of the killer and his likely motivation. No doubt in due course there will be clinical psychologists spouting a load of bullshit about my likely character traits and habits. I'll be described as a loner, some-one who lives alone, a person who indulges obsessively in strange hobbies. And they'll all be wrong. Because I'm a goddam married vicar.

Sure enough, my killing is the first story on the 7pm local news. Some little ratbag reporter stands outside the woman's house. There's the obligatory cordon, tent and forensic guys walking around in white suits. It occurs to me that wearing one of those suits might be the ideal way to dress for future murders. Apparently my victim was a Rebecca Paulson, twenty-seven, a local teacher who was engaged with a marriage date set for next week. Hearing this annoys me. This little twist will add to the media inter-est in the story, and make the police try that little bit harder to solve the case. I replay the sequence of events before and after the murder, trying to comfort myself that I didn't make any elementary errors. I'm pleased to find that I can't think of any.

'Dreadful, just dreadful,' my wife comments half way through the report. 'I bet it's the fiancé. It's normally always someone the victim knows.'

'Probably,' I say. 'A week away from her marriage date. Fancy that.'

You can imagine my surprise the next morning when I receive a telephone call from the dead girl's parents. They want me to take her funeral. I almost drop the phone, before getting my shit together and saying, 'Well of course. I'd be happy to take it.'

'We're not regular church attendees,' the father explains. 'But my mother Ethel was a member of your church before she passed away some years ago.'

'If only regular church attendees had church funerals, then there wouldn't be many church funerals at all,' I say soothingly. 'Now, when would you like to pop in for a chat so we can discuss your preferences for the service?'

A date is set for four days hence, and I'm able to return to my thoughts. I'm agitated, excited, and a little bit scared. I have an urge to tell someone about my murder, but know it's the last thing I can do. I think about saying something to Joey. He's a Mafioso with a lot more blood on his hands than I have, and he definitely wouldn't go to the police. Well, he wouldn't go to the police straight away; but there might come a time when he would. At any rate, by telling him about my murder it would give him power over me. I'd always have to factor him into any thoughts I have about my ongoing liberty. I can see now why so many serial killers engage in games with the police. Part of it is probably intel-lectual arrogance, but a bit of it can I'm sure be explained by a desire to be caught and feted as the badass the indi-vidual thinks he is.

That afternoon I'm acutely aware of any police sirens that I hear. I tense up straight away and wait anxiously to see if they are getting louder or fading away. There's a knock at the door at about three o'clock and I jump up straight away and stare fiercely at my wife. I open the door nervously, my heart racing, sure I'm going to see a couple of uniformed policemen on my doorstep. Instead it's my son's friend, Jack. Never in my life have I been so pleased to see the kid. I have to control the urge to hug him before inviting him in.

Is this what I'm going to have to put up with for the rest of my life? I've only killed one person, and already I'm a bag of nerves. I tell myself that once I've seen the police fail in their attempt to solve this first murder I'll probably start to relax, but I only half believe it.

\* \* \*

A couple of days later I'm driving with Courtney in his car. Courtney needs to pick up some ammo for his handgun from a Czech living in Ilford, after which he wants me to show him one of my favourite whorehouses. I'm not needed for the ammo pick-up, and I could quite easily have just given the Jamaican the address for the knocking shop, but I get the impression he likes the company. As a crook without the daily banter most nine-to-fives involve, I guess I'm as close to a workmate as he has.

On the way to Ilford we don't talk much, largely because Courtney's stereo is outputting at a volume that makes my skull vibrate. After picking up his bullets he seems to forget to turn the stereo on, so the drive back to Hackney is blissfully quiet.

'I got a funny email this morning,' Courtney tells me as we wait at some lights.

'Yeah?'

'Yeah. I got one of them Google Alert things set up. Meant to send me an email every time there's new information about Peyote cactus on the web. I love Peyote buttons – grow them at home and everything. Anyways, I get an email with a link to a site that has this story about a big cactus. Weren't Peyote cactus, but sooo funny.'

'What was the story?'

'This is meant to be true. Some guys back about twenny years ago were out in the desert in Arizona, taking pot shots at big cactus. This guy fires so many shots at one that it topple over like he'd cut it down with an axe. He tries it again, with an even bigger cactus, but this time he stand too close to it, and when it topple it fall on him and kill him!'

I laugh. 'You really think that happened?'

'Article had a scan of the local paper reporting it. Looked pretty real to me ...'

This tale gets me to thinking about the web generally, and how it's changed our life so much in twenty years. I remember porn sites back in the early Nineties, when it took about two minutes for a single jpeg to load.

I find Google much more than a source of restaurant reviews and the way I look for dirt on members of my congregation. The facility whereby Google suggests a search query after no more than a word or two typed, and which is based on the popularity of past searches, seems to serve as a great insight into the minds of users of this search engine. I've noticed that if you type 'why am I' into Google, the site suggests searches such as 'why am I so tired?', 'why do I feel sleepy?', and 'why do I keep putting on weight?'. Typing two words into Google tells you that a good proportion of its users are tired and fat, something a walk down a busy road in the United Kingdom or the United States readily confirms. Interestingly, if you type in the words 'how can I tell', top recommendations are 'how can I tell if an egg is bad?' and 'how can I tell the sex of a goldfish?'. The human race, capable of putting a man on the moon and, yet, en masse, seemingly more interested in the freshness of eggs and the sex of goldfish than many other things. I feel justified in the killing spree I'm embarking on.

I share this insight with Courtney, but he doesn't seem too interested, saying in reply, 'You gonna take me to that slapper place?'

'No problem,' I reply. 'Bottom of this road and do a left. Carry on until I tell you.'

It takes about five minutes to get to our destination. I tell Courtney to pull over opposite a parade of shops. 'You see that little alleyway between the charity shop and the hairdresser's?' I say, pointing.

'Yep.'

'The second door – it's a blue door – is the one you want. Whatever you do, don't knock on the first door. I made that mistake once and a big homo answered.'

'Really?'

'Yeah, it was an awkward moment. I'll give you the place's number. I normally ring first to make sure there's a girl free.'

'Thanks, man.'

Just then Lucy calls, wanting to know where I am. 'Just with a friend,' I say.

'Did you not think of telling me you were popping out?'

'I know, sorry. Back soon.'

'Who was that?' Courtney asks after I finish the call.

'Wife. Wants to know where I am,' I tell Courtney. 'Should probably head back.'

Nearing my home, we stop at some lights. Just as they're flashing amber in anticipation of a change to green, we feel an enormous thud as another motorist crashes into the back of us. 'What they fuck?' I shout, turning around in my seat. For a fat man, Courtney shows amazing speed in getting out of the car. 'Cho! A wha di bloodclaat di yuh?' I hear him shout. A voice replies, but I can't hear what is said. I'm about to get out of the car myself, when I hear two gunshots ring out in quick succession. A second later Courtney jumps into the car and we tear off.

'Fucking jerk,' Courtney says as he drives away.

'What the hell just happened?' I ask. I can't be sure I'm not dreaming this whole sequence. I hope I am.

'He called me a fat nigger and gave me the bird. Well, let me tell you, he said nigger for the last time. Got him once in the neck and once in the chest. Guy's a gonner.'

'And what about us?! You can't just shoot people who piss you off in this country!!'

'You give the cops too much thought, man.' Courtney corners with a squeal of tyres. 'The only crimes they solve are the ones they can't help solving. Look at what just happened now. No witnesses. I take this car and store it somewhere for a few weeks. They won't catch us.'

'Catch *you*. I didn't have anything to do with it.'

'Well yes and no. You didn't pull the trigger, but you ain't going to the police either, which makes you accessory.'

I decide not to argue this point.

Courtney is driving even faster now, trying to put as much distance as possible between the crime scene and us. Memories of past crime shows I've watched return to me. Shell casings. Shell casing can give away a murderer, and must at all costs not be left at a crime scene. 'Shell casings!' I shout.

'What?'

'Did you pick up the shell casings from the bullets you fired?'

'Course I did. You think I'm an amateur?'

'No, I'm just checking. What about CCTV? There might not have been anyone else around, but the police can probably track you with cameras. Use forensics to get DNA samples from both of us.'

'Car isn't registered to me.'

'Yeah, but your DNA is registered to you.'

'I've never been busted for a crime in this country, so they don't have a sample from me.'

'Yeah, well I do have a record and a sample of DNA on file …'

'Maybe you got a point. We might need to burn this baby. I'll stop at a gas station and get some fuel.'

'You can't do that! All petrol stations have got cameras! Find a petrol station and stop a couple of hundred yards beyond it. I'll go back on foot and get the petrol.'

Courtney grins. 'You know you've got some street smarts for a preacher man? You sure you've always been a Bible thumper?'

'It's called common sense.'

We near a Shell garage. We stop some distance from it as planned and I scamper back to the petrol station. I have no way of disguising myself, so want the transaction to go as smoothly and quickly as possible. Walking into the petrol station's store I almost collide with Jennifer Patterson, a member of my congregation. Stifling the urge to swear, I arrange my features into as pleasant a mask as possible and greet her.

'I can't see your car,' she comments, looking over my shoulder.

'I'm just out for a walk,' I reply. 'Popped in for a bottle of water.'

'You're a long way from home. Can I give you a lift back?'

'Well, thankyou, but I'm fine. Part of my new exercise regime to put in a couple of long walks a week.' I laugh nervously. 'You know how it is. Get to a certain age and the fat just seems to cling to you!'

'Well, yes. I suppose you're right. Anyway, enjoy your walk. I'll see you on Sunday!'

I pretend to browse the shop's shelves for five minutes – long enough to ensure Jennifer Patterson isn't going to return – before picking up a plastic petrol container. I pay for it, before heading to the pumps to fill it up. Back to the cashier to pay for five litres of petrol, then I set off for Courtney and the car.

'Man, I was beginning to think you'd run off to the police,' Courtney says as I slide into my seat. 'Thought I was gonna have to come and shoot you as well.'

'Just took a bit longer than expected,' I explain. The smell of petrol fills the car.

Courtney starts the engine, and we set off. 'We're looking for somewhere hidden,' he explains. 'But not too far from places. I don't want to be walking for hours to get back home.'

'How about just up there?' I say, pointing at a building site.

'Could be worth a look.' Courtney pulls the car onto a muddy track that leads between the shells of eight detached houses. The builders have got as far as constructing breeze-block inner skins, but judging by the lack of building materials on site and the rusted condition of the two skips present, it's been a while since labourers last laboured on the buildings. The houses back onto a railway bridge.

'Pull in behind,' I say. 'We won't be overlooked.'

'I think you're right,' Courtney agrees. A few moments later he's sploshing petrol on the seats of the car. When the container is empty he throws it onto the back seat and pulls out a box of matches. 'I should have trickled some gas away from the car,' he comments. 'I'm gonna get my eyebrows burned now.'

I stand well back as Courtney pulls a match from the match box. He lights it and throws it into the car, but the fuel fails to ignite.

'The match was probably out when it landed,' I say.

Courtney grunts. 'This should do it.' He picks up a muddy piece of newspaper. Without rain for the last few days it's dry. The man strikes another match and holds it to one corner of the paper. Flames rapidly take hold, and Courtney has to move quickly to throw it into the car before burning his fingers. This second attempt works, and within seconds flames have filled the interior of the vehicle. 'Get well back,' Courtney shouts. 'It's got a full tank of gas.'

I move backwards, marvelling at how quickly the flames are taking hold.

'Let's get out of here,' Courtney says. 'We should go different ways so we're not seen together.'

'You head left at the bottom of the road,' I say. 'I'll give you five minutes then go right.'

'Okay my man. Be in touch. Keep safe.'

Twenty minutes later I've put half a mile between the burning car and myself. I jump on a bus that takes me to within ten minutes walk of my house. I'm not quite ready to go home, though. The excitement of the last few hours hasn't left me, and I can think of only one way of quickly dissipating it. I'm going to get laid. My experience enables me to quickly navigate to a good brothel; I even have a good idea who's going to be on this afternoon. I press a door buzzer and a crackly voice says, 'Hello?'

'Hello,' I say in return.

'Push the door, darling.'

I do as instructed, and find myself in a whore-lock. A short stretch of corridor separates the outer door from an inner door. A sign on the wall instructs visitors to look up at the camera above the inner door, which I duly do. Image of my face captured, the inner door is released and I push through to a flight of steps that takes me up to the flat's first floor.

A middle-aged maid wearing a stained T-shirt greets me at the top of the stairs. 'Hey, babe.'

'Hi there.'

'Haven't seen you in a couple of weeks … How you been?'

'Bearing up.'

'Come on through. Yes, into that bedroom there. I'll get the girls to come and introduce themselves.'

I sit on the bed in a room that is quite neutral in its decoration. Apart from the pile of condoms and tube of KY Jelly on the bedside table there is little to suggest I'm in a brothel. After a couple of minutes the first girl appears. 'Hello, I'm Monica,' she says, with a smile that seems quite genuine. She's about five foot eight with shoulder length brown hair and a nice figure. Accent suggests she's Eastern European.

'Hello,' I say. So far so good.

The next girl in is called Sandy. She's shorter than Monica, with quite big arse. Very pretty face, though. Blonde hair and blue eyes. She sounds like a Londoner.

The maid appears shortly after Sandy leaves. 'So, sweet-heart. Either of our girls appeal to you today?'

'Yes, I think I'll go with Sandy.'

'You won't be disappointed. I'll send her in.'

Sandy walks in a couple of moments later with a smirk on her face. She does a little jig in the in the centre of the room and performs a mock-curtsey. I like it when whores are in a playful mood like this. It normally means the sex is going to be good.

'So, what's it going to be?' she asks.

'Straight sex for half an hour should be fine. If I'm having lots of fun I might extend.'

'Oh, you *will* be having lots of fun.'

'I hope so!'

I hand over the agreed payment, and Sandy walks out to deliver this to the maid. I use her brief absence to disrobe and make myself comfortable on the bed, lying face down. Soon I hear the door squeak, and footsteps making their way towards me. A hand slaps me on the arse, making me start. The blow doesn't exactly hurt, but I certainly feel it.

'That woke you up,' Sandy says, straddling me. She gets to work on my neck, massaging it firmly. Every time she leans forward I can feel her nipples graze my back. I groan appreciatively.

'How long you been doing this?' I ask. I can't help making small talk with working girls.

'About three years. I only work two days a week. Putting some money aside to start my own business.'

This is what they all say. They're all doing it part-time to fund their Big Dream. The reality is normally that they're doing it full-time to fund their Big Habit.

'How about you?' Sandy asks.

'Me?'

'How long you been doing it?'

I laugh. 'Of course. Longer than you. About ten years. It's just so much more convenient than wining and dining women.'

'I guess …' Sandy falls silent as she concentrates on massaging my back. After a few minutes of digital manipulation she says, 'The house I worked at until a month ago had the weirdest thing going on …'

'How so?'

'There was a woman working there in her forties. Really pretty. She could have passed for thirty-two. Anyway, one of her regulars was her son!'

'What?'

'Yeah. Her son was blind and used to come every two weeks with a friend. He really liked this woman who happened to be his mother. Used to keep coming every second Friday when she was on. We couldn't believe she would fuck him. She *was* pretty screwed up. We couldn't believe the son didn't figure out who he was screwing either. You know, blind people are meant to have a really good sense of smell and all that. You'd have thought her smell and her voice would have given her away.'

'That's sick,' I say. 'She must have gotten a kick out of it. And the son must have guessed who he was screwing. You wonder why they just didn't just do it at home and save all the hassle.'

'Yeah …'

We fall silent as Sandy concentrates on my back. Her massage technique is a rough and arrhythmic. She alternates between being too hard and too soft. My mind wanders to the blind punter. And I think I'm fucked up …

'You ready to turn over?' Sandy asks.

I oblige, grabbing a handful of tit in the process.

'Naughty!' Sandy says. 'Do you like my labia reduction?' She lifts herself up to make her groin region more visible.

'Your what?'

'I used to have a big labia that flapped around. Some men liked it, but it always used to bother me. Got it reduced to about half its original size.' She leans back and splays her pussy.

'It's looking pretty tidy now,' I concede.

'Wanna suck it?'

I don't normally like going down on whores, but what the hell. While I'm slurping away I think 'forget whorehouse, I'm in a nuthouse'. I come up for air and say, 'Did they put you to sleep to do the reduction?'

'No, local anaesthetic. They stick a needle into your flaps – which hurts like hell – then ten minutes later you don't feel anything. Only took about fifteen minutes.'

'Pretty quick.'

'Yeah. Took about two months to heal up properly. Couldn't work during that time – obviously.'

I stare down at Sandy's pussy for a second, before giving it another lick.

Sandy continues, 'I screamed like hell when they put the needle in me. It was kind of weird, 'cos I'm used to screaming when men put long things that squirt liquid in my pussy, and there I was, screaming when a man put a long thing that squirted liquid in my pussy.'

'Interesting observation,' I say. Then I fuck her properly.

\*\*\*

The phone rings soon after I get home. It's Marcus, an old acquaintance from university. 'You'll never guess what,' he says.

'What?'

'Jake's out.'

I allow a few seconds for this news to sink in before saying, 'How do you know?'

'James got a call from him.'

'Shit. I mean, that's great.'

This isn't unexpected news, but I thought his release date was a few months off. Everything seems to be happening at the same time, I think to myself. I make small talk with Marcus for a few minutes before ending the call with an excuse about needing to go to the toilet.

Jake's release gives me plenty to think about. I don't want to have to kill him, because the connection between us is too strong and too well known. At the same time, if I have to make a choice between killing and being killed, I know which one I'll go for.

That night I'm surprised to see a report on the news about another killer who has been operating in East London. He's been dubbed the Bouquet Killer, because he always leaves a bunch of flowers on the torso of his victims. The news item says that he's killed five times, and that there are no solid leads as to his identity. An obvious thought occurs to me. Why don't I imitate this person? Kill and leave a bouquet of flowers? It will muck up the police's investigation by introducing a random element into any pattern identification they've been trying to use as part of their attempt to catch this person, and might make my capture less likely as well.

This thought develops over the coming days until I feel I'm almost ready for action. How, then, to select my next victim? From visiting an elderly woman who attends my church I know of another lady who lives alone in the bungalow next to hers. She's in her early eighties, quite infirm, and gets very few visits. My parishioner once even mentioned that she keeps a spare door key under a flowerpot by her front door. And why wouldn't she mention this in passing? How's a vicar going to abuse this information? An ideal target in many respects. I settle on the following Monday evening as my kill date. I decide to buy my wife a large bouquet of flowers the next day (Friday). That way if the purchase of flowers is traced to me I'll have the perfect explanation for my actions. The flowers I leave on the old lady will come from Lucy's bunch.

Monday evening arrives, and I'm pretty much ready to rock. My excuse to Lucy for being out in the evening is a spot of night fishing – something I am genuinely fond of but haven't done for many months. Having a tackle box to load into the car is useful, as I can pack my killing paraphernalia away in it. 'Shouldn't be more than five or six hours,' I tell Lucy before leaving the house. 'Depends on how busy the fish are.'

I park my car a good two minute walk from my target's house. I take facemask, surgical gloves, snooker ball, a pair of shoe protectors, bunch of flowers and large knife from my tackle box – then return the knife. My intended victim is elderly and I should be able to send her on her way with my bare hands if I need to. Better to leave potential evidence behind and rely on knives I'll be able to find at her house. I pack my stuff into a Tesco bag and head off.

Approaching the house, I'm pleased to see that the lights are off. Some of these old coots are night owls, and I don't want to have to hang around until four am. I head to the rear garden where I'm pretty much hidden from neighbours and passers-by and prepare myself for entry. On go shoe-protectors (cheaper than discarding every pair of shoes I wear on these sorties), facemask, surgical gloves and cap. I'm wearing a long waterproof coat designed to protect decorators from paint. Each of these items are designed to protect me from shedding DNA evidence, and will be burnt after I'm done.

Looking like a cross between a doctor and painter, I walk around to the front of the house. I should have checked that the key I'm expecting to find is actually there before donning my killing garb, but I locate it easily enough, under the flowerpot as expected. Looking around to check I'm not being observed, I unlock the front door and enter the house.

The house has a musty, old-lady smell about it. It reminds me of summer homes that aren't lived in much. I guess at eighty-two my target isn't living in it as much as she would have been thirty years ago. There's less movement, less laughter, less consumption, less of a future. The front door opens onto a big open plan living area. I peer around nervously, heart thumping, making out plenty of dated furniture, but not the house owner. There are two doors to the left, both closed. I begin to turn the handle of the first, when I realise I haven't armed myself. Scanning the living area, I see a serving hatch that indicates the location of the kitchen. I creep into this room, quickly locating a large carving knife. Returning to the living room, I place my bouquet of flowers on the carpet, then turn the handle of the door nearest the front door. It opens to reveal a bedroom, but obviously a spare bedroom, as it contains a single bed, which is unoccupied. I move onto the second door, which opens with a squeak. A lump under the duvet and the sound of snoring indicates I've hit gold. I turn the light on. The old lady doesn't stir, so I walk over to her and say loudly, 'Your time has come!'

The woman jerks and sits up in bed. 'Who? What? Who is this?'

'It's time for you to be reunited with Ethel and Audrey and Rose,' I say. My voice is somewhat muffled by my face-mask.

'Who are you?' the old woman asks. She still hasn't screamed, I have to give her credit for that.

'I'm a full stop.'

'A what?' She draws the duvet up, covering her face from the nose down.

'A full stop. Your full stop. You know the punctuation mark? I'm going to bring you to an end. Now!' I lift the knife high, and bring it down with a smooth sweeping action, its point connecting with the woman's throat.

The old lady tries to scream, but the sound comes out as a gargle. I jump excitedly, then hop around to the other side of the bed. The woman tries to get out of bed, but collapses face first on the carpet. I want to be able to see my victim as I stab her, so I roll her over, then start to stab her in a frenzy. Pretty soon her face and torso are reduced to a bloody pulp. Torn shreds of nightdress mingle seamlessly with scraps of pulverised flesh. I don't clock the moment she expires, but

I imagine it's pretty quickly. Her face is so mashed up it wouldn't easily reveal the moment of her passing.

When I'm finished I stand up, panting. The woman's motionless body lies in a pool of blood. I can really smell the iron in the blood. I look down at my own body and see plenty of blood spattering my clothes protector and hands. I feel a wonderful stillness, like the world's suddenly stopped turning. Before I forget, I open the woman's mouth and pop a yellow snooker ball into her gob. I then retrieve the bouquet of flowers from the living room and throw them on the dead lady's chest. Figure that one out, plod.

On the basis that the newly deceased woman is unlikely to get visitors in the early hours of the morning, I don't rush my departure. I first of all grab a toothbrush from the bathroom, after which I decide to have a bit of a snoop around. I go back to the woman's bedroom and open a cupboard door. It's full of old lady clothes. A shelf at the top is stacked high with shoe boxes, and I pull one of these down. Opening it up, I see it's full of old black and white photographs. I tip them on the floor and spread them out. Most of them are boring snaps of people, with a few of coastal scenes – Devon or Cornwall at a guess – but I'm surprised to see a couple of nudes and even some showing sexual activity. I pick up one which shows a buxom woman kneeling before a man with a scar running down his thigh. She's giving him head. Could this woman be the old lady I've just killed? If so, I'm not sorry for her, but I do have more respect for her. We're all young once. The wrinkled face deceives. It suggests an innocence and incapacity for action that is misleading.

I pull down another shoe box. This one contains several old books – early Aldous Huxley titles complete with their dustwrappers – along with a handgun. What the fuck? I swing the chamber open and see it contains six bullets. I decide I'll keep the gun. It might come in handy later.

I almost help myself to a large sherry before leaving, but realise that leaving DNA on a glass wouldn't be a clever idea.

I make a final sweep of the house to check that I haven't left any evidence behind, then make my way to the front door. I open it a crack and spend a few moments watching the road for anyone that might be walking around. When I'm sure I won't be observed I leave.

# Chapter Six

The next Sunday I make an announcement at church, asking for volunteers to take in kids from Haiti for a week. The kids will actually be in the U.K. for two weeks, but I figure I'll get more takers if I say a week to begin with. I'll let any families that come forward know the proper stay length after they're committed. 'These children have had a truly traumatic time,' I explain to my congregation. 'Since the earthquake they've been living in camps, with little food and no sanitation. What's worse, crocodiles have moved in, snapping up anyone that isn't fast enough to outrun them. The reptiles particularly like albinos, whom scientists think they mistake for fish that walk on land.' This, of course, is bullshit, but I want plenty of hands up for this one. 'So please, remember the privileges we enjoy living in this country, and consider whether you'd be willing to help these poor children ...' By five o'clock that afternoon I have eight emails from people with a bed to spare.

The next day I head over to Joey's place for a business meeting. We have the whores to talk about, plus the coke-smuggling nuns. Joey's particularly concerned about the girls who have been staying at the convent. Some of them are getting a bit stroppy about being kept there, and not all of the nuns are convinced about having them as guests either. 'I want you to go over and smooth things over with everyone,' Joey says to me. 'Use the Bible, use money, use your dick. We need to be able to store those bitches there. Those whores

I had in my cellar drove me crazy after about a week. The place stank.' Turning to Courtney he says, 'Can you hurry up some of our buyers? If they place an order for women, I want them picked within a week. If they're not ready to take delivery of the girls they shouldn't be ordering.'

Courtney and I nod our understanding.

'I don't want to have to get New Jersey involved in the logistics here,' Joey continues. 'We have to be able to show that we can handle things on our own. Which leads me to another thing. We probably need some more manpower. Anyone know of someone who might be able to help out?'

'I can put a sign up on the church noticeboard,' I suggest impishly.

'Very funny. But seriously, if someone comes along you think can help, have a word with them.'

The next morning I drive to the nunnery, located a couple of miles from Dorchester. I've spoken to the Mother Superior by telephone, and have arranged to meet her, then see a group of the girls that are her guests. Arriving at my destination I see that the nunnery is a grand old stone building with leaded windows. Ivy covers much of the front elevation. I climb steps that lead to a large oak main door, press the doorbell and wait. A minute later the door is opened by a nun in her twenties. She's wearing a habit, and to my mind very attractive. I would love to corrupt her. It occurs to me that she might already have been corrupted. I'm guessing a lot of women become nuns to do a dramatic U-turn in their lives.

'Hello, my name is Reverend Cuthbert, and I have an appointment to see your Mother Superior,' I say.

'Oh, yes. She's expecting you. Come in.' The nun has a strong Brummie accent, which clashes with her appearance.

My interview takes place in the Mother Superior's office, high ceilinged with large, framed photographs of present and past Popes on the wall. The room has a large desk, but we take armchairs on the other side of the room.

'Thanks for seeing me,' I say when we're seated. I don't know if there's a title I should be using to address her with, but I figure she'll forgive any slips in etiquette on account of me being an Anglican. How many Hail Marys would you have to say to be forgiven for being a serial killer? I wonder idly.

'My pleasure,' the MS says. I'd put her in her mid-sixties; very slim with eyes that are too large for her face, giving her a permanently startled look.

I clear my throat. 'As I explained on the phone, Joey, I mean Father LaMotta, wanted me to have a meeting with you, firstly to thank you for looking after the poor girls you've given shelter to, and also to find out how they are getting on.'

I catch a whiff of disinfectant, which is gone as soon as I detect it.

'We're very happy to help with giving the girls somewhere to stay. My only concern is that the first group have been here for almost three weeks now. My understanding was that individual girls would only be staying a couple of weeks at the most, before they move on to their fruit-picking jobs. And also there has been some squabbling amongst them. And we did catch one with a bottle of vodka, which we had to confiscate, I'm afraid.'

'I'm sorry to hear that,' I say. 'Obviously some of these girls come from quite disturbed backgrounds. That's why we've taken it upon ourselves to try and help them start new lives in the United Kingdom. But I can assure you that I've spoken to the farmers who are keen for the girls' help, and I'd hope to be ringing in a couple of days to organise the collection of the first group.'

'Well, I'm pleased to hear that. May I request that Maria Gunzele is in that first group? She's the one we caught with a bottle of vodka, and I fear her continued presence here may be disruptive.'

'I'm sure we can arrange that,' I say. 'Can I ask you

about the two girls that have disappeared? Still not sign of them?'

'No. This was four days ago, and I doubt we'll be seeing them again. It's odd, because I understand you're holding their passports ...'

'Yes. For safekeeping. We don't want them losing them and not being able to go home for a holiday. I'm wondering if it might be possible to dissuade the girls from leaving the nunnery? The village only seems to have a pub and a service station. It's not as if there's much for them to see locally.'

'I'm afraid that wouldn't be possible. We're giving the girls accommodation, but I don't know if we could legally prohibit them for going out when they wish. Also, a number of them smoke. We don't allow them to smoke here, so they have to go out for that. Then of course they need to be able to buy cigarettes, sweets and toiletries.'

A few minutes later I'm introduced to seven of the girls, in the convent's library. They look at me suspiciously as I enter the room. One, I immediately note, has amazing legs. She is going to make someone a packet.

'Hello,' I say. I feel surprisingly nervous. 'I'm a friend of Joey's.' I look at my audience to see if they're following me. 'You know Joey? The man who brought you here?' I get a nod from a girl with dyed blonde hair and focus my gaze on her. 'I'm here to check that you're comfortable, and tell you that you'll soon be moving on to those jobs we've promised you.'

'It take very long time,' the girl with dyed blonde hair says. 'We wait almost a month already.'

'I know. And I'm sorry. But this time next week you'll all be earning money.' And how you'll be earning money, I think to myself.

'I don't want to work farm,' a girl whose prettiness is slightly marred by an overlong nose says. 'I work shop.'

Knocking shop – no problem. 'We'll see what we can do,' I say. 'You may have to do some farm work for a while –

fruit picking – but after that maybe we can move you on to something else.'

A girl with a stunning body but a face that has been acne-scarred says, 'Man in Bulgaria say we stay in hotel before starting job. This is crazy nun place. No men.'

This last comment gets a laugh from several of the girls. 'Don't worry, you'll be meeting plenty of men soon,' I respond, grinning broadly. 'Now, I've got some money for you people. You need cash for cigarettes and things?' The girls crowd forward, and I put a twenty pound note in each outstretched hand.

'Mugs,' I think to myself as I drive away later. How can people be so naive as to think that individuals would go to the trouble of bringing girls all the way from Eastern Europe, putting them up and giving them money, just so they can pick strawberries? Trafficking has been going on for long enough that stories must be circulating in Romania and Bulgaria about the dangers of promises about work abroad that seem too good to be true. A good example of wanting to believe defeating common sense.

My drive home is interrupted by a stop at a whorehouse. It's pre-planned, and the mix of nuns and slags I've just spent time with has really put me in the mood. I stop the car outside the house, the top floor flat of which is the knocking shop. From the back seat I pick up what to most people looks like nothing more than a white FedEx box, about a foot long and four inches deep. It is indeed a FedEx box, but I've altered it so that a sleeve of cardboard inside the empty box will hold my iPhone. When positioned inside the package my phone's camera lens lines up exactly with a small square hole in the box. I've written 'Fragile' in huge black letters on the outside of the box, and the hole is positioned exactly at the top of the downstroke in 'F', meaning that it would only be spotted on close examination. My converted box is designed to allow me to capture my fucking of prostitutes on film, something I've decided to do partly to give me a souvenir of such visits, and partly for later erotic entertainment. I'm thinking of filming my next murder as well, despite the dangers such a record would present.

After being shown to a bedroom by the maid, I position the box in what I think will be the best spot to capture the action. The camera is towards the top of the box, as I'm not interested in filming the carpet, but it's hard to tell how wide a field of capture my phone camera has. I take my pick of the two girls on offer – a dark-haired girl with a pretty face and a huge but shapely butt. She doesn't pay any attention to the box as we get undressed, but I can't help looking at it. I can see why there are so few men that can perform as porn actors. Knowing there's a camera pointed at your willy is a bit of a distraction.

Everything is going fine, and I'm really getting in to banging the slapper from behind, when the iPhone in my special box starts to fucking ring. It wouldn't be so bad if I'd left a bag or something next to the box, but I haven't, so it's pretty obvious that the phone is in the box. Things get even worse when the vibration from the ringing phone topples the box. The hooker turns round and then breaks off screwing me to go and pick up the box. Maybe she's clocked the word 'Fragile' on it and thinks she's doing me a favour. In the process of righting the box she clocks the little hole in it, and the lens visible behind. The next thing I know she's out of the room, screaming for the maid. Fucking hell. A couple of moments later the pair of them enter the room. The hooker has pulled some pants on, but is still topless.

'Are you police?' the maid demands to know. 'Why are you filming?'

'I'm not police,' I reply, and immediately realise my mistake. If I'm not police I'm just a pervert, and fair game.

The maid lunges at me. She's quite stocky. Probably a dyke who gets off on seeing naked whores all day. Without thinking about what I'm doing I pick up a desk fan sitting on a bedside table and clobber her over the head with it. Hard. The cage that contains its blades breaks open on impact, and I can see immediately that I've drawn blood. The maid goes down clutching her face, whilst the hooker hollers like a wounded animal. Suddenly I think about a huge pimp who might be dozing upstairs; a pimp who might get woken up by all this racket and come down and attack me. I quickly pull my boxers on, scoop up the rest of my clothes, my shoes and the FedEx box, and flee. I run out of the building with nothing more than underwear on, leaving the front door open. A woman pushing a pram is walking down the street towards me, and mindful of how ridiculous I look I shout 'Fire!' and carry on running.

When I get home Lucy immediately notices that I seem flustered. Ironic that I've come home after murdering and been more relaxed than I am on this occasion. 'Everything okay, honey?' she asks me. She's ironing clothes in the hall-way, the picture of domestic contentment and industry.

'Yes. Yes, I'm fine. Why do you ask?'

She puts the iron down and looks at me directly. 'You just look like you've had a big shock, that's all.'

'No, no. The only shock I had today was finding I didn't have to queue at the bank.'

Just for a moment, I catch a glimpse of what it would be like to have a normal relationship with this woman. I don't really understand emotions, but I can sort of get them intel-lectually. I understand that my wife could make a man very happy.

Later that night I dream again of murder, of hidden bodies, and the fear of discovery. I wake from the dream and have a strange moment of knowing I'm not respon-sible for the dream corpses, but am responsible for two real ones. Fact and fiction, life and death, it's all becoming pretty blurred.

A couple of days later I'm back at the convent, picking up two girls for delivery to a Turk who runs brothels in North London. 'Maria and Elena,' I say when asked which two girls I'm collecting by a Sister Veronica. 'I rang yesterday to let someone know, so hopefully they're packed and ready.'

'I hope so too,' the woman says frostily. 'Come through.' I'm left to sit in a lounge with tatty carpets and paintings on the walls depicting rural scenes of Tuscany. After about fifteen minutes Sister Veronica returns with Maria and Elena, the latter pair carrying heavy bags. 'Well, the girls are ready to join you,' Sister Veronica says.

'Thanks,' I reply. Turning to the girls, I say, 'Ready to begin your new lives in England?'

I don't think they understand me, but one of them mumbles something.

As we're walking towards the main door, the convent's Mother Superior rushes up to us. 'You're off girls?' she chirps.

'Yes, we're off,' I reply for the women. 'Thanks again for your help. I'll no doubt see you again shortly.'

'Our pleasure. I have a little something for the girls.' She hands each girl a small Bible. 'Something to read to help you with your English,' she explains. 'And with life.'

'Thankyou,' one of the girls says. 'I will read.' I bet you'll read, I think to myself. You'll be on your knees giving blowjobs, then you'll be on your knees praying for deliverance and reading that little book for any scrap of encouragement it might offer you.

Two hours later we arrive in Turnpike Lane, and I park up outside a unit on an industrial estate. 'Ezmet & Sons, Industrial Ducting Manufacturers' a sign above large shutter doors reads.

'This is where the man that owns the farm you will be working on works,' I explain, turning around to look at the girls. 'Wait here,' I say, before getting out of the car.

I knock on the door to the right of the large shutter and quickly encounter a short, fat man in his mid-fifties. 'Mr Ezmet?' I ask.

'Yes,' he says, looking over my shoulder at my car. 'You have them?'

I nod.

Ezmet walks over to the car and looks inside. He gives the girls a wave. 'No deformities?' he asks.

'No.'

'They're pretty enough. Not fat. You have their passports?'

By way of answer I pass them over to him. He flicks through each briefly, before sticking them in his back pocket.

'We said three grand each, didn't we?' the Turk says.

'No, it was four. Definitely four.'

'They're not bad, but one has a grumpy face. Six and a half.'

'You can have both for seven and a half,' I reply.

'Six two hundred?'

I shake my head.

'Okay, seven and a half. Let's do the money inside.'

We walk into the industrial unit, where a scene of hammered metal and sweaty activity greets us. There's an office off to the right, and we enter this. Ezmet reaches into the top draw of his desk and brings out a petty cash box. Opening it, he counts a hundred and fifty fifty-pound notes and hands them over to me. I verify all the money is there, then say, 'Good stuff. Thanks.'

We walk back out to the car. 'Where are you going to keep them?' I ask. 'In there?'

'Just for a couple of hours,' the man replies. 'Then I take them to their new home.' He laughs hoarsely.

I open one of the car's back doors and say, 'Okay, you can get out girls.' When they're both out of the car I say, 'This is your new boss, Mr Ezmet. He'll look after you now.'

As I'm driving home I consider my next murder victim. How I'll choose them, what they'll be like. It occurs to me that I seem to have been favouring the female sex up to now, and realise that there may be some unfairness here. I'm an equal opportunities killer, and when the story of my crimes is written I don't want people to fixate on my hatred of women. I love women. Fucking them, anyway.

A week later I'm about to execute the first step in a two-step plan that will see me force someone to kill someone else. For some time I've become fixated with the idea of putting someone in a position where they have no choice but to murder an innocent person, and on a blustery Wednesday morning I'm parked on a road that borders Victoria Park, waiting for one of the many dog walkers that use the area to exercise their canines. I've hired a Ford Transit van, which will enable me to transport my victim without fear of them escaping or attracting other motorists' attention, and I have the use of a remote seaside house that was left to me by an uncle in which to stage the event I have planned. My uncle was a right-wing nut and survivalist, who spent most of the Sixties and Seventies convinced that a nuke was about to be dropped on his head. This lead him to purchase a property in Essex which met his criteria of being at least fifty miles from the nearest civilian or military target, in the grounds of which he built a nuclear bunker. The bunker was designed to keep radiation out, but it will also serve to keep prisoners in. The person I capture will be the first of two I hold in the bunker.

After waiting for about fifteen minutes, a dog walker appears. She's about fifty, a little on the chubby side, and her companion is a light-coloured terrier. She'll do, I think to myself.

I get out of the van and approach her. 'Hi there,' I say. 'You don't know the way to the A12 link road do you?'

I allow about three words to emerge from her mouth before taking the truncheon I've been hiding in my coat pocket out and cracking her on the head. She's clean out, and collapses on the ground. I know she could come to very quickly, so waste no time in grabbing her under the armpits and dragging her towards the van. Her dog follows me, barking excitedly. I put the woman down on the ground before opening the back doors. The dog licks her face, but the woman doesn't come to, and seconds later she's in the van. I drive off, then promptly bring the vehicle to a halt. I haven't checked to see whether my hostage has a mobile on her person. I get out and open the rear doors of the van. My prisoner is still out, and I quickly rifle her handbag, locating a smartphone. Smart phone; dumb criminal. It shocks me that such a simple error could have unravelled everything for me.

An hour and a half later I'm at the house. I know from the thumps I've heard from the back that my captive is now fully awake, so before opening the van's back door I pull out the gun I took from the old lady I murdered's home. Pulling the door open, I peer in with the gun held in front of me. The woman is sitting inside, and shields her eyes with a hand as the sunlight streams in. 'Get out.' I say. 'And don't try any funny business.' This sounds terribly clichéd to my ears, but I think you're allowed to come out with the odd corny line when you're holding a revolver.

She scrabbles to her feet and walks to the door, crouching. 'What are you doing with me? I don't know you do I?'

'All will be explained in good time,' I reply. 'You're not in any immediate danger. Now jump out of there and walk this way.' I point in the direction of the house with my revolver.

The bunker is situated about fifteen yards to the right of the house, its location indicated by a hinged slab of concrete with a D-shaped iron handle.

'Lie on the ground, please,' I instruct the woman. She duly sinks to her knees, then lies face down on the grass.

Keeping her under observation out of the corner of my eye I pull up on the heavy concrete hatch. Directly beneath it is a concrete-walled vertical shaft. Steel rungs spaced at regular intervals allow descent to the bottom.

'Alright, stand up.' I say to the woman. She obliges. 'I want you to climb down through this hatch. When you're down I'm coming in after you.'

She whimpers softly, but does what I ask of her. When she's down I follow suit, until we're standing together, cramped, at the bottom of the shaft. Directly in front of us is a heavy steel door, for which I have the key. Inserting key in lock, I turn clockwise. I meet nothing but resistance initially, but after jiggling the key around manage to turn the lock. Pushing the door inwards, we're met with a rush of stale air. As far as I'm aware this bunker hasn't been entered for over twenty years. Pulling a torch from my pocket, I shine its beam into the space in front of me. I can make out two single, wood-framed beds, a table and chair, and shelves occupying all of one wall, each stacked high with tinned food.

'Alright, in you go,' I say.

'You're just going to leave me here?'

'No, I'll be back very shortly. I'm just off to get water and food for you. And a bucket.'

'Why have you brought me here?' the woman asks. 'Why me?'

'You'll find out in due course. Now get in.'

A few moments later I'm pushing open the front door of the house. It's a familiar hallway I'm confronted with – up until a few years ago my family and I used to stay at the house on a regular basis. Even so, it's got that cold, musty smell of an unloved property. There's no food in the house – despite what I've just told the woman – but I will be able to get my hands on a bucket and fill it with water. I wander about the building for a few minutes, as if looking for something I don't know I've lost, before snapping out of my reverie and heading towards the kitchen. Five minutes later I'm back at the bunker with a bucket full of water. The woman will have to decide between drinking from and pissing in the bucket.

As I drive away from the property a short time later I realise I've really only got about a week to find the second victim in this experiment and return.

# Chapter Seven

The following day I see Joey and Courtney. Joey's in an ebullient mood, full of humour and well-concealed menace, as he talks about how pleased he is with the first shipment of girls. 'This is going to be a great earner,' he informs us matter-of-factly. 'The guys in New Jersey will really be liking this when I tell them how well it's going.'

'I thought the Mafia wasn't that into prostitution,' Courtney says. 'You're all Catholics and stuff. Family values.'

'Like fuck,' Joey retorts. 'If it made money they'd sell babies bombs.'

I laugh.

'In fact,' Joey goes on, 'I'm wondering if we can't really be pioneers in this whole trafficking/prostitution thing. Maybe there are some new things we could look at.'

'Like what?' I ask.

'Well, everyone's got a different thing they like, right?'

'Whatdya mean "different thing"?' Courtney says.

'You know, some people like fat ladies, some people like young ladies, some people like *men* that look like ladies ...'

'You're talking about catering to people's fetishes?' I ask.

'Yeah. Yeah, exactly. All the other traffickers are doing the same thing, bringing young, attractive women to this country. Let's be more imaginative. Plus we won't have to pay as much for some of the freaks that might appeal to people.'

'Yeah, but we probably wouldn't get as much for them when we sell them on, either.' I say.

'Maybe, maybe not,' Joey says. 'The point is, no-one else is doing it …'

Joey is interrupted by the sound of scraping furniture coming from the other side of the room, a sound that makes Courtney and I jump.

'What was that?' Courtney wants to know.

'Oh, just a friendly poltergeist,' Joey replies. 'Been here since I moved in.'

'You shitting me?' Courtney asks.

'No. It's absolutely real. I call it Ed. Ed's been pretty quiet recently, but when the mood takes him he can really cause problems. You wouldn't believe how much I spend on cups and plates every year.'

I study Joey closely, looking for the grin that will reveal he's joking. It doesn't come.

'You're a priest,' Courtney says, 'why don't you exorcise this critter? I'm not coming here no more if there's some ghost hangin' around.'

'Ohhh, the big gangster, scared of a little poltergeist,' Joey taunts affectionately. 'Bullets don't scare him, but a bit of scraping furniture and he pisses his pants.'

'I grew up with all that shit,' Courtney protests. 'I believe in it, man.'

'You're looking very white,' Joey says to the Jamaican. 'Maybe that's how Michael Jackson should have lightened his skin colour. Should have scared himself pale.'

Courtney walks over to the table that has just moved and inspects it closely. He runs his hand over the top, pushes it slightly, knocks on one of the legs.

'It's just a normal table,' Joey comments. 'No ropes, no string, no tricks.'

'Fuck,' Courtney swears. 'Can we go to the kitchen? I don't wanna stay in this room anymore.'

'That won't help you,' Joey says. 'Poltergeist moves all over this house. Ed goes where he wants.'

'Well give me a large Scotch then,' Courtney demands.

'I'll have one as well,' I say, not because I'm scared but because a Scotch cheers you up at any time of day.

'Scotches all round,' Joey says, heading over to his drinks cabinet.

'Pour one for the ghost as well,' Courtney says. 'It might keep him quiet.'

'Alright,' Joey says. 'Real voodoo stuff this is.' After he's tipped a generous measure out for each of the three humans he fills a fourth glass right to the top and places it on the table that had moved earlier. 'If I wake up tomorrow and that glass is empty I'll know I've got an alcoholic poltergeist on my hands,' Joey cracks.

'A spirit who likes spirits,' I come back with.

After this the mood lightens, and we get back to discussing business. 'I've got a good dealer network ready to take all that coke we're going to be gettin' our hands on soon,' Courtney informs us. 'Serious guys who can move a lot of product. And keep their mouths shut.'

'Good. Very good,' Joey says, nodding sagely. 'The mouths shut bit is the most important part.'

'These guys killed off all the idiots who were trying to sell the white stuff in their areas. Only the big boys left.'

'When did they get rid of them?' Joey wants to know. 'I didn't read nothing in the papers.'

'That's because they did their killings without a fuss. Nobody knows they're gone, apart from family and friends, and they know better than to talk. Police don't know about the bodies.'

'The only bodies I've heard about recently are the ones due to that serial killer that's been in the news,' Joey says.

'The guy seems to have a big hate for women,' Courtney says.

'All serial killers do,' Joey responds. 'Or most of them anyways. You ever heard of a serial killer that killed old men?'

I want to say something, tell this pair of pricks that

they've got it all wrong about me hating women, or hating them more than men.

'They kill instead of having sex,' Courtney says. 'That's how they get their rocks off. And 'cos most serial killers are men, they want to get their rocks off by killing a woman.'

'What about that Dahmer guy?' Joey says. 'He's one that *did* only kill men.'

'He was a fag,' I say. I didn't want to join this conversation, but my comment just slips out.

'Was he?' Joey says.

'Yeah, a fag and totally wacko. He wanted sex slaves – he wasn't that into killing people apparently. He killed mainly to stop his victims going to the cops. He tried to make a zombie out of one guy by drugging him up, then drilling a hole in his skull and squirting acid into his brain. Didn't work, so the guy had to die.'

'You seem to know a lot about this,' Courtney comments.

'I've got cable. Plenty of crappy crime shows on all the time.'

'Whatever ...' Courtney says.

I decide to change the subject. 'Hey guys, I stitched this guy up pretty badly twenty years ago. He went to jail because of a stunt I pulled. He's out now, and I'm worried he might try something stupid. Either of you able to help me sort him out if I decide that's what's needed? Or can you recommend someone who can step in and take care of him?'

'What happened?' Joey wants to know.

I explain briefly, drawing a shocked reaction from Courtney: 'I always told you we had to watch this one, Joey,' he says. 'Got crime in his veins.'

'I'm impressed,' Joey says. 'And you're right to be worried. Only problem for you is that if a hair on this guy's head is touched, police are going to come straight to you for answers.'

'That's why I'm asking for help. I can't pull the trigger or draw the knife.'

'He been around hassling you?' Courtney wants to know.

'No, but I know him well enough to know he isn't going to let this one lie.'

'If he's been locked up for twenty years he probably doesn't want to go back to jail anytime soon,' Joey says. 'Keep your eyes peeled. Carry a knife at all times. If he shows up in person, that'll be the time to act. I wouldn't recommend doing a pre-emptive strike, though. We've got too much going on at the moment to want to draw heat unnecessarily.'

'I can lend you a piece if you want,' Courtney offers. 'You haven't got one, have you?'

'No,' I lie.

'I'll drop one round to you tomorrow. I've got a nine you can have.'

\* \* \*

The next day I wait until I've taken delivery of the gun, then head out to finish off my hostage plan. Ever mindful that I've been picking on women up to now, I decide to kidnap a man. I drive around for about half an hour looking for a victim, but then realise that this is the wrong tactic. I park the van on a street that has a construction site on one side and an industrial estate on the other. Fewer prying eyes to witness what I'm about to do. I go to the rear of the van and open its doors, then sit inside the vehicle waiting for the right person to walk by. The first pedestrian to pass is a teenager and I decide to give him a break. The second person to appear is a stocky builder in his late twenties. He gets a pass on account of the fact that he'd likely break my neck if I tried anything with him. The builder is followed by a woman pushing a pram. Totally unsuitable. Finally, a thin man in his forties approaches. I jump out of the van, quickly scan my surroundings to ensure there isn't anyone else about, then prepare for action. When the man draws level with the van I say, 'Hey there, you wouldn't mind helping me to get this box out of the van?'

The man stops and looks at me for a few seconds, blinking rapidly, before saying, 'Yes, alright.'

'It's just in here,' I say. I move behind the man, and when he's right by the vehicle, I quickly reach into my pocket, pull out the gun Courtney has lent me, and pistol whip him. The open doors of the van shield me from anyone apart from someone bearing up from behind. The man isn't knocked unconscious with this single blow. He emits a muffled shriek, and tries to turn around. I raise the gun and bring it down for a second time on the man's skull, this time with much more force. This follow-up blow achieves its purpose; the man slumps against the van. I grab his jacket by the shoulders and force him into the vehicle. As soon as his feet are fully inside, I jump in and grab his mobile from his trouser pocket, then jump back out and slam the doors shut. I quickly get into the cab.

Nearing my destination I catch a whiff of smoke, and wonder if the house is on fire. Rounding a bend in the road I see the property through a stand of trees, and am pleased to note that flames aren't engulfing it. I park the van right by the shelter hatch, and walk round to the rear. Gun in one hand, I use the other to unlock the doors. I open them and quickly step back, holding the revolver in both hands. My new hostage is lying down, but raises his head as light streams into the vehicle. He's been totally quiet on the drive down, and I begin to wonder if I've caught the most passive man in England. 'You,' I shout. 'Get out of the van.'

The man gets to his knees, then feet, and stooping, walks to the rear of the van. After looking around hesitantly for a few moments, he jumps onto the grass. I see that he has vomited down his front. Fright, or carsickness? I wonder. His face is a shade of green.

Still the man says nothing, and I begin to wonder whether being taking hostage is a weekly occurrence for him. 'Over to that thing that looks like a man-hole cover,' I command, waving my gun in the direction I want him to walk. 'Now lift it up, using the handle.' The man does as instructed. 'Okay, I want you to climb down the rungs until you get to the bottom.' I say. 'I'll be following you down, and I won't be leaving the gun behind.'

When my captive has reached the bottom of the shaft I throw the keys to the door down after him. 'I want you to unlock that door,' I instruct him. 'Open it up and enter the bomb shelter, then stand against the wall opposite the door. Get the woman who's in there to do the same. Don't try anything clever, because it won't work.'

My captive complies wordlessly. Is he mute? I wonder. When he has entered the shelter I begin my descent. I enter the room to see a truly wretched pair of prisoners. The woman is sat with her back against the wall. She looks like she's lost about half her body weight. The man is standing, looking at his feet as if he's expecting a stern reprimand. The room smells of piss.

'What do you want with me?' the woman asks. 'I have a family. They're going to be worried sick about me.'

'I have a little game I'd like you both to take part in,' I explain. 'Do you like games?'

The woman looks at me blankly.

'You,' I say, turning my attention to the man. 'I haven't heard a peep out of you since I picked you up. Don't you have a tongue?'

'I don't see how talking is going to help my predicament,' the man replies, revealing a Yorkshire accent. 'What will happen will happen.'

'True. And I admire your philosophical approach. Some things we just don't have any control over.'

'Will you let me go now?' the woman asks. 'I can give you money if that's what you want.'

'I have a game we're going to play,' I explain. 'A game which will lead to freedom for one of you. This is how it works. I'm going to give each of you a revolver, though only one will be loaded. You're each to take aim at the other and fire. One of you will kill the other, leaving one of you to go free. If you refuse to play, I'll shoot both of you. Now, how does that strike you?'

The woman breaks down and sobs. 'Please, please let us both go! Or if you won't do that, just shoot me.'

'What about your family?' I ask. 'There's a fifty-fifty chance you could be back with them tonight. Given that not playing the game will result in you both dying, wouldn't it make sense to have a go? You're going to condemn an extra person to death if you don't.'

'How do we know you will let the survivor go?' the man asks.

'You don't. But that makes participation all the more essential. You have nothing to lose.'

'I can't do this!' the woman wails. 'Just shoot me, and let him go.'

'That's not an option,' I state calmly, deriving an almost sexual pleasure from the woman's mental torture.

With a suddenness and energy belying her age, the woman makes a sudden dash for the door behind me. I react pretty swiftly myself, turning and catching her by her top just before her hands reach the door. She struggles violently, and quickly I realise there is only one way to restrain her. I whack the woman with my gun, catching her firmly just above her left ear. She responds as I hoped she would, crumpling to the floor. I grab one of her ankles and drag her back to where her fellow hostage is standing, the latter's face a mask of terror.

'I hope what you've just seen has provided you with evidence that you won't be getting out of here without my consent,' I say, looking at my one conscious hostage.

The man nods almost imperceptibly. He appears to have given up any hope of surviving the hour, and looks extremely unlikely to try anything adventurous.

I suddenly feel overcome by boredom, and consider just shooting the pair of them so I can get on with my day. The man's lack of a reaction to his predicament is deeply disappointing. If the fear of death doesn't motivate him, what does?

Instead of doing this, however, I opt to let them stew for a couple of hours. Maybe they'll fuck each other, and that will give them the lift they need to play.

'I think you two need some time to ponder your next move,' I tell the man, backing towards the door. 'I'm going to leave you two alone for a while, and I want you to think long and hard about whether you really think two deaths are better than one. Talk about it, discuss fully, and I expect to see a change of attitude when I return.' With this, I step out of the bunker, slamming its door firmly shut.

I walk towards the house after reaching ground level. The weather has changed since I ventured underground. Strong winds accelerate black clouds across the sky, and bend grass and tree branches. A couple of large raindrops fall on me before I reach the front door. The house is situated in an isolated spot about half a mile from the nearest dwelling, accessed by a rough track that runs from the nearest tarmacked road. Stands of trees shield the house on three sides; on the other side slopping grassland leads to a coarse-pebbled beach some two hundred yards away.

After entering the house I feel suddenly weary, and decide to get some sleep. Climbing the stairs I make straight for the room that used to be mine as a child. My uncle never married, and I was a regular visitor as a kid. As I'm nestling under the covers I see the room's bookcase still holds sev-eral of the books I used to read as a ten year old. It occurs to me that my life has turned out very differently to how I imagined as a kid of nine or ten. I'm married – that much is as anticipated – but instead of being an astronaut or police-man I am a serial killer. Seconds after putting my head on the pillow I fall asleep.

I awake an hour or so later, refreshed and ready to see my hostages.

When I enter the room containing my prisoners they're both awake, sitting next to each other with their backs against the wall. 'So,' I say, 'are we ready to play?'

'We have a suggestion,' the woman says. 'What you're asking us to do means that one of us will live for no reason other than blind luck. Why don't you just toss a coin and decide on that basis which one of us lives and which one of us dies?'

The man nods his agreement.

'Ah,' I reply. 'But that isn't how this game works. You see, I want you both to be taking an active part in it. If I just wanted to kill someone on the basis of a coin toss, what would the point have been in bringing you both here? You see, I'm invested in you both now. No, the game is played according to the rules as outlined.'

'We're not going to play,' the man says. 'We'd rather both die.'

'So you'd find it preferable to be responsible for two deaths rather than one? Think about the life whichever one of you is released will have. Another twenty years with your family. Twenty years you could spend doing good, as I'm sure whichever of you survives today will have their outlook on life transformed.'

'Twenty years of guilt at having killed another person,' the man replies. 'You must be joking.'

'Well I'm glad you've found your tongue,' I say. 'What you need to find now is your courage.'

'We're not going to change our minds,' the woman says.

'Do either of you have families?' I ask.

Both the man and woman nod.

'Hold your hands out. Both of you.'

The pair do as I ask, and I immediately see that both are married.

'Throw me your wallets,' I say.

'If this is just about money we can get you that,' the woman says. 'I'm quite well off.'

'Nothing to do with money. Now come on, wallets.'

The man reaches into his trouser pocket and retrieves a black leather wallet that has been deformed to match the shape of his thigh. He throws it to my feet. The woman reaches into her handbag and pulls out a large brown purse, which she lobs in my direction. I retrieve driving licences from purse and wallet, and place them on the ground in front of me.

'I'm not interested in whether either of you can drive,' I say, 'but I am interested in where you both live – information I now have. You see, chances are that your spouses and kids live at these addresses. Now, are we going to play the game, or do you want me to shoot the pair of you, and then go and shoot everyone that lives under your respective roofs? Don't think for a second that I'm bluffing. I assure you that I'm not.'

The man and woman look at each other.

'Are you going to stick to your silly principles,' I say, 'or save the lives of what, maybe four or five people?'

'He's bluffing,' the woman says.

'You really want to take that risk?' I ask. 'What would your kids think if they could see you gambling with their lives right now?'

The man looks more uncertain. I can see my words are working on him.

'Have another chat,' I say. 'I'm going up for some fresh air. Something one of you could be experiencing in a couple of hours if you make the right decision.'

I lock my prisoners up and head up to ground level. The air is wonderfully fresh as I stand looking out to sea. I unzip and stand urinating, enjoying the freedom of being able to take a piss outdoors without fear of being seen. I sit on a tree stump and rest awhile. I figure on giving them half an hour or so to change their minds.

'So, what's it to be?' I ask after returning to the bunker.

'We'll play,' the man says.

'Good choice! I'm genuinely surprised. I thought we were going to end up doing this the hard way. Right, first up a little task for you both.' I drop an envelope in front of them, followed by a felt tip pen. 'Before we get started I want you each to draw a toothbrush on the back of that letter. Try and make it look like the toothbrush you actually use.'

'Whatever for?' the woman asks.

'Never you mind. Just humour me.'

The woman draws a toothbrush in profile, then holds it up for me to inspect.

'Very good. Now buddy here's turn.'

The woman passes envelope and pen to the man, who duly obliges.

'Great, now I want you each to sign next to your drawing.'

The pair comply with my request.

'Good stuff. Pass it back.' The man slides the envelope over to me and I put it in a back pocket.

'Right, let's get on with things. I'll just go and get the other gun.'

I go to the van and retrieve the second revolver. I check that one gun is unloaded, and that the other has a single bullet, chamber rotated ready to fire. Returning to the bunker I put the guns on the floor and say, 'Ladies first. Which gun do you want to use?'

The woman takes the revolver nearest her. I slide the other firearm over to the man. 'Okay, so you know the drill? Get nice and close to each other as I'm guessing neither of you is a good shot. Aim for torsos – less chance of missing that way.' I move back towards the door. The pair each pick up their gun, and, holding them with hands that are trembling, raise them to chest level. 'I'm going to count you down,' I say. 'Backwards from five. Ready? Five, four, three, two, one!'

As I shout 'one', both the man and woman swing towards me and pull triggers. I have barely enough time to react, ducking just in time. The sound of the gunshot in such a confined s pace i s d eafening. I r un a t t he w oman, w ho i s standing nearest me, and wrestle the handgun from her hands. I load it quickly with bullets from my pocket, take aim and shoot, striking her in the chest. Without waiting for her to fall I swing and shoot at the man. I catch him in the arm with the first bullet, necessitating a more accurate shot that hits him in the upper chest. He collapses. I take a step back. Both of my hostages are on the ground now. I move over to the woman who is lying face down and put a bullet in the back of the head, then cross to where the man is lying and put a bullet in his forehead. Six shots in the space of a minute leaves me wondering if I've ruptured an eardrum. The smell of cordite is overpowering.

I'm fucking mad that they pulled the stunt they did, but accept I would probably have done exactly the same thing. I go to the house and retrieve black plastic bin bags and tape. Back in the bunker I slide two bags onto each body, one going over their feet, the other going over their heads. The tape secures the bags. I can now get rid of the bodies without dripping blood all over the van. It takes a lot of effort to haul each body up to ground level, but after fifteen minutes I've done so. I slide both bodies into the back of the van and slam the door shut.

A storm breaks shortly after I set off. Rain batters the van and winds buffet it whenever the winding road I'm follow-ing loses its shelter. The weather matches my mood. I feel like breaking over someone. The road straightens out for a lengthy section, and in the distance I see what looks like a car accident. It seems a tree has come down on the road, landing right in the path of an oncoming vehicle. Behind the car that has smashed into the tree is another car, but I can't tell from this distance whether it has collided with the car in front, or has stopped to help.

As I get nearer I can see that the occupant of the second vehicle – a tall man wearing a check shirt – has stopped to aid the leading driver. He turns to wave at me when he hears me approach. I'm going to stop alright, but not to lend assistance. I halt my car, and, fumbling under my seat for the knife that is hidden there, jump out and run at the Good Samaritan. The look on his face is a mixture of surprise and fear as I lunge at him with the blade. 'There's a ...' he begins, but steel pierces flesh before he can finish his sentence. My first thrust hits him in the upper arm. It's by no means a fatal blow, but it disorientates him sufficiently to allow my second strike to be more precise, aimed at his heart. Although by no means an expert on human anatomy, I think I'm on target. I hit home hard, twisting the knife's blade as I remove it. The man puts a hand to his chest and staggers forward, mouthing silent protests. He slumps to the ground, resting his back against the body of the crashed vehicle.

I immediately turn my attention to the occupant of the crashed vehicle, a blonde man in his thirties. The car's crash impact has pushed its steering wheel up against the man's torso. He looks trapped, but his eyes are open and he's obviously still alive. I slap his face, and he reacts by grimacing. I don't want to risk having another motorist come along and spot me, so I act quickly. I reach through the smashed glass of the driver's window with my right hand, and slice the throat of the injured man. Blood spurts from his severed jugular. Not quite as dramatically as I had hoped, but then I guess he may have already lost a fair bit of blood.

I don't have time to watch the man fade away; getting spotted would totally ruin my day. Nor do I have spare snooker balls to plant, but I'm not sure I would leave them even if I did. Too close to the house, which is in my name. I race back to the van, start its engine, and manoeuvre around the two stationary vehicles and fallen tree.

I travel another twenty miles before turning the van off onto a private road that leads to a farmhouse. I follow the dirt track for a couple of hundred yards, before steering the van into the field of barley that borders the road on the right. The suspension just about copes with the rough ground; the crop folds under the front bumper of the van with ease. When I'm far enough into the field to not be visible from the road I stop the vehicle and get out. I open the rear doors of the van and pull the plastic-wrapped corpses out, letting them fall unceremoniously onto the ground. I break open the plastic on both bodies around the head area, then pull out the two snooker balls in my right pocket, one green and one brown. I decide to pop the brown ball into the woman's mouth, as it matches her outfit. The green ball goes in the man's mouth. He isn't wearing green, but looked a bit green when I pulled him out of the van at the house.

# Chapter Eight

Two days after the bunker killing Joey, Courtney and myself head off to Heathrow to pick up the first group of Haitian orphans. We've hired a van that seats twelve – it will be a squeeze, but we should just about get everyone in. There are three kids scheduled to stay with families from my church, and a further four going to families from Joey's; Courtney's going to put his cousin and another Sister along for the trip up at his place. I feel nervous as we park the van on the second floor of a multi-storey at Terminal Three. I accept that smuggling coke using orphans from a disaster zone is a pretty novel and low-risk way of doing it, but even so … cocaine – it's heavy shit if you get caught with this stuff.

The orphans' flight is due to land at ten past eleven, and by the time we get into the terminal the screens are already displaying the flight as landed. We gather by the arrivals exit and wait for nine black faces.

The plan is to take all the kids for a meal at a Pizza Express in Hackney straight from the airport. While the kids are eating Joey's going to drive the van and suitcases back to his place and remove the drugs. Courtney's Haiti contact reckons the coke can be removed without wrecking the cases. If there are any that are too badly damaged they will be replaced prior to the return flight.

'Where are these fucking kids?' Joey says after we've been waiting for about twenty minutes. 'They should be out by now. Courtney, why don't you ring your cousin and find out how long they're gonna be?'

'I'm not ringing no-one,' Courtney replies. 'What if they've been caught and they're with customs people right now?'

Joey's silence indicates he cedes this point.

'Maybe we should split up,' I say. 'If they get nabbed they'll be trying to find out who was waiting for them.'

'Hey, who's doing the smuggling here?' Joey says. 'We're just priests doing a good turn. Nothing anyone can pin on us.'

Twenty minutes later, when there's still no sign of the kids, even Joey's beginning to get nervous. Finally, just as we're about to leave the terminal, a black woman with a trolley piled high with luggage appears, followed by seven skinny black kids. Another black lady dressed in a habit brings up the rear. She also is pushing a trolley, also heavily laden with bags.

'That's them,' Courtney says, moving forward to greet his cousin.

After hugs and hellos we make our way to the van. We seem to be attracting quite a bit of attention from others in the terminal as we walk. Two men in their clerical garb, two nuns in habits, seven excited kids and a fat Rasta. The luggage falls off both trolleys several times before we get to the van. Eventually bags are stowed, everyone's on board and we set off. Courtney, Joey and myself occupy the front seat, Joey at the wheel. During the drive into London Courtney talks with his cousin, using a combination of English and some sort of pidgin French. All I catch is that the flight went well, but the cousin is tired and looking forward to sleeping. The kids seem to find the drive enjoyable, pointing and shouting excitedly as they're treated to the sight of roads without pot-holes, traffic lights that work and shops that haven't been looted. The volume of their voices rises steadily, until, arriving at the Pizza Express restaurant, I find I have a throbbing headache.

We all hop out of the van, apart from Joey. I pray for strength as our throng enter the restaurant. A startled looking waitress greets us. 'Table for eleven,' Courtney says.

The meal is the chaotic affair you'd expect. The kids eat their pizza as if it's the first meal they've had in a year. A fight breaks out at one point over a piece of garlic bread with a fork used to settle the argument. A girl who obviously isn't used to sitting on chairs falls off hers and brings her plate of food to the floor in the process. Courtney and I exchange glances at one point. I'm not sure what he's thinking, but I'm thinking 'there'd better be a big payday in this for me'.

After what seems like two hours but is more likely forty-five minutes, Joey enters the restaurant. He has a broad smile on his face. 'How we doing people?' he asks the table.

Courtney stands up, saying, 'Take my seat, Joey. Going outside for a cigarette.'

Finally everyone's finished eating and fighting and the bill has been paid. We shepherd our charges to the van. I see Courtney pulling his cousin aside for a private chat and wonder what they're discussing. We drive to Joey's church where those offering accommodation have agreed to meet their new houseguests. By seven pm everyone's been taken to their new residences, including Courtney's cousin and her fellow nun. Joey walks over to where I'm standing in the car park with a hand raised, palm out. I hi-five him. 'Good work,' he says.

'Yeah?'

'Very much "yeah". Each case had about a key. Just shy of seven keys, baby. Time you thought about buying some new clothes, maybe upgrading your wheels …'

I drop in on Joey and Courtney two days later. Courtney opens Joey's front door, and I'm surprised to see he's sporting a black eye. That's not the best way of putting it, I guess, because strictly speaking he always has *two* black eyes. He's obviously been punched in the eye, however – that or collided with a fist-shaped object.

'What happened to you?' I ask as I cross the threshold.

'I was going to ask you the same question.'

'Me? I think I'd remember if I'd punched you ...'

We walk in to the living room, where Joey is staring intently at his mobile phone. He's so engrossed he doesn't even look up to acknowledge my arrival.

'I stopped at your place just now – to see if you needed a lift,' Courtney starts to explain. 'There was a man lookin' in your big downstairs window ...'

'What ...?'

'When he saw me he turn round real quick. Looked guilty as hell, so I asked him what he was doing.'

'A burglar?'

'He didn't look or sound like one. Sounded and looked a bit look you. But he looked like he knew I knew he shouldn't be there. I tell him to get lost and he hit me.'

Knowing that Courtney wasn't the sort of guy most men would dare to touch, I can't keep the surprise out of my voice: 'He *hit* you?'

'He hit me. I knocked him down. Then I left 'cos I knew he was going to stay down and I didn't want no police trouble.'

'You didn't kill him?'

'I don't think so.'

'Shit.' I fumble for my phone and dial the home number. 'Darling? Everything okay?'

'Sort of. Except a man's been found in the front garden. I just got back from Christine's.'

'Found?' What's he doing there?'

'He seems to have been injured, but how I've absolutely no idea. There's an ambulance here now, and I think they're going to take him to hospital.'

'What does the man look like?'

'What does he look like?' Lucy snorts a brief laugh. 'Why should you care what he looks like? You can't possibly know him.'

'Tell me what he looks like. He might be one of the alcoholics I drop in on at that halfway house.'

'I don't think he's an alcoholic. Too smartly dressed. He's quite a handsome chap, actually – or would be without the bruising. About your age ...'

I finish up the conversation, then turn to Courtney: 'I think you slapped someone who very much wants to slap me – or worse.'

'Huh?'

'Guy I was telling you about who did a long stretch thanks to me. He's out now, and probably wants to get even.'

Joey walks towards us. 'Did I hear the words "get even"? One of the most beautiful phrases in the English language.'

'Just that guy I was telling you about who doesn't wish me well,' I explain.

'Only one way to deal with that sort of thing,' Courtney explains. 'You gotta get to him before he gets to you.'

'Don't know where he lives ...'

'Then you'd better find out. He sure as hell knows where *you* live.'

'I'm really impressed at the way you fixed that guy,' Joey says. 'Not the sort of thing you college boys normally get up to.'

'They don't normally get involved in bitch-smuggling, either,' Courtney chips in. 'But our guy is different.' I'm given a playful punch on the arm by Courtney to punctuate this remark.

I grin. It's true. I'm *very* different.

We exhaust the subject of Jake and move on to discuss our Haitian mini-mules. 'All going well so far,' Joey informs us. As Joey fronted almost all the money for the deal he's taken charge of the whole operation. 'One kid took a dump in the back garden of the house he's staying at, but apart from that everything's cool. Main thing is they got through. Should have most of the powder sold by next week. Kerching!'

'You reckon you can get some more kids over soon?' I ask Courtney.

'Should be cool,' the Jamaican says.

Conversation turns to whores. Joey has managed to source some 'exotic' Moldovan prostitutes, and he wonders which of us wants to take delivery of them the following day. 'We've got a one-legged one,' he explains, 'one, that's about thirty stone, and one that has three breasts ...'

'Bullshit!' Courtney exclaims. 'No woman was ever born with an extra titty!'

'This one was,' Joey says tetchily. 'I've got a photo of her.' He gets his phone out, and we're soon looking at a tri-titted lady, naked from the waist up. 'We should be able to get good money for her. I bet lots of men will pay top dollar to sleep with this freak.'

'You'd have to pay *me* top dollar to sleep with her,' Courtney says, a grimace on his face.

'Don't be such a snob,' I say. 'I don't think she looks too bad. Better three tits than one. *One* would freak me out.'

'None of yous are going to be sleeping with her,' Joey says, 'cos she's going to be busy sleeping with Johns, but Adam, as you seem to have more interest in her than Courtney, maybe you'd like to take care of her collection. Her and the other broads.'

'I don't mind. As long as you don't want it done on a Sunday.'

We move from talking about the details of the pick-up to discussing money. 'We haven't done too bad this last month,' Joey says, reaching into a holdall. 'One of these for each of you,' he continues, throwing Courtney and I a bundle of cash each. 'That's ten grand for you. If we keep on top of things I think it might be twenty grand next month.'

I look at the wad of notes I'm holding, and think about all the screws that have happened and are going to happen to pay for this money. I feel happy. It is fitting that I earn this way. Not only am I holding proper dirty money, it's also a lot of money. I'm holding over a third of my annual wage in my hands. At this rate, maybe I can soon move on from the Church. I'll be financially capable of doing so soon, I figure, though I would miss abusing my position in the way that I do.

Just then the sound of smashing glass makes us all jump.

'Fucking poltergeist!' Joey says, getting up as if he wants to physically confront it. 'If it had a body, I'd wring its neck,' he adds.

'Aren't you going to tidy that up?' Courtney asks, pointing at the broken remains of a coffee cup that are lying on the floor.

'No point,' Joey responds. 'Fucker'll break something else soon. Breaks things in threes, so I'll wait till he's finished.'

'How do you know it's a "he"?' Courtney wants to know.

'It's gotta be a "he". Female sprite wouldn't go round making such a mess. She'd want to live in a nice environment.'

'I don't think spirits necessarily confirm to normal gender stereotypes,' I say.

'What does that mean in English?' Courtney asks.

'Poltergeists are troubled spirits,' I say. 'They're not "normal", so you can't expect them to act normally.'

'Okay, let's stop talking about poltergeists,' Joey says. 'Stupid thing causes me enough aggravation without spending the whole day giving it our attention …'

The next day I drive to a shabby house in Maidstone where our three ladies are waiting for me. In a bag on the front passenger's seat is six thousand pounds in fifty pound notes, money given to me by Joey the day before to settle the transaction. I walk up a short pathway that divides an overgrown front lawn and knock on the door. After a couple of minutes a fat man wearing tracksuit bottoms and a stained vest opens up for me. He looks Eastern European; Georgian or Azerbaijani I guess.

'I'm Joey's friend,' I inform him, and by way of reply he opens the door fully. I follow the man into a living room that has stained carpet and worn sofas. 'I bring the girls,' he informs me. 'You have money?'

'I do.'

The man leaves the room, and I'm left alone for about ten minutes. I can hear the sound of voices coming from upstairs; the man talking harshly, softer replies from the women. Then I hear the sound of footsteps coming down the stairs, and four people walk into the room.

They are the motley assortment I've been primed to expect. They're all wearing jeans, so I can't tell which one has but a single leg. I figure I should be able to work it out by figuring out which one has three tits, as the fatty is obvious enough. One of the women has a very large chest, but I can't be sure whether it's because she has three boobs.

Ten minutes later we're on the road. The three women are in the back chattering away in whatever stupid language they have the misfortune of speaking. I turn the volume on the radio up – I'm tuned into a station that seems to play nothing but Eighties classics. My mind starts to wander: killings, the topic I'll choose for my next sermon, whether I prefer big butts or big tits … My thoughts are interrupted by an incongruous sight. There's a car approaching me, but on *my* side of the road. For about a second I find the arrangement of vehicles merely intriguing – *that's not where the car is meant to be.* Then the reality of what's about to happen grabs me, and I swerve wildly. Too late. The front of the van clips the front of the oncoming car, and suddenly we're spinning and sliding. With a crash the van collides with a low wall, and it's at this point I lose consciousness.

I have no idea how long I've been out for when I come to. Could be hours, but I'm guessing minutes or seconds. What I do know is that my ribs and head hurt like hell. I lift my head from the steering wheel and look up to see a smashed front windscreen. Turning around to check on the girls I'm horrified to see they're not in the vehicle. An open passenger door indicates how they exited. I can't open the door on my side as the van is wedged up against the wall it collided with. Wincing with pain I edge over to the front passenger door. With some difficulty I get it open, and jump down onto the road. Despite being mentally foggy, I'm aware that it's an offence to leave the scene of an accident. I need to find the girls. Joey and I have never exchanged angry words, but I've got a feeling that's going to change if his cargo goes missing, accident or not. As I'm scanning my surroundings an elderly man approaches. 'Are you alright, son?' he asks me. 'I've called an ambulance. You should sit down until they arrive.'

'Thankyou,' I reply. 'Tell me, you didn't see a number of women leave the vehicle? I had three passengers, and now they're gone.'

'No. I live over there.' The man points at a house across the road. 'I came out as soon as I heard the bang, but I didn't see anyone walk away.' The man wipes his nose with the sleeve of his shirt. 'They must have scarpered pretty quickly. Can't have been more than a minute after the crash that I first popped my head out the door.'

I sit down on the pavement, my back against a wall, and try and figure out what to do. I feel okay; I doubt I have any serious injuries. The question is whether to wait for the police and ambulance to turn up, or to start looking for the girls right away. I can't see the car I collided with, and can only assume the driver didn't bother stopping. I turn to the old man. 'You wouldn't mind waiting here for a second until the cops turn up, while I go and have a quick look for my passengers? I'm worried about them. They don't speak any English, and I guess they could be injured.'

'I can do that for you. Don't be long, though. I expect we'll hear sirens any second now.'

I walk in what I can only hope is the right direction. It's a pretty seedy part of town, all off-licences and kebab shops.

I pull out my mobile as I progress, debating whether to call Joey. It makes sense to – if he and Courtney turn up quickly enough the chances of recovering the girls will be that much higher. Fear of his anger holds me back, however. Another couple of minutes; they could be just ahead.

Five minutes later I spot the one I think is the one-legged girl. She's leaning against a streetlight as if drunk or exhausted after running a marathon. Approaching her, I put a hand on her shoulder and ask, 'You okay?' She jumps as if I've just given her an electric shock, and spins around. 'You okay?' I repeat. 'We had an accident.'

The woman looks dazed. She seems to be staring straight through me. I can see a small cut on her forehead, and wonder is she's suffering from concussion. 'Come with me,' I say, pulling her in the direction of the van. 'Do you know where your friends are?'

I don't get an answer to any of my questions, but the woman seems happy to be led. I decide to call Joey. At least I've recovered one of the women.

'You fucking did what?' Joey shouts a few moments later. I explain briefly what has happened, and give him my location. 'Give me half an hour,' he says, before hanging up.

When I get back to the van both the police and an ambulance are on the scene. I approach an officer who is standing beside the van, writing in a little notebook. 'I was involved in this accident,' I explain. 'Just went to look briefly for some passengers who wandered off after the crash.'

The cop waves one of the paramedics over, before asking, 'Is anyone seriously hurt?'

'We're okay, but there were two other women in the van and I haven't been able to locate them yet.'

'If they're able to walk they're probably not too badly injured,' the officer says. 'Let the paramedics take a look at you, then I'll take a statement.'

The girl and myself are checked over – we're both going to live – and then I give the police a statement. The cops ring the car rental company to arrange the removal of the van. Five minutes later the emergency services leave – I'm told to take the missing girls to hospital if they show up in a bad way. Shortly afterwards Joey and Courtney pull up, with the two missing girls sitting in the back seat of Joey's car.

'That was quick work,' I say, addressing Joey through his wound down window when he pulls to a halt.

'You was lucky,' he says. 'They were walking away along the route I took to get here. I spotted them 'cos they weren't walking straight.'

I glance at his passengers. 'Are they hurt?'

'Nah. One's got a bruise on her arm, but that's about it. Anyway, hop in. Your girl will have to sit on a lap.'

The next day I drop by Joey's to pick up some coke. 'Mr Cuthbert!' Joey says happily as he ushers me in. I'm pleased he's in a good mood. Seems the whorecrash of the day before is forgotten. 'What can I do you for, you limey prick?'

'Ten grams of your finest,' I say, throwing my coat over the armrest of a couch.

'You wouldn't be developing a habit, would you?' Joey asks, a smile on his face. 'You know the rules – we profit from it, other people fuck up on it.'

'No chance of that,' I reply. 'Pity the same can't be said for some of the call girls I've been hiring recently. I throw in a gram of your white gunpowder and the hour's half price. Seems most dealers cut their stuff to fuck.'

'That they will do,' Joey agrees. 'That they will do. Talking of coke, we've run into some trouble with our Haiti connection. Seems the Home Office are tightening up on visas for poor orphan kids.'

'Shit …' I'm aware how much we made from our first shipment.

'But fear not. Working on something else – could be even more lucrative. I'll let you know about it when it's been firmed up.'

Joey brings me a bag that looks like it contains more like a hundred grams of coke. 'This should keep you popular for a couple of weeks,' he says. 'Now I'm going to have to ask you to scoot. Little lady's going to be pressing the doorbell any second now.'

# Chapter Nine

The next day I decide it's probably time to sort out Jake. I have a feeling he won't go away, or forget about what I did to him, and I can't stand the thought that he might try to harm me at some point. It's just a distraction; one I can do without. I'm aware that killing him might risk getting myself onto the police radar, but I'm banking on my status as a vicar and thoroughness in not leaving an evidence trail to keep me safe.

My first task is to find out where he's living. A Google search turns up the phone number of the business I know his father owns, and soon I'm talking to Jake's old man, pretending to be a friend called Bob. 'Yeah, I used to visit Jake in prison every couple of months. Got back from a trip abroad a couple of weeks ago and found out he'd been released.'

'I'm please you found the time to visit him,' the father replies. 'I wish all of his friends had been as good as you. You say your name is Bob? Are you a university friend?'

'Yeah, we were on the same course. Absolutely tragic what happened. Your son should never have gone to jail, as everyone with a brain knows.'

This last comment seems to eliminate any lingering scepticism the father might have had about my status as a real friend. Seconds later I'm taking down a phone number and address.

After putting the phone down I spend a few minutes thinking about my options. Jake lives only about a twenty minute drive from my home, in Tufnell Park. That's convenient – for both of us.

That night I have a strange dream. I'm standing in front of a huge Jake, who lies before me on his front in a dark, cavernous space. His chin is on the ground and his mouth open wide, presenting me with an entry point to the man's body. I clamber over Jake's lower lip, and onto his tongue, as big as a trampoline, and covered with a thick film of mucus. The roof of the giant's mouth is higher than the ceil-ings in my house. I feel afraid, worried that Jake's mouth will shut and trap me in his huge gob.

I move forward into Jake's throat, where I find t hat instead of being surrounded by moist tissue I'm in a chrome tunnel. Concave TV screens are set into the tunnel at irregular intervals, and seem to be showing random scenes from Jake's life. I catch a clip of my former friend and myself whilst we were at university, the two of us sitting in a lecture. I really don't understand why people don't have more lucid dreams – become aware during a dream that what they're witnessing couldn't possibly happen in anything other than a dreamscape – but like most people I accept this outlandish environment I find myself in as perfectly normal.

After traversing a section of Jake's 'throat' area I reach a gate. It is totally dark on the other side of this barrier, and I consider turning back. I'm about to do so, when a regular sized Jake steps up to the gate from the other side. Grabbing an iron bar in each hand he says, 'Hello, Adam.'

'Hello,' I say. 'Are you trapped there?'

'Not as trapped as you are. Not half as trapped as you are. You need to see the astrologer.'

'The who?'

'The astrologer. The only person that can save you, and maybe even me.'

'I'm not interested in saving you,' I respond. 'No remotely interested.'

'I know that, Adam, but he's still my only hope.'

I'm about to reply, when a huge fireball rushes towards us from behind Jake. It engulfs both Jake and myself. I wake up, sweating and confused.

The following afternoon I'm scheduled to pick up some more whores-to-be from the nuns. I'm fervently hoping this collection goes more smoothly than the previous one. Courtney is scheduled to accompany me, something I could get offended about, but frankly it will be a relief to have him with me.

With a morning free of other commitments, I decide it might be an idea to get on with a bit of murdering. I'm aware that I seem to have floated away from my original cashpoint method of target selection, and decide to return to it.

An hour later I'm sitting in the same coffee shop where it all began, sipping a flat white, a copy of a broadsheet spread out before me. As before, my seat allows me to look outwards, towards the cashpoint machine. At my feet is a shoulder bag that holds my killing tools; in my head are thoughts of slashing and gashing.

I decide to finish my coffee, after which I will choose the fifth person to come along as my victim. A few minutes later I return an empty cup to my table, and look out at the cashpoint machine. No one uses it for about ten minutes, after which two people arrive in quick succession – first a builder-type wearing a hardhat, then an elderly woman holding a leash to which is attached a small dog. After these customers leave there is a wait of about five minutes, after which a man in his twenties turns up. He stands in front of the machine for a few moments whilst searching his trouser pockets, before, presumably having discovered he has left his wallet elsewhere, leaves. I debate whether to count this person as customer three, quickly deciding that I will. A five minute wait, then the same man returns. Hooray, you've found your wallet, and how lucky you found it when you did and not a few minutes later. I count him for a second time. The next person to come along will be my victim.

The next person to come along is my wife. I know her body so well, not to mention her wardrobe, that even at fifty yards I'm in no doubt as to who I am looking at. Lucy is wearing a pale blue dress, and I was with her when she bought it the previous year in Marks and Spencer's. On her head is a straw hat, one she wears when out throughout the summer months on account of her fair skin and a fear of skin cancer that even her Christian faith can't overcome.

What to do? I'm in no doubt that I have to kill her, but here and now? I accept immediately that this would be opening me up to risks that are wholly unnecessary. I've found my next victim; the key now is to despatch her without risking imprisonment. I pay and leave, checking when I step out onto the pavement that I'm not spotted by Lucy. I decide to take an unhurried walk home – it will give me time to think about how and when to kill my wife.

In the end I get distracted by my dick on the way home, and end up calling on one of my favourite whorehouses. It's not until I'm sitting over the dining table from Lucy that evening, tucking into pork chops and mashed potato, that I return to the question of how to despatch my wife. I marvel at how alive she is, as she lifts fork to mouth, and talks her normal inconsequential waffle, and how soon she could resemble my pork chop, should I choose to butcher and cook her after murdering her. I've heard human flesh tastes quite like pork, and wonder whether Lucy would be good eating.

I could smother Lucy, I decide. In some ways this might be the best way of getting rid of her. It could be done in bed when she's asleep, with minimal noise and no blood. Blood seems to get murderers into no end of trouble; avoiding its spillage could be a good move. How to explain her disappearance, though? She's so gullible I could probably stage a creative writing exercise for her, wherein she has to write an imaginary 'I'm leaving you' note. That could work.

I wonder how I would cope post-Lucy. I'd have to do housework for a change and pretend to be a father. That could be quite tedious. Then again, I could probably find another wife quite quickly. The 'widowed father' routine would probably be quite effective at snaring a new partner.

Ben walks into the room, trailing a teddy bear to which he's attached what looks like a dressing gown cord. 'Gordon's dead,' he informs us, referring to the teddy bear by name.

'Why is he dead?' Lucy asks, feigning concern for the toy.

'Someone killed him,' Ben replies. 'I think it might have been Dad.'

I swallow uncomfortably. 'How did I kill Gordon?' I ask my son. 'I bought you that teddy. Why would I want to kill him?'

'You gave him one of those bad looks. Like you give mum sometimes.'

I exchange a glance with Lucy. Her expression suggests this isn't as strange a comment as I might have hoped.

'Bear'll be fine,' I say. 'He wasn't alive to begin with, so I can't really have killed it.'

'Adam!' Lucy rebukes me. 'Try and remember what it is like to be five ...'

'I remember only too well. Plenty of beatings and no pocket money.'

Ben screams and runs from the room. I turn my attention to my food, glad that the interruption is over.

'Adam, I wish you'd be more human sometimes,' Lucy says.

Correction. The interruption isn't over. 'Leave me in peace, Lou. I've had a hard day.'

'Hard day? I saw you come out of a café at about eleven. Don't tell me, you were blessing the place?'

I'm taken aback at having been spotted. 'I was meeting

Peter Simpkins,' I lie. 'Not able to meet my parishioners now?'

'Course you are. Just don't pretend you're breaking rocks from dawn till dusk.'

Suddenly Lucy's despatch seems a much more straightforward proposition.

The next day I decide to go and take a look at Jake's residence, to see whether getting him on his home patch is viable. Before leaving I make sure my mobile phone isn't on my person. I've just seen a crime programme which highlights how people can be tracked by their cell phones. Seems they should be a long way from an individual before he does anything the police might later take an interest in.

I drive through dull suburban streets on my way to Jake's place. The houses I pass seem to be sinking on their foundations with boredom, almost crying out for something to happen to enliven their neighbourhood. I promise them I'll do my best.

Jake's house is a non-descript semi-detached Edwardian affair. Front lawn well, but not obsessively tended. Woodwork in good order. It could belong to anyone other than a gypsy or benefit trash. I park my car a hundred yards from the target property, then get out and give it a closer inspection by walking slowly past it. I rely on the passage of time and the flat cap I'm wearing to protect me from being recognised should Jake be at home and observing the footpath in front of his house.

The good news: a flimsy gate guards a path that presumably leads to the rear garden. Getting into the property by kicking the back door in would be preferable to taking the front door route. Additionally, I can only see one doorbell by the door, indicating the property hasn't been sub-divided. Less chance of near neighbours hearing me rumble. The bad news: there's protected housing for the retired opposite Jake's house, meaning plenty of snoopers who rarely leave their flats. Overall though, it's definitely do-able. I return to my car to do a bit more driving around. I want to get a better feel for the area, and locate my best exit routes.

As I drive I'm reminded of an incident that occurred when Jake and I were students. We'd gone into the West End to do some shopping. Jake had been supplementing his grant by donning rags and begging at tube stations – he reckoned that he made about eight pounds an hour, much more than a job in McDonalds would have paid back then. I hadn't joined him in this endeavour, but had stolen some money from my sister the preceding weekend, so we both had dosh to spend. We spent a few hours browsing and buying in record and bookshops, before taking a side road off Oxford Street which Jake insisted led to a great but affordable Italian restaurant. We were both starving. A hundred yards down the road we saw what at first looked like a couple having a lover's tiff, but which we quickly realised was a mugging in progress. A well built man wielding a knife was trying to grab a woman's handbag, the latter holding grimly to the bag's strap while her attacker held the bag by its base, flashing his knife at the woman as he did so. I was interested in the scene unfolding before us, in the same way that a zoo visitor might witness lions mauling each other in their cage. Jake, however, had other ideas. As soon as he became aware of what was happening he dropped the bag he was holding and ran to the imperilled woman's aid. Although a good few inches shorter than the mugger, Jake barrelled into the man with such force that they both fell over. The woman took this opportunity to flee, without so much as a 'thankyou' to Jake.

I strolled over to where the two men lay. Jake quickly got to his feet, but the other man seemed to have been concussed or worse – he lay motionless. 'You haven't killed him, have you?' I asked my friend.

'I hope not,' Jake said. 'Reckon we should call the police or ambulance?'

'Could do. Or we could just walk on. He's only a mugger.'

At this point an elderly man walked up to us. 'What's happened here?' he asked.

'He was trying to mug a lady,' Jake replied. 'I knocked him over and now he seems to be unconscious.'

'Oh,' the old man said. 'Well, good work. I hope you're around when I'm next mugged.' With that he walked on.

'Come on, let's go,' I insisted. 'If we hang around we'll probably get charged with assault. Fucked up way things work in this country.'

I observed Jake wavering between following my suggestion and the impulse to see the man right. Before he had time to decide the attacker emitted a groan and shifted his legs. 'Here we go,' I said.

The man slowly lifted himself to his feet. He looked at us strangely, as if he'd never seen fellow human beings before. 'Thanks a bundle,' he said. 'You just cost me fifty grand.'

'What do you mean?' Jake said.

'That woman. She's my ex-wife, and she stole fifty grand from my safe. By now she'll be on her way to an airport. I'll never see her or my money again.'

'It looked like you were trying to mug her,' Jake said.

'Exactly right. *Looked* like.' The man rubbed his face with both hands. By now we could both see indicators that he wasn't a mugger. A Rolex watch. Expensive clothes.

'Sorry, man,' Jake said. 'Why don't you call the cops? They can get her before she gets on a plane.'

The man batted away this suggestion with a lazy air slap. 'Can't be bothered. She's going west. Like my old man used to say, if you go west far enough, you'll end up east.'

Jake and I soon moved on, but I've often wondered what the man meant by this remark. It's stayed with me, for some reason.

In the course of reliving this memory I have driven down several roads in the vicinity of Jake's house. Nothing I see perturbs me – no likely traffic bottlenecks, police stations or Wanted posters with my face on them. It's doable. It will be done.

When I get home I get a call from Courtney. He sounds frantic, which is very unlike Courtney. 'You need to come over now,' he shouts down the phone. 'Joey's going crazy!'

'Joey's been crazy for a long time,' I point out.

'No, I mean *really* crazy. He's smashing things up in his house. We don't want the police coming over, but they will if he doesn't shut up and calm his shit down.'

'Has he been taking drugs?'

'I don't think so. He's bangin' on about that ghostie. Polterheist or whatever you call it.'

'Poltergeist.'

'Yeah. I …' The rest of Courtney's sentence goes unuttered as a huge cry and crashing sound come from somewhere in Joey's house.

'I'm on my way,' I say, putting the phone down before Courtney has a chance to reply.

I pull up outside Joey's house about half an hour later. As I walk up to the front door I see that it is open. I don't bother knocking – I'm straight into the house. 'Arrgh!' a cry erupts. I follow the direction of the sound, entering the living room. In the centre of the room lies Joey, face down. Courtney is sitting on his back.

'Thank the Lord you're here,' the Jamaican says when he sees me.

'What's happening?'

'Look around you,' Courtney replies, gesturing with a hand.

I scan the room. The sofa is out of position, a couple of feet forward from where it would normally be. A ceramic vase lies smashed on the floor. Scatter cushions have been scattered all over the place.

'What the hell happened?' I ask.

'The sofa moved on its own a while back. Joey freaked out. He said he could see something moving in the room.

Started shouting so loud I thought neighbours would come to see what happening. After he been shouting for awhile he said he was gonna get his gun, shoot the ghost. That's when I sit on him …'

'Joey,' I say, crouching by his head. 'Are you okay, buddy? There's no ghost.'

'There fucking is. Tell that fucking oaf to get off my back, or I'll shoot him as well as the poltergeist.'

I struggle to keep a straight face. 'We're just looking out for you. You'll thank us after you've calmed down.'

'Lemme go!'

I look at Courtney. He seems to know what I'm thinking: 'If you want,' he says. I nod, and Courtney releases Joey.

Joey rises and stamps his feet. He walks over to a coffee table and opens its drawer, producing a handgun. Holding it with both hands he points it in the direction of the sofa. 'Come on, you motherfucker!' he shouts. 'Show yourself you cowardly piece of shit.'

'Joey,' Courtney says. 'If it's a ghost you ain't going to be able to shoot it. Put the gun down.'

Joey swings around, and for a second I think he's going to shoot Courtney. Whilst Joey's back is turned to the sofa, the piece of furniture moves violently with a shriek. Joey swings back and lets off two quick shots. My ears ring, and the smell of burnt chemicals fills the room.

'I think the sofa is dead,' I say, risking Joey's wrath. 'Come on. Put the gun away.'

Joey looks at the pistol as if he can't explain its presence in his hands, then shakes his head and throws it on the sofa. 'Fucking poltergeist …'

'You need to get a priest in,' Courtney says. 'A proper one.'

'You can laugh, you guys. I have to live with this thing everyday. How's about I move into your house Adam, and you spend a week here?'

'I'm not saying you haven't got a problem, but if the

worst this thing can do is move a piece of furniture around, what's the big issue?'

'You think anyone heard the shots?' Joey asks.

Before anyone has a chance to answer, the doorbell rings. 'Fuck!' Joey exclaims. 'That's probably the cops …'

'They wouldn't have got here that quickly,' Courtney whispers. 'Not unless they was just walking past when you fired.'

Joey places the handgun under the sofa and opens a window to try and remove the smell of cordite from the room. 'If they ring again I'll have to answer,' Joey explains. 'I don't want the door kicked in.' No sooner has the man uttered these words than the doorbell rings for a second time, this time a long, insistent burst.

Joey walks to the front door. Courtney and I stay in the living room, looking at each other ominously.

'Mrs Jones!' we hear Joey exclaim loudly, the relief evident in his voice. 'Come on in. Come on in.'

A few moments later Joey walks into the living room, followed by an attractive blonde woman in her mid-forties. 'This is Mrs Jones, one of my parishioners,' Joey says by way of introduction. 'Mrs Jones, meet Jim and John, two homeless men I'm currently helping.'

Mrs Jones looks me up and down, obviously impressed at how well turned-out I am for someone sleeping rough. Courtney has his mouth open, apparently about to correct Joey, but Joey is too quick for him. 'Why don't you two go upstairs and help yourselves to some of the clothes I've laid out in the spare bedroom? I'll drive you over to that hostel in half an hour or so.'

Courtney isn't standing for this. 'I don't need no clothes,' he says, before plonking himself down on the shot sofa. I decide to follow suit, sitting beside the Jamaican.

Joey glares at us but doesn't comment. Turning to Mrs Jones he says, 'Take a seat over here.' He gestures towards an armchair. 'Can I get you something to drink?'

Mrs Jones sits before saying, 'I'll have a cup of tea – if you'll join me.'

'Back in a second,' Joey says and leaves the room without offering either Courtney or myself a drink.

Mrs Jones smiles at us when we're alone. 'How are you chaps getting on?' she asks. 'Homelessness must be a truly horrible experience. I find camping for a weekend pretty traumatic, and that's with on-site toilets and showers.'

'Yes, we're pleased Joey could escape that life, and now he's helping us do the same,' I reply. Courtney chuckles.

'Joey was homeless?' Mrs Jones asks, her face lighting up with curiosity.

'Yes, shortly after he came over from the States his mother died. He hit the bottle pretty hard, and his life started to unravel.' I can sense Courtney shaking with restrained giggles as I talk. 'But his faith in God helped him back onto his feet, and look at him now!'

Mrs Jones opens her mouth to say something, but before she can the sofa Courtney and I are sitting on jerks violently in her direction. 'What the hell?' she exclaims. 'How did that happen?'

I jump off the sofa, quickly followed by Courtney. Seconds after we're on our feet the sofa shifts left, colliding with a side table and sending the magazines it's holding tumbling to the floor. This movement also exposes the gun that Joey has recently hidden.

Mrs Jones starts gabbling – I can't really make out what she's saying. It's at this point that Joey walks back in, and I take this opportunity to take my leave. 'Seems your sofa's playing up again,' I say. 'Don't worry about that lift to the hostel. I'll walk.'

'Yeah, I'll walk as well,' Courtney says.

We make our way to the front door, leaving Joey to explain homelessness, poltergeists and a handgun to Mrs Jones.

On the way home I see a woman wearing a bright pink top. It sparks a memory from early childhood that is almost painful in its clarity. I think I had a bunch of plastic blocks, one of which was exactly the same colour as the woman's clothing. I can't figure out why this recollection occurs now, given I must have seen this colour many times before, but it does. The memory isn't just of the toy, but of the whole emotional climate I was experiencing at the time. Excitement and fear both seem to feature prominently, but what either the excitement or fear relate to I can't remember. The memory of the blocks triggers a memory of a childhood friend; I think his name was Charlie. I recall play in my back garden, and the play leading to a squabble. Now I'm punching Charlie, and I really don't care that he's being hurt. He's my friend, but I'm hurting him, and I acknowledge this fact without any sort of emotion. It's just happening, and that's the way things are.

Was I born this way, I wonder? I have to acknowledge that my parents gave me a pretty good upbringing. I don't think I was every dropped on my head, or suffered an illness that might have messed with my mind. The only death in the family before my eighteenth birthday was of a grandfather who lived in Australia and whom I had only ever met two or three times. Strange. I sometimes wish I was like other people, but only out of curiosity as to what it would be like. I don't feel a moral obligation to act in accordance with society's expectations. Morals to me are like signs on a motorway. I have to behave in certain ways to avoid trouble, but not because I really want to.

I stop the car outside my local newsagent. I need to buy some King Size Rizla for my nightly cannabis habit. In all our time together Lucy has never picked up on my need for a daily smoke, something I find shocking. Admittedly I go outside to toke, but all the same. My excuse that I like to watch the night sky for ten minutes every evening is lame, given I even go out when there's heavy cloud cover. And the smell! I must reek of smoke when I come in.

There are several scrawny white kids wearing hoodies

hanging around outside the shop. A comment's made as I pass them, followed by raucous laughter. I can feel my jaw clench. When I leave the shop they're still there, mock-fighting, and generally behaving like the feral shits they are. 'It's stopped raining,' I find myself saying to them. 'You can take your hoods off now.'

Two boys who are jostling each other stop and look at me. 'What did you say, tosser?' the taller of the two asks.

'No more rain. Why've you still got your hoods up?'

'Maybe it's 'cos we don't want to be recognised on CCTV when we beat the shit out of you.' It's the same boy speaking.

'But that's not going to be an issue,' I reply.

'Why?'

'Why? Because I'm going to be the one beating the shit out of *you*.' I'm running towards the boys before I've finished this utterance. Along with the cigarette papers I've also bought two cans of peaches. All of my purchases are in a plastic bag, which is transformed into a very effective weapon. I twist the handle as I run and slam the bag into the kid I've been exchanging words with. The cans thud into his left temple, and he falls like a stone. The boy standing next to him looks at me in horror as I turn my attention to him. Instead of looking he should have been running. Too late: the shopping bag fells him as well. I look around for the other kids, but they haven't hung around to suffer the same fate as their friends. I watch their backs as they run as fast as their junk-food-fed legs will carry them.

The shop owner steps out onto the pavement at this point. He looks down at the two boys and says. 'I've been wanting to do that for a long time. You go now. I'll wait five minutes then call an ambulance.'

When I'm back in my car I see that the bag has torn and my Rizlas have fallen out. 'Fuck,' I say, then start the engine.

Later that night after getting stoned I wander downstairs and turn the TV on. I'm greeted with the beaming mug of the anchor of a rolling news station. I would change channels, but I'm feeling too lethargic. Within ten minutes I've learned two very important things. Firstly, it's very hazardous to be a nice person. The anchor has told me about a soldier in Afghanistan who was killed earlier that day, and as ever, he was 'a wonderful soldier and a loving husband'. He will, apparently, be deeply missed by his colleagues, friends and family. Why is it always such people that get killed? Why don't we ever hear that so-and-so has been killed, and that he was 'a right arsehole, and it couldn't have happened sooner'? I'm tempted to ring up my life insurance company and ask them if they'll cut my premiums on account of me being a total cunt.

The second thing I learn is that the media is a poisonous quagmire of quicksand and lethal gases. Actually, I knew this already. Open yourself up to more than five minutes of exposure to its horrible influence and you're certainly doomed. I witness the anchor asking a colleague of his to comment on a rumour about an alleged crime. News nowadays, apparently also includes extensive reporting on the goings-on at other news organisations. The news making the news. Self-referential, recyclical, fart-harvesting shit-heads. I've always thought I was in favour of the freedom of the press, but now I'm thinking it might be better to live in a country with a State-controlled media. At least you'd know from the off that everything said and reported was bullshit.

# Chapter Ten

'Whadya mean you're outta Scotch? You gotta have some left.'

The speaker is a fat New Jersey Mafioso called Vinnie, and he's sitting to my left. There's nine of us gathered around Joey's dining room table, the occasion a reunion between host and his criminal brethren from the States.

'I'll have a look,' Joey says, rising from his chair. 'But if we're out, we're out. I'm not gonna go cruising the neighbourhood looking for a liquor store. You'll have to do with brandy ...'

In the company of his fellow hoods Joey's voice broadens and slackens into a fruitier Brooklyn accent.

'We fly all this way to see you, and this is the hospitality you show us?' Gino, a small man with a cleft palate says as Joey leaves the room. The grin on his face reassures me he isn't about to pull his gun out.

The joshing is interrupted by the arrival of another pasta dish, carried to the table by a buxom woman in her fifties who is wearing pounds of makeup and jewellery. Joey follows her into the dining room. The Americans pile spoonfuls of sauce-laden linguine onto their plates, and then into their mouths, until almost all of them have white tentacles hanging from their chins.

Courtney is amongst the guests. He's sitting to my right and looking very uncomfortable in a jacket that isn't big enough for his broad shoulders. Whenever one of the

Italians tries to engage him in conversation he answers in the minimum number of words. Seeing that Courtney isn't showing himself in the best possible light, and perhaps uncomfortable at how this might reflect on him, Joey tries to draw him out: 'Hey, Courtney, tell these guys about that fucking ghost thing. Tell them about what happened the other day.'

'Joey shot up his sofa,' he says.

Joey chuckles. 'It's the way he tells them. But he's right. Some kind of poltergeist thing keeps moving stuff around this house. I went crazy the other day and shot up the couch. I don't know if I got the fucker. There was no blood.'

A blonde fortysomething called Janice says, 'My mom used to tell me about a ghost that was meant to haunt her home when she was a kid.' Turning to her husband, Louie, she goes on: 'You saw our old place on Neptune Avenue, didn't you?'

'If I was a ghost I'd choose a better neighbourhood to haunt,' Louie comments. 'If I could walk through walls, I'd just have kept walking until I got somewhere more upscale.'

'The only spirits I believe in come in a bottle,' Vinnie declares. 'Have you found my Scotch already, Joey? I'm your goddam guest remember. And someone, pass the calamud.'

'All out buddy. Cognac? You should wait until you've finished the main courses before you hit the spirits, anyway. That's the way it's done over here.'

'Listen, fratu, do you think I give a fuck how it's done over here, or anywhere for that matter? The only interest I have in this crummy country is how much money you can make for me here.'

'You guys have done pretty good so far with this hooker racket,' Louie comments. 'You think you can expand the action there?'

'Not in front of the ladies,' Vinnie reprimands Louie.

'Yeah, not in front of us,' one of the wives echoes. 'I don't wanna know about any prostitution activities.'

'Yeah, but you don't mind spending the money we make from broads,' Gino says.

'Enough,' Vinnie says. 'Let's change the subject. So, Adam, Joey tells me you're a priest as well.' A gurgle of chuckles erupt.

'I am indeed,' I reply. 'Like generations of priests before me, I find it important to spread lies, instil guilt and fear, and profit personally from the gullibility of my flock. Something you guys can, I'm sure, relate to.'

'We've got a fiery one here, Joey. With the exception of Father Bernard, who married me and buried my mamma and papa, I agree with you. In fact, you've got me to thinking. There *are* quite a few similarities between the Church and the Mafia. We both swear an oath ...'

'We both take a weekly collection!' Gino chimes in.

'You're both big in Italy,' I add.

Laughter interrupts what threatens to become the elicitation of an almost endless list of similarities between the two institutions.

'What about this poltergeist thing?' Louie asks, looking in my direction. 'What's that all about?'

Being asked this question forces me to quickly examine my own thoughts on the matter. 'I don't know,' I say. 'I felt the sofa move. Joey wasn't even in the room at the time, so he can't have been yanking on fishing line. I don't know whether what happened is supernatural. It's probably something very natural, just a something Science doesn't understand yet.'

'There you go, Joey,' Vinnie says. 'No need to try and shoot the poltergeist. It's just a natural thing Science doesn't understand.'

'Whatever ...' Joey says, seemingly unimpressed.

In due course the women take themselves off to the living room, leaving the men to talk business. 'So you're doing well,' Vinnie says to Joey after a long pull on his drink. 'Do you need some extra bodies? Some more help?'

'We're okay at the moment. Maybe in six months or something, depending on how things develop.'

Stroking his glass, Vinnie continues: 'You thinking of expanding into other stuff apart from whores?'

Joey nods, before replying: 'Yep. Thinking about doing more of the white stuff …'

'Coke or heroin?'

'Coke. I've got a pal who lives in Galicia in Spain. Has lots of good contacts with Colombians. Half the coke that comes into this country come through that part of Spain.'

'Yeah?'

'Yep. Long stretches of deserted coastline with lots of little inlets and bays. If you look at a map that bit of Spain is the closest part of mainland Europe to South America. And Spanish. The Colombians like being able to talk in their native language.'

'Makes sense,' Vinnie says. He glances at Louie before adding: 'Do you need us to front you some cash to get things started? I'm guessing you're looking at moving tonnes not kilograms.'

'Well, maybe not tonnes, but a lot of kilos. Some financing might help. I'll know more after I've been to see this kid in Spain. We'll talk numbers, and I'll get a clearer picture of things.'

'How you going to get the stuff from Spain to here?' Vinnie wants to know.

'Couple of possibilities,' Joey says. 'One involves Courtney here driving it over in a van on his own. The other involves Adam driving it over in a van on his own.' Laughter from everyone at the table apart from Courtney and myself. 'No, I'm working on that. If it works well, I'll let you know all about it.'

\*\*\*

During the drive home my mind is occupied with thoughts of murder. I've already got my wife and Jake to get rid of, but a copy of 'Hello' magazine I flipped through at Joey's has made me want to kill a pop star called Kim Catcheside. I'm filled with hatred for this woman – for her imbecility, for her lack of any discernible talents apart from looking good, and for the fact that this non-entity will be remembered long after I'm forgotten by my small group of friends and family. Just as natural disasters like earthquakes and volcanoes are the result of the build-up of forces that can't be resisted, so I think this woman elicits a justifiable loathing that can only be sated by her annihilation. It seems just and equitable that she be wiped out.

If Catcheside was a celebrity of any real status killing her would probably be difficult, but she's one of those nonentities that's been recently scooped up by a desperate media, and from what 'Hello' tells me, still hasn't had time to trade in her trashy cheap house for a trashy expensive one. There'll probably be a Neanderthal boyfriend lurking around, but despatching him would be kind of fun. So many people to kill, so little time to do it ...

My thoughts are interrupted by the ringing of my phone. It's Janet, a dark-haired strumpet I fuck from time to time. 'Hey, Janet. How you doing?' I say, trying to avoid driving the car into a lamppost.

'I'm alright. Just haven't heard from you for a while.'

'I'm sorry. Just been really busy with work. Deliveries up and down the country.' Janet thinks I'm a truck driver. It's a totally implausible lie given my demeanour and accent, but she's stupid enough to have bought it. If I can't be available for a period of time I can conveniently blame my driving schedule. As for why she can never come to my place, that's been taken care of by a crazy mother I supposedly live with.

'You want to meet up this weekend?' Janet asks.

'Erm. I think that's doable. I've got a load of turnips I

need to deliver to Shropshire Friday, but I could come over to yours on Saturday morning …'

'*Morning*? Can't you do an evening? You make me feel like a floozy.'

Just then I see another incoming call. It's Jane, who I like fucking more than Janet. I'm reminded of those old Ladybird books. *John fucks Jane. Jane fucks Jim. John, Jane and Jim like fucking.* 'Hang on a sec,' I say, before switching callers. 'Hey, Jane. Good to hear from you! How are you?'

'Good, but I'm late.'

I think I know what she means, but decide to try humour: 'Well if you're late for something, maybe you should hurry up and not be ringing me …'

'No, I mean *late* late. My period …'

'Ah …' I feel like an air traffic controller, keeping planes in a holding pattern while he co-ordinates their landing. Once in a while a plane declares an emergency and has to be cleared for immediate landing. 'Shit,' I say.

'Can I see you Saturday morning? We need to talk.' Jane's declaring an emergency landing. She's wrong about needing to talk, though. We don't need to talk, we need to get her an abortion. Still, I have to be seen to be playing the game. 'Of course,' I say. 'Come over to yours about ten?'

'Yeah. Adam, what are we going to do?'

'That's what we need to talk about on Saturday,' I say, adopting my warmest voice. 'We need to consider everything, and make the right decision.'

'I knew this was going to happen,' Janet goes on. 'How could this happen?'

'Well, we *did* stop using condoms. It's not a total surprise. We've just proved we're still fertile.'

We talk for a few more minutes, during which I run a red light, before I remember Janet and make my excuses. 'Janet!' I say, after Jane rings off, but she's gone. I decide to wait until I'm parked up before ringing her. 'You're such a cuntster,' I tell myself. 'A proper vagi-tarian.'

# Chapter Eleven

It's my own stupid fault – I've underestimated the threat that Jake poses, and he has managed to land the first real blow. It doesn't come in the form of violence, as I have anticipated, but in the form of a sheet of A4 paper that he places on the windscreen of every car parked in the church car park the following Sunday. I've got to hand it to him; the boy's done his homework. The sheet of paper contains two photographs of me. In both, I'm leaving massage parlours – 'Aqua Massage' and 'Annabelle's'. The paragraph of text beneath the photos outlines the surveillance the unnamed author has undertaken, and states that these two photos are just a couple of fifteen possessed. It's further stated that 'your cherished vicar' on each occasion spent over half an hour in the massage parlours, making it unlikely that I was dropping off 'religious tracts'.

What to do? If I kill the cunt now I'll be even more of a suspect than I would have been previously. Driving back from church Lucy still isn't aware of the leaflet – but she will be soon, along with most of my congregation, the local paper and the Anglican Church. I take three calls that afternoon from concerned members of my congregation. I've had long enough to think of a response, which is that I have been visiting massage parlours in an attempt to reach out to fallen women. I know this explanation alone will not suffice; I'll need to produce witnesses that can testify to my unusual ministry. I'm going to have to pay hookers to say that that's what I haven't been doing. This will immediately open me up to the risk of being blackmailed by these whores, but it's a risk I'm going to have to take.

'Lucy, I need to have a word with you,' I say after taking the last of my phone calls.

'What is it honey?'

'There's someone trying to blacken my name. He's aware of an attempt I've been making to reach out to women working in ... er ... massage parlours, and he's ... uh ... trying to make out that my intentions are not ... pure.'

'Massage parlours? What?'

I have to think fast. 'Yes,' I say. 'I haven't told you about this, but an old girlfriend of mine got into trouble with drugs, and ended up working as a call girl. Ever since hearing about what's happened to Kim I've felt it my duty to try and help people who've gotten into this sort of trouble ...'

'For Goodness Sake,' Lucy replies. 'What a stupid thing to be doing. Who's found out about this? Can you imagine the possibilities for misinterpretation?' She pauses, and I sense she wants to accuse me of telling a pack of lies. 'Well, why do you think someone's trying to make you look bad?'

I explain the car park paper distribution.

'Who could be doing this?' Lucy asks.

'I don't know,' I say. 'I really don't know.'

I decide to tackle the problem head-on. The next Sunday in church, after the opening hymn, Greeting and initial readings, I address my congregation: 'Brothers and Sisters, I'm going to take the unusual step of addressing directly the allegations made by an unnamed individual, that my ministry to the needy in our community has ... gone astray.' A pause. 'Many of you will have had a leaflet placed on the windscreen of your car last Sunday, and those of you who didn't will I'm sure have heard from others about it. It would appear that someone seeks to discredit me, and is going to some effort to do so.

'Why this individual should wish to blacken my name, I have no idea. Perhaps the Forces of Darkness have such a hold on him that he will go to any lengths to try to diminish the good I have tried to do for those who live amongst us. The plight of women trapped in prostitution has long been a source of sadness to me – partly because I personally know someone who fell into this trap – and it is true that I have been trying to reach out to such people, to try and deter them from continuing to work in an industry that not only endangers their soul, but also the health of their bodies …' Looking around I see the entire congregation giving me their undivided attention. They clearly haven't expected this.

'I feel it appropriate, given the extraordinary allegations that have been made, to go to extraordinary lengths to refute them. To that end, I've invited Mandy, one of the women I've been trying to help, to come to church this morning and speak to you directly. Mandy, would you mind standing up?' Mandy, 36-32-38, £100 per hour, will consider anal, stands up. She's occupying a seat in one of the front pews. She's about five eight, with long brown hair. Pretty face. Late twenties. 'Mandy, thankyou for coming to church today. Can you tell me – and my congregation – how I've been working with you over the last few months?' Don't blow it, I think. Don't blow it.

Mandy clears her throat and says: 'Yeah, you've been helping me a lot recently. Telling me about God, and how I can have a better life.'

All it will take is for her to start giggling and I'm fucked, I think to myself.

'Have I on any occasion behaved inappropriately whilst trying to help you?' I ask the girl.

'Sorry?'

'Have I done anything other than speak to you about ways in which your life could be improved?' I say.

'No. You never tried to sleep with me or anything.'

'And the other women you know who I've also tried to help – would they say the same thing?'

'I think so. I mean, yes. They would say the same thing.'

'Thankyou Mandy. You've been very helpful.' Mandy stays on her feet for a few more seconds, before sitting down. Directing my attention to the congregation I say: 'I hope Mandy's testimony will help to clear things up for you all. I'm aware that this is a somewhat unusual deviation from the normal order of service, but I hope you understand that these are quite extraordinary accusations that have been made ...'

As I'm greeting my parishioners as they exit the church at the end of the service, I sense my introduction of Mandy into proceedings has done more good than bad. Those who refer to the massage parlour scandal mainly offer words of encouragement. Marjorie Sanderson, who could probably turn tricks herself quite profitably, bats her eyelids and puts a hand on my arm as on the way out. She says, 'We feel dreadfully sorry for you at this time.' I make a mental note to see if I can offer her a more personal ministry in the near future.

The following day I receive a phone call from the bishop responsible for my diocese. He doesn't tell me who has tipped him off about the massage parlour stink, which I resent, as I'll now have to mistrust everyone in my congregation. 'I'm sure there's nothing to it,' Bishop Green, a balding homo tells me. 'Nevertheless, I'd like to pop in for an hour at some point in the next week. I have to be seen to be taking this matter seriously, even if I'm happy that you're just the victim of some poisoned soul.'

'Sure,' I reply.

Sure. Sure, sure, sure. One thing's sure, and that is that Jake is going to pay for this. He was going to get bumped anyway, but now there's revenge to throw into the mix. I can't kill him yet, though. This one has to be really well planned. And I can't kill my wife just now. I'm too distracted to have to deal with a domestic upheaval. Plus, if she were to 'disappear' just after this church fuss, it would look too odd to too many people. No, it has to be someone else. My thoughts turn to Kim Catcheside. I fire up my computer and punch her name into YouTube. I'm presented with seemingly endless pages of thumbnails of clips featuring her. I click on the third one down and a moment later I see her being interviewed on a breakfast TV programme. It's all hair flicking and pouting, and she seems to speak a language called Bullshit quite fluently:

Interviewer: 'So, Kim, you must be really excited about the release of your last album?'

Kim: 'Yeah, well it's like amazing. I mean it's great. This album really speaks to my heart ... I mean speaks from my heart. It's a thankyou to my fans, it's a come-on to people who aren't my fans. I'm just so pleased about it.'

Interviewer: 'You created quite a stir in New York recently, when you appeared at the premiere of "A Forgotten Promise" wearing *that* dress. What do you say to people that claim you were being deliberately exhibitionistic?'

Kim: 'What do you mean?'

Interviewer: 'Exhibitionistic – that you wanted to show flesh for the sake of it, to get a reaction.'

Kim: 'Oh, well I think if you've got a good body you should be happy to show it off.'

I switch off in disgust. This bitch is definitely going to get it. I type 'Kim Catcheside address' into Google, and what do you know, an article comes up that gives her address. A second website confirms that Wensley Road is where she lives – either that or they're both wrong. I chuckle, and write down the address.

At midnight of the same day I park my car on a road that runs parallel with Wensley Road. My bag of tools is on the passenger seat beside me, and I retrieve a knife from it and step out onto the road. I'm aware that there's precious little planning that's gone into this kill – I don't even know if the bitch is going to be in – but I'm desperate for the smell of freshly spilt blood. It's like I've been walking around with a boner for a month.

I walk past Catcheside's house. Confirmation that I've got the right place comes in the shape of a Porsche Cayenne parked in the driveway – just the sort of silly car a silly star would want to be seen in. There's one light on, on the ground floor, coming I guess from the living room. I carry on to the end of the road, then turn and walk back the way I've just come. The street is quiet; no people, nor cars on the road. When I reach Catcheside's house I take a quick look around me, then crouch and run to the window with the light on, ducking beneath it. I wait for about a minute, listening for footsteps, then rise to peer into the window. I'm in luck. Catcheside is sitting on a sofa facing me, painting her nails. Beside her a large, well-built man is asleep, his head back, mouth open. I'm guessing this is the boyfriend.

That wonderful American term 'home invasion' springs to mind. Catcheside's home is about to get invaded, and its occupants terrorised. How to approach this challenge? I could knock on the door and start slashing as soon as it's opened. A possibility, but I'd lose the element of surprise. The house's occupants could even just not open the door. I decide to try one of my favourite sexual practices, the rear entry. There's a gate between the right hand side of the house and a fence. Keeping low, I creep over to it and try the latch. It's unlocked, and I slowly open the gate. I slink down the narrow walkway between house and fence. When I reach the back garden I check the windows at the back of the house, and am pleased to see that there aren't any lights on. I check the ground for water bowls or bones – anything to indicate a dog in residence – and see nothing of this nature. The rear of the house has double doors opening onto a wooden deck on the right hand side, and a regular sized door on the left. I try this latter door's handle, and to my delight discover that it is unlocked. Holding my breath, I open the door a fraction. It scrapes a tiled floor, making a sound that to my ears seems deafening. The door opens onto the kitchen, that much I can tell even in the dark as I open the door fully. I creep into the room, checking as I do so that I still have my knife – one with an eight inch blade – in my pocket. The kitchen's other door is open, and leads onto what must be a hallway. A left turn should take me straight to the room I'm after.

As I enter the hallway I can hear the sound of the television. It sounds like some sort of chat show is on. Catcheside is probably watching herself on television. If so, I don't care; the sound is helping to mask the sound of my footsteps. When I get to the door to the living room I pause for thought. I'm going to have to knock two people out very quickly, and I don't thing I've had a former life as a ninja and certainly haven't had martial arts training in this lifetime. I decide to go straight for the big boyfriend, who I'm hoping is still asleep. Slit his throat, and then, while he's trying to keep blood off the floor, go for the idiot. I raise my knife, take a deep breath, then spring into the room. The oaf is nearest me as I run in, and I've slashed his throat before he's even had time to open his eyes. As I'm using the knife Catcheside starts screaming, but not for long, because within moments I'm on her, and I quickly manage to catch her jugular. I step back. The boyfriend has by now got to his feet, but he's bleeding profusely and doesn't look very steady. Catcheside stays seated, making a gurgling noise as she tries to stem the flow of blood. It looks like she's wearing a bright red scarf.

I've got the better of them; the question is whether to flee or wait until they've died. I decide to wait. It won't take them long to bleed out, and I can't risk a freak rescue or survival resulting in me being identified. The man moves towards me, an arm raised. I use a leg to keep him at bay. A few seconds later he collapses backwards onto the floor. I look at Catcheside, who seems to have lost consciousness. 'Caught in a trap …' I sing softly. It's the title of Catheside's most recent hit. I hope she appreciates being sung out with her own lyrics.

Five minutes later I'm satisfied that the couple are dead. They're both lying in pools of blood, eyes open. I retrieve two snooker balls from my pocket. By sheer coincidence the next two in the series are blue and pink, making their allocation easy. I open Catcheside's mouth and pop the pink in, before moving over to the boyfriend and giving him a big gobstopper to suck for eternity. I decide to torch the house. It'll bring the emergency services to my victims sooner than otherwise, but also ensure that any forensic evidence I might have left is destroyed. I haven't taken my normal precautions on this sortie. I look around for a cigarette lighter. Not finding one I head into the kitchen to see what there is there, returning shortly with matches. There's a huge stack of 'Hello' magazines on a coffee table, and I start tearing pages out of a bunch of them, crumpling these up. When I've got about twenty balls of paper I pile them in a stack next to one of the fabric sofas and start applying lit matches to it. Soon flames are jumping high, licking hungrily at the sofa. I run upstairs to the bathroom and grab both toothbrushes. As I'm coming back down the stairs I hear a phone in the hallway ringing. On a whim I pick  up, answering with, 'Hello? Angel of Death speaking.' The caller says, 'What?'

I laugh, put the phone down without disconnecting the call, and leave the house.

# Chapter Twelve

Thoughts of Jake are interrupted for a week by a trip to Spain with Joey. Courtney doesn't come because he doesn't like flying much and anyway, has overstayed his UK visa and is only going to be making one-way trips from England until he solves that problem. We fly into Vigo and on the drive from the airport to the hotel I'm surprised by the greenery of the landscape. The outskirts of the city look like Wales without planning controls, with cheaply-built concrete houses clinging randomly to steep hills amidst plenty of signs of small-scale agriculture. I'm thinking this place looks a bit fucked up, until, turning a corner, I'm rewarded with a view of the bay of Vigo. It's one of the many rias that rip gashes out of the coastline of this part of Spain, the result of glaciation millennia ago. I feel giddy when I realise how high we are, the road descending steeply towards the city and harbour. In the distance the other side of the bay is just visible, mainly discernible by green slopes at higher altitudes. The logic of this area for drug smuggling becomes visibly apparent. The coastal incursion I'm looking at will undoubtedly extend, narrowing, for miles, offering plenty of convenient unloading points.

'Impressive, huh?' Joey says.

'I read something about the British and Spanish navies having a big battle here a couple of hundred years ago,' I reply. 'I can kind of understand that now.'

As we near our hotel in the older part of town the city

takes on a more conventional European feel. Lots of older stone buildings, wooden shutters and smart apartment block entrances wedged between cafes and pharmacies. There are lots of pharmacies. Pharmacies every hundred feet it seems.

'Pharmacies everywhere,' I say to Joey. 'Is this a nation of hypochondriacs?'

'I know they like their drugs,' he replies with a grin.

As we're waiting to check in I do what I normally do when I'm waiting in public, checking out tits and bums where worthy. It is like any other mid-priced hotel; lots of glass and marble and tacky staff uniforms – uniforms worn by the uniformly unctuous. I'm looking at the arse of a women who if you'd asked me to guess I would have said was thirty-two when there is a blur of movement out of the corner of my eye and a man walks past me and out of the main entrance. Something about the shape of his back strikes me as being familiar, but I can't immediately say why. My attention moves back to the arse.

It's later that evening that it suddenly hits me. From behind, the man who walked past me in the hotel lobby looked like Jake. I marvel at how a back can contain enough original characteristics to link it to a single individual. Question of course is, was it Jake that I'd seen? Impossible, I tell myself. Even if he was keeping an eye on me, there'd be no way, without the help of a major intelligence agency, that he'd have known that I was going to be going to a certain city on a given day and staying in a certain hotel – he'd even have had to know when we were going to check-in. An alarming thought occurs to me. Granted, he couldn't know all this, but if he *did* – if he did then he'd be capable of finding out all about my crimes. The thought distracts me sufficiently that I don't hear Joey address me. 'What?' I say when I realise he's trying to communicate with me.

'I was just telling Jose here about that hooker with three breasts, and how you almost lost her.'

'Oh, yeah. Close one.' I grin briefly.

We're sitting in one of Vigo's better restaurants. Around the table are five men, including myself. Apart from me there's Joey, Miguel and Jose – the latter duo our Spain cocaine contacts – and Jesus – Miguel and Jose's Colombian contact. We're munching pretty passable food and talking – mainly about nothing in particular but occasionally business. Business talk has caused the odd bit of confusion. The Spanish speakers keep referring to coke as 'salt', which causes problems when I actually want someone to pass me the salt. Jose tells me to wait until later, that I shouldn't snort coke at the table.

After dinner we move on to a bar. Most of us start drinking spirits. Jose passes me a wrap of coke within ten minutes of arriving. Poor chap seems quite concerned I might have taken his earlier caution the wrong way. Within half an hour the booze we've consumed, added to the wine we've had at dinner, loosens our tongues. Jose, who with his round glasses and slight frame looks more like an accountant than drug smuggler, airs the moral conflict he's having with drugs. 'Do you ever wonder if we are doing a wrong thing selling drugs?' he wonders.

Joey's hoarse laugh shows where he stands on the matter.

I don't have any morals, so I really couldn't give a shit, but I know what to say if I want to pretend to be normal. 'My view is that the State shouldn't be interfering with the right of the individual to consume whatever he wants,' I say. 'That being the case, I don't have a problem helping people to do something I think they should have the right to do legally.'

'So you think …' Jose begins, his accent making a real mess of 'think', 'you think if you don't agree with a law you don't have to stick to it?'

'Pretty much …'

'Yeah, but if everyone think that way, then there would be riot in the street.'

'I'm relying on the fact that most people don't think like I do,' I reply.

'What if everyone start thinking like you tomorrow?' the Spaniard asks. 'Would you then stop selling drug and obey the law?'

'If that happened I'd buy as many guns as I could and take to the hills,' Joey butts in. 'Fucking damn right.'

'Good point,' I say, addressing Jose. 'But it's a hypothetical scenario, so I'm not going to lose too much sleep thinking about it.'

Jesus takes a hit of whichever drink he's drinking and chips in: 'There is the world of priests, and there's the real world. Where I grow up, if you follow the Bible you don't live past the age of twelve.'

'Ah, but we *are* priests,' Joey says with a grin.

Jesus laughs. 'Very funny!'

Miguel says, 'No they really are. Crazy, hey?'

'Really?' the Colombian says. 'What went wrong?'

'Something went very right,' Joey says.

Jose says something to Jesus in staccato Spanish, then turning to Joey and myself says, 'I was just telling Jesus here about the whores. Your import game.'

'Oh, yeah,' Joey nods. 'You know, you gotta diversify in business.'

Jesus' face lights up. 'Where these women come from? What part of the world?'

'Mainly Eastern Europe,' Joey says. 'They all come from there, actually.'

Jesus: 'When they come to England, why don't you get them to carry drugs? Take care of two things at the same time ...'

'I never thought of that,' Joey concedes. 'But Eastern Europe isn't Colombia. It's not Drugs Central.'

'Heroin,' Jesus says. 'Much easier to get heroin to somewhere like the Ukraine than to England. Closer to Afghanistan. Customs officer who can be bought off.'

Joey looks at me. 'Never thought of that,' I say.

'Hey, hey, I've just had a thought.' Joey draws himself up in his seat. 'What if we were to bring girls over from Colombia? Then we could get them to bring some really interesting packages!'

'Yeah, but customs officers are going to be all over girls from Colombia,' I say. 'Coming in with little English and not much money.'

'What if one of us travelled with them? Wearing our robes and stuff.'

'Maybe,' I reply. 'Though personally I think we should keep the two activities separate. If our friends here can provide us with good quality product in good volumes, why look elsewhere?' A sudden thought occurs to me. 'I wonder what Courtney's up to?'

'Probably listening to those Rare Groove records of his with a huge bag of weed,' Joey replies, stubbing a cigarette out. Smoke trails from his mouth like a dragon that's given something a good blast. 'I don't really know why he gets involved in crime, to be honest. His needs are pretty simple – weed, music and the occasional woman.'

I laugh. He's right. 'You said he was introduced to you through some of your mob pals?'

'No, they introduced me to Desmond, but Desmond got arrested before he could be useful. Courtney is Desmond's brother.'

'You trust him?'

'As much as I trust you.' Joey looks at me meaningfully for a few moments before slapping me on the back and laughing.

We turn our attention to the other three. They're talking in Spanish, but switch to English when they realise we're back. Even drug dealers can have manners, I guess.

Miguel says: 'We were just talking about finding some women.'

'Paid for or seduced?' I ask.

Miguel gives me a confused look.

'You talking about prostitutes?'

Miguel looks at me as if I'm totally dumb. 'Of course! Much easier.'

'I'm up for it,' I say.

'Not for me,' Joey says. 'I'm pretty beat. But don't let me stop you guys …'

I look at the other three, their expressions indicating general willingness.

'What are you going to do?' I ask Joey.

'I think I'll head back to the hotel and get my head down. We've got a busy day tomorrow.' He gives the Spanish speakers a meaningful look.

The evening's mild as the four of us stroll to a 'place' Jose knows of. At about half past ten it's still early by Spanish standards, and I see plenty of kids out walking with their parents. The cafes seem full, as are most of the bars we pass. I wonder what the Spanish talk about during the seemingly endless hours they spend in drinking establishments. We stop at a set of pedestrian lights, waiting for green. Before we get the signal to walk a man crosses right next to us, timing his passage carefully to avoid being hit by a car. At first I pay him little attention, but then I notice his back, and realise it's the same person I saw in the hotel foyer. What the fuck is going on? I want to follow after him, but as soon as I have this thought the traffic really piles up and I can't cross. I lose sight of the man in the crowd on the other side of the road.

It seems I'm either going crazy, or Jake is in Vigo, shadowing me. Neither is a scenario I relish. I have an idea. I have Jake's home telephone number saved on my mobile. If I ring it and he answers I'll know I'm going mad, not about to be attacked. I begin to manipulate my mobile, trying to keep up with the others as I do so. They seem to have increased their pace, no doubt spurred on by desire. I get a ringing tone. Jake's phone rings for about a minute before an answerphone kicks in. Inconclusive.

The next day Jose and Miguel pick up Joey and I from our hotel. We climb into a brand new Land Rover Vogue and begin the twenty minute drive to our destination, a small village in the hills above Vigo called Rodondela. Leaving the outskirts of the city, and with the nose of the car firmly pointed upwards, we take new, EU-funded roads, through heavily wooded terrain comprising mainly pine and eucalyptus trees. The sun burns off cloud as we climb, and by the time we reach the village the day looks like it's going to turn out fine. Down the village's main road, a left and then a right, and finally we stop in front of large gates that guard the entrance to an impressive estate, dominated by a large neo-Colonial mansion. I half expect to see tigers on the other side of the gates. Jose gets his phone out and makes a quick call. Seconds later the gates are opened remotely.

A few minutes later we're being given a tour of the grounds of Jesus' property. The house is rented, he explains. No point tying up cash in something he can't put on a plane, but why shouldn't he enjoy the fruits of his labour? The villa is set back about fifty yards from the main gates, and to the rear of the property are landscaped gardens that extend at a downward angle for at least a hundred and fifty yards, terminating in well-established woodland. A large fountain, marble statues, a swimming pool – it's ticking all the boxes as a drug-dealer's lair.

'What do the locals think you do?' I ask Jesus.

'They know but they don't know,' he replies. 'There are plenty of houses like this in the area. All the same people live in them. I give money to local charity, employ people from the village, pay off some policemen. This makes for easy life. As long a no gunfights or murders, people leave me alone.'

'You live here on your own?' I ask.

Jesus chuckles. 'No, my wife and two kids are here for half the year. I have people from my group in Colombia staying very much of the time. Security, two of them. Any burglar who try to rob me gonna be in for a big surprise.'

After walking the perimeter of the grounds – a perimeter made very clear by a high wall – we move inside. Jesus takes us to the room he calls his 'office' – about the size of most apartments, with lots of mismatched furniture, a huge LCD television bracketed to one wall, and four computers.

'Sit down,' he instructs us, pointing at several leather sofas. 'You guys wanna drink?'

It's at this point that I switch on the video record function on my iPhone, then discretely scan the room and its occupants. Call it paranoia, but I've long wanted a little insurance policy against death should Joey and I have a falling out. I let my phone continue to capture sound and image.

The drink orders come in, and Jesus opens a fridge that's positioned against one wall. I sit next to Joey on one sofa; the two Spaniards share another sofa to our right, both sofas facing another sofa that is separated from the other two by a glass coffee table. Glass clinks against glass as our drinks arrive, then Jesus settles into the empty sofa, the cushions sighing with expelled air.

'Down to business,' Jesus says. He reaches for a small wooden box that rests on the coffee table and swings open its lid. Retrieving a bag of white powder – I'm guessing it isn't icing sugar – he proceeds to empty a large pile of its contents on the glass top of the table. 'This is the product. I can get you anything from two kilos to two tonnes. Available pretty much straight away. Try some.' Jesus takes several short plastic straws from the box and places them on the glass. Taking a credit card from the same place he cuts up four fat lines.

Joey goes first, making plenty of noise as he vacuums up the powder, followed by Jose, Miguel and then me. Seconds after the powder hits my nostrils I feel like I've doubled in size and tripled in perceptivity. Everything is good. Everything. My life couldn't be better if I'd just won the lottery. I put the straw down and grin at the others in the room.

'Good, hey?' Jesus says with a big smile on his face.

'I haven't had stuff like this since Miami in about '86,' Joey comments, wiping his nose. 'What's its purity?'

'About ninety-seven percent,' Jesus replies. 'You never get a hundred percent. Ninety-seven is about as close to pure as you ever get.'

'What's the price for this stuff?' I ask. The drug has made me chatty, and I'm talking where I'd normally stay silent.

'Price depends on how much you take. Tell me how much you want and I'll give you the kilo price.'

I look at Joey, who takes over. 'We're thinking maybe a hundred keys to begin with. If the people I have lined up to shift it do what they say we'd be back for a lot more pretty quickly. Have to make sure I'm not dealing with bullshiters before we get too loaded up.'

Jesus leans back in his seat, putting his hands behind his head. 'One hundred kilo? I charge you fifteen thousand U.S. a kilo. Now if you take five hundred kilo, that price would fall to about eleven thousand.'

None of this means anything to me, but Joey's pedigree as a lifetime crook becomes evident as he says: 'That's a *good* price. My old boss was paying that kind of money about twenty years ago …'

'Of course it's a good price. You can thank your friends Jose and Miguel for that. And I think we can do a lotta good business together in the future.'

'Cash upfront?' Joey queries.

'Yes, unless you wanna leave your wife with me as a deposit.' The Colombian laughs. 'Not because I don't trust you, but if you guys get busted that leave me with a problem.'

'That's fair enough,' Joey says. 'Just outta interest, how much would you charge to deliver that quantity to England?'

'Wouldn't even a try and do it my friend. My job is to get the stuff across the sea and to this place. The rest is up to you guys.'

'Have you figure out how you going to get it back to England?' Jose asks, looking at Joey.

'Yeah, but for operational reasons I'm not going to tell you.' He flicks a grin. 'It's not that I don't trust you, but what you don't know you can't tell – even if you come under a lot of pressure to do so.'

'That's okay,' Jose responds. 'But if you want some tips or help, I can give. Miguel and I know the best ways.'

'Thanks.' Turning to Jesus, Joey says, 'When can we collect? I'm going to hire a van tomorrow, and I've got the cash already. Can we do the transaction tomorrow?'

'Get the van today,' Jesus responds. 'I call you when everything ready. Maybe tomorrow, maybe day after. You gonna pay in dollars or euros?'

'Euros if that's okay. I'll convert at the exchange rate on the day.'

'Dollars are better, but euros okay.'

Joey's phone starts to ring. 'It's Courtney,' he says, before answering. 'Courtney, you fat cunt, you missing us?' he asks. There follows an exchange that involves Joey saying 'really?' twice, 'no way!' twice and 'wear a crucifix' once. Joey puts the phone down and turns to me. 'Seems that poltergeist is bugging Courtney'. He laughs.

'It's turned up at his place?' I ask.

'No, he's housesitting at my place.'

'The amount of weed he smokes I'd have thought the poltergeist would be too stoned to cause any problems.'

Joey looks suddenly serious. 'That's a fucking point. He better not be burning holes in my carpet or furniture ...' Breaking off from his domestic concerns, he says, 'Sorry guys, just a call from someone in the U.K.. Okay, well the gear is good, the money is ready. You call me when the stuff's ready to collect.'

We talk trivialities for a few more minutes, before walking with Jose and Miguel to the car and heading back to Vigo.

'So how are you going to get the stuff back?' I ask Joey back at the hotel. He's followed me into my room and is standing in the bathroom, stroking his hair whilst staring at it in the mirror, ever vigilant against the appearance of grey hairs.

'All taken care of,' the American replies. 'We're gonna drive up to Calais and then Irish Jim's gonna fly over and pick us up. The coke's going to go into ten ten kilo tubes, and we're gonna drop them over Jim's farm near Colchester. He'll then fly on to a little air strip near Dunmow, and that's where we get off. The only risk is going to be the drive between here and Calais – and that's low – and picking up the stuff from Jim's farm – also pretty much zero risk.'

'Nice. I didn't know Jim had a plane.'

'You didn't know he had a farm either, but he does.'

'You trust him to keep his mouth shut?'

'As much as he trusts me to keep mine shut. He's buying twenty kilos of the stuff.'

I begin to wonder why exactly I'm along on the trip. It seems Joey could have done everything without me.

We meet Jesus at his villa on a Tuesday morning. The following Thursday afternoon we're flying low over the Essex countryside, preparing to 'bomb' Jim's farm. Joey stopped at a big hardware store on the drive back from Spain and bought a whole bunch of large diameter plastic piping. Using a hacksaw he chopped it into two-foot lengths. Plastic-wrapped cocaine parcels were shoved into these, and the ends sealed with caps. The result is shockproof and waterproof missiles.

'Get ready,' Jim says over the radio. He cuts the speed of the plane and Joey slides back the window of the passenger door. I'm sitting behind the other two, and my job is to feed missiles to Joey.

'Now!' Jim says, and Joey launches the two tubes he's been holding on his lap. As soon as the last one is out I lean forward with a third, which Joey jettisons. We get another two off before Jim says, 'Okay, that's it for this pass. I'll bring her around again.'

The second pass seems to go smoothly, but after the last tube goes out Joey shouts 'Fuck!' loudly and turns to Jim.

'What's up?' the pilot says.

'I owe you a cow,' Joey replies. 'One of those bombs hit a cow on the head.'

\* \* \*

Tumbling slowly, the cratered, potato-shaped mass of iron-nickel, cobalt and gallium drove forward on a course determined by gravity and chance. Travelling at fifteen miles per second, you might be forgiven for thinking the object was in a hurry to get somewhere, but this rocky lump has no destination, and had been travelling without arriving for over three billion years.

We'll call this asteroid Albert. That isn't a name an astronomer would recognise, but then the asteroid wouldn't recognise the astronomer, and there isn't an astronomer alive that is aware of Albert's existence. Currently arcing its way through the sky some two hundred and fifty one million miles from Earth, it is occupying a position in the sky that is approximately half way between Mars and Jupiter. If Albert possessed self-awareness he might appreciate the significance this portion of this particular orbit held for the asteroid, as it was just a few hours from a momentous collision.

# Chapter Thirteen

Joey gives me twenty grand for my help with the cocaine importation. I've never really had expensive tastes, but now I'm thinking I'm going to have to develop some. I'm also going to have to think of somewhere to hide all the cash I'm accumulating. There's no way Lucy is going to believe my congregation have started giving six-figure sums on a Sunday. Talking of Lucy, the money I'm now making does make getting rid of her a bit easier. I can now afford to hire a live-in nanny – preferably one who does 'extras'. The immediate priority, though, is Jake. Whether I was hallucinating my sightings of him in Vigo or not, I want to know soon that any future sightings of him are of his ghost.

How best to get rid of him, though? The inner psychopath wants to wield the blade himself, but I wonder whether that's wise. I think of asking Joey to do it. He's got bodies on him; he's done hits. My worry is having anyone other than myself knowing about Jake's fate. People talk. People can use information against you. I don't like that. In the end I decide to go and do a bit of a stakeout. Keep an eye on Jake's place and see if I can detect any sort of pattern to his comings and goings. I also want to see if he lives with anyone. That could be quite significant in making the final choice regarding the way I get rid of him.

That afternoon I hire a car, and the following morning it's parked on the opposite side of the road from Jake's house, with me inside it. The rental was a necessity – Jake will know what I drive – and I'm wearing a flat cap and shades in case he comes near my vehicle. Time passes. I read for a period. I watch a dog do a shit. I skip through a bunch of radio stations. I've brought food and a bottle to piss in so I don't have to leave the car. I eat the food. I piss in the bottle. After three hours there's been no sign of Jake. I ring his home telephone number to see if I can catch him in, but it clicks through to the answerphone straight away. Fucking hell, I think to myself. Thank God I'm not a police detective having to do this on sort of thing on a regular basis. I wonder if cops are ever going to camp themselves outside my place, watching my comings and goings.

After about four hours of fruitless waiting I decide to risk getting out of the car and stretching my legs. I walk up and down the footpath for a few minutes before getting back into the car. It occurs to me that any local residents who have seen me sit in the car for the whole morning might well wonder what I'm up to. The last thing I need is for the cops to come and start asking questions.

At a quarter past four in the afternoon, just as I'm about to give up and go home, a car pulls up outside Jake's place. There's something familiar about the vehicle, but I can't say what. Then the driver's door opens, Courtney steps out, and it all becomes clear. 'What the fuck?' I say audibly. I hold the paperback I've brought up to my face, sink a little lower in my seat, and watch with disbelief as Courtney walks up to Jake's front door. He hits the doorbell, and about a minute later the front door is opened by someone I'm ninety-nine percent certain is Jake.

My mind's spinning as I stare at the spot on which Courtney had stood until being admitted to the house. What in the name of all the divinities that have ever been and ever will be, is that fucking Jamaican doing visiting Jake? My brain struggles for traction; there just isn't anything remotely plausible about what I've just witnessed. After a couple more minutes of sitting in the car with my mouth open I realise the only possible way in which the two men could have become acquainted is by Jake making contact with Courtney. He must have figured out who my buddies and associates are. This realisation leads to further questions. What's he trying to do? Why hasn't Courtney told me anything? The whole thing reeks of treachery. How fucking lucky that I decided to turn up on this particular day.

I have to fight the urge to burst into the house right away and have it out with the pair of them. After resisting this idea I have to the control the desire to wait until Courtney emerges and say something to him. Neither idea is good. I know something they don't know I know, even if I don't know what, if anything, is being planned. I have to hang tight, think hard and bide my time. I pull my hat off and start the car.

The house is empty when I get home. While munching on a sandwich in the kitchen I notice a two-day-old copy of the local paper. Flicking idly through it, I spot an article covering the on-going investigation into the death of Kim Catcheside. The media have really caught on to the snooker ball thing, and the connection with my other murders has been made. It's with a glow of pride I see that I'm being described as 'The Snooker Ball Killer'. I've arrived as a serial killer. I have been awarded eternal life in the form of a steady stream of TV specials and trashy paperbacks devoted to my legend. It occurs to me that I only have the colour 'Black' to go. What happens after my next killing? Do I start from red again? The article informs me that a man is in custody, being detained for questioning in connection with Catcheside's death. Unlucky fucker! It comforts me that the police are so devoid of proper leads that they're hauling old boyfriends or local wackos in. Saying that, if one tenth of the population feel a tenth as hostile towards her class of individual as I do, there has to be a huge list of potential suspects.

Thinking of a past killing makes me think of an intended one. I've promised myself the murder of my wife, and I don't like to renege on promises. My original thought had been to smother Lucy, and then stage her 'disappearance'. On further reflection, I decide that this would be inadvisable on account of the need to dispose of a body. I decide, therefore, that a 'suicide' will need to be staged. In the absence of witnesses to my involvement, I don't see how the murder could ever be pinned on me. There might be suspicions, but suspicions alone wouldn't be enough to convict me.

I decide that Beachy Head is the best place to stage Lucy's 'suicide'. To that end I suggest an afternoon out there the following Saturday. I come up with some guff about wanting to spend some more quality time with Lucy – she laps that up – and tell her that Beachy Head has always been a special place for me – that it was on a visit there when I was in my early twenties that I first felt drawn to a life of ministry in the Church.

Lucy's parents are booked to come over to look after the kids on the appointed day. To add credence to what I'm going to say after Lucy tries her hand at flying, I engineer an argument on the morning of our date. I want her parents to see her upset. About an hour before her parents turn up I 'confess' to her that I'm sexually attracted to Yvonne Williams, a member of my congregation. 'I just feel I have to be honest with you about this,' I explain. 'I have no intention of doing anything about this feeling, but I feel honesty is what's needed here.'

'Yvonne?' Lucy responds angrily. 'She's fat! How can you fancy *her*?'

'That's not a very Christian attitude, Lucy,' I reprimand her. 'As I said, I'm only telling you this as part of an effort on my part to be more honest with you. Do you prefer me telling you these sort of things, or keeping these desires hidden?'

'Hidden, actually. Who else have you got the hots for?'

I pause deliberately, then shake my head and say, 'No-one. No-one, Lucy.'

'You tell me this after all that stuff with the massage parlours? I can't believe you.' Lucy slams her hands down on the table we're sitting at. 'Look, forget today. I'll ring my parents. I don't think I want a day out with you.'

I put my hand on Lucy's shoulder. 'Come on, let's not cancel today. It'll be a good opportunity to talk about some of the things in our relationship that could be improved ...'

Lucy removes my hand from my shoulder. 'I'll go, but only because it will get my parents talking if we cancel at such short notice.' She gets up and walks off with angry footsteps.

When the parents-in-law turn up soon after this exchange, Lucy lets them in. One of those telepathic mother-and-daughter-moments occurs on the doorstep, and without Lucy having to say anything her mother is left in no doubt that I've been beastly to her firstborn. The father, Arthur, is blissfully unaware of any of this, and greets me warmly when I walk into the living room. The mother, Gloria, glares at me evilly. The kids quickly burst in, running between legs and making lots of noise. 'Let's go,' I say to Lucy.

'We're off,' she says to her parents. 'Should be back by about four. There's pizza in the fridge for lunch.' Turning to Ben and Chloe she says, 'Are you going to be good for your grandparents? Remember granddad's got a bad back, and can't carry you ...' Her last words to her kids.

An hour and a half later we're nearing Beachy Head. The evil thing that seems to inhabit me has spurred me to make plenty of references to gravity during the drive. I've asked Lucy whether she's had any significant falls in her life, whether she knows about Isaac Newton's eureka moment involving a falling apple, and whether she thinks a tonne of bricks or a tonne of feathers would fall faster. If she finds my obsession with falls and falling strange she doesn't let on.

We park in a car park about two hundred yards from the chalk cliffs. I'm pleased to see just one other car in the lot – I'm relying on no-one else being around to see my wife's maiden flight. Getting out of the car the first thing I notice is a strong breeze. I grab a shoulder bag from the back seat that contains sandwiches and drinks – a Last Supper for Lucy – and we set off for the cliff. I take Lucy's hand as we walk. Her hand is warm and so evidently part of a living body. I find it strange to think that in twenty minutes or so this same hand will be cold and lifeless.

We reach the drop-off and spend a few moments admiring the view. The rocks below look far, far away. I can see a couple of large tankers out on the horizon; nearer to shore there's a much smaller boat, presumably belonging to a fisherman. I try to gauge whether the owner of this craft could see me giving Lucy a push, and decide that without binoculars this wouldn't be possible. It's a risk I'll have to take.

We spread a rug and eat a sandwich each. I don't have much of an appetite, but Lucy gobbles her food hungrily. 'Unlike you to suggest something like this,' Lucy comments with a full mouth. 'You're not about to tell me you're gay and planning to leave me for your boyfriend?'

'No. No confessions pending.'

'Do you love me?'

It's a simple question, but as I don't really get love one that I can't answer truthfully. 'Of course I do, honey.' I say. 'Why would you ask me a question like that?'

Lucy moves a strand of hair from her forehead to behind an ear. 'I don't know. Sometimes you don't seem to really be … present. It's as if you're here in body but your mind or soul are elsewhere.'

'Oh, I'm here alright,' I reply. 'Maybe sometimes I'm a little distracted with work.'

'You've always been like this. Even before you were ordained.'

'I don't know, sweetheart. I'm just the way I am. Not away with the fairies most of the time as far as I can tell.'

'Why did you marry me?'

'Well, why do most people marry each other? Because I wanted to spend my life with you. Why did you marry me?'

'Because I loved you.'

'Loved past tense?'

'You know what I mean.'

This is all becoming a bit too uncomfortable for me. I decide it's time for Lucy to fly. 'Stand up,' I say, rising myself. Lucy looks at me with suspicion, but complies. We stand facing each other, with her looking inland. Lucy's about three yards from the cliff edge. I put one hand on her waist and grab one of her hands, as if we're going to dance. The hand on Lucy's waist moves to my pocket and I take a handkerchief that is white with black dots and place it in the back pocket of Lucy's jeans. It's as near to honouring my murder signature as I deem safe. She doesn't notice me do this. The hand returns to Lucy's waist and I edge my wife back. I look over both shoulders to check there's no-one in sight, then utter the last words Lucy will ever hear: 'I've always despised you. It's always been a struggle to look at you without retching. It's time we parted company.' Lucy's eyes widen as she hears these words. I sense she's about to bolt, but before she can I rush her forward and over the cliff. There's a muted cry as she tumbles, then silence. I don't hear her hit the rocks below. A minute after her fall I crawl to the edge of the cliff and peer over. I can't see a body, but can only assume she's perished in the tumble.

I find I'm trembling slightly as I move back from the drop-off. This is the first time I've killed someone I've had a relationship with, and it definitely feels different to the stranger killings. I pull my mobile out of my pocket and dial 999.

Half an hour later a police car turns up and two officers disembark. It's time to go into acting mode as the cops walk towards me. I make my lower lip tremble and pretend to stifle sobs.

'Mr Cuthbert?' the taller of the two officers says.

'Yes.'

'You reported your wife jumping from the cliff?'

'That's right. From just over there.' I point towards where we had our picnic. 'I'll show you.'

'Was there anything to suggest your wife was feeling suicidal?' the other officer asks as we walk.

'We had an argument this morning, but otherwise no.'

The radio on the lapel of the taller officer crackles. The cop leans his head towards it and says, 'Yeah, come in Mark.'

A tinny voice says: 'Coastguard on the way. Are you at the normal jumper spot?'

'Roger. Normal spot. I'm with the husband at the moment. Keep me posted.'

'Coastguard?' I say.

'There's a chance your wife will still be alive,' tall officer says. 'If she is she will be badly injured, so we need to get someone to her as soon as possible.'

My heart sinks. 'Is … is that possible? Oh, please may she have survived! We have two young children.'

'It's unlikely she's survived the fall, I have to be honest with you. But there is a chance.'

We reach the site of our picnic. 'So talk me through the last few moments before your wife jumped,' short officer says.

'Everything seemed normal,' I reply. 'We were eating our sandwiches, talking about nothing in particular. After we'd been here for about twenty minutes Lucy stood up, saying she had a cramp in her leg. She got up, and just ran towards the cliff. Didn't say anything.'

'Whose idea was it to come here for a picnic?' tall officer asks.

'Lucy's,' I lie.

'And you didn't think this was a strange place to come?' Short officer.

'We've been here before for picnics,' I lie. 'She was saying that as we weren't going to make it to France on holiday this year the next best thing was a picnic with a view of France. I did point out you can't actually see France from here ...'

The two police officers look at each other.

'I'm not feeling too good,' I say. 'Do you mind if I go and wait in the car?'

Another exchange of looks between the officers. 'Okay, PC Summers will go and wait with you,' short officer says. 'We'll need to take some details if that's alright.'

I nod my assent.

Back at my car I give PC Summers my name, date of birth, address and contact numbers, then settle down to wait to see what the coastguard find. I sit in the front passenger seat of my car, with the door open. The cop paces up and down a few feet from me. We don't talk.

After I've been sitting in the car for about forty minutes Courtney rings me on my mobile. I look at PC Summers for direction as to whether to take the call. He nods assent, and I connect . 'Courtney,' I say. My voice sounds somehow altered to my ears. 'What's up?' What I want to say is 'What the fuck were you doing at Jake's place?' but for obvious reasons I don't.

'Joey wanted me to call you,' he says. 'He's got a job for us.'

'Not a good time right now,' I reply. 'Can I ring you back?'

'What's up?'

'Can't explain now. I'll have to fill you in later. When's the job for?'

'Tomorrow.'

'I don't think I'm going to be able to help, but listen, let me speak to you later.'

Courtney rings off. I don't want him to think I'm on to him, but I don't have time to worry about this as just then the other police officer approaches the vehicle. He walks straight up to where I'm sitting and says, 'I'm sorry to have to inform you that the coastguard have recovered your wife's body. She didn't survive the fall.'

I experience a sudden urge to start laughing, and my mouth even begins to form a smile. I have to snap out of this fast. I force myself to think of what would happen if I were ever convicted of my wife's murder, and the urge to giggle passes. I put my head in my hands. 'Oh, no,' I whimper. 'This can't be happening. We've got two small kids ...'

'This must be a dreadful moment for you,' PC Summers says, putting a hand on my shoulder. 'We don't want to keep you too long, but you're going to have to come with us to the station. We'll need to take a formal statement.'

I lift my head and do my best to splutter pathetically. 'What'll I tell the kids?'

'Where are your kids now?' Summers asks.

'With their grandparents. I ... I can't face telling them. We argued this morning. Oh fuck, oh fuck ...'

'We can ring your parents if you like,' the unnamed policeman says. Turning to Summers he says, 'I'll drive Mr Cuthbert to the station in his car. I don't think he should be driving right now.'

Summers nods. I'm driven to a police station in East-bourne. The cops treat me gently, but I know at the back of their minds is the possibility that Lucy's fall wasn't an accident. I'm taken into an interview room where Summers and another cop take my statement and question me. Has there been anything unusual about Lucy's behaviour recently? Was my wife on anti-depressants, or had she ever been treated for depression? Has she ever previously tried to harm or kill herself? I wonder what sort of expression Lucy's face bore after hitting the rocks. Would a look of terror have been frozen on her features, incriminating me? I can only hope her head was pulped on landing.

When the questions are over I'm told that I'm free to go, but that I will need to go to the local morgue to identify Lucy's body. I feel exhausted, and think about asking them whether this can be done another day, but I figure this might strike the cops as a strange reaction. A grieving husband would want to see the body of his dead wife. I *am* a grieving husband, I remind myself, emitting a phoney sob that sounds like a small mammal's squeak.

The morgue seems strangely familiar as I enter it, led by a man whose name I fail to catch. Too much Hollywood, I guess. It's all there – the gurneys, the autopsy tables, the banks of morgue freezers. I'm taken to a gurney that holds a sheet-shrouded body. The sheet is lifted from the top half of the body, and there lies Lucy, looking very dead. Her corpse isn't as badly damaged as I would have expected. Apart from a gash to her left cheek the head looks pretty unscathed. Lucy's eyes are open, and in the manner I've often heard described but never witnessed, the expression on her face is one of mild surprise. 'So that's what dying's like,' it seems to say. 'Not such a big deal really.'

'That's my wife,' I say.

On the drive back home, I feel slightly nauseous. I'm not looking forward to facing Lucy's parents, who I've now spoken to briefly. Well, I've spoken to her father; her mother was too hysterical to talk. I feel a wave of exhaustion. I really enjoy killing, but it all seems to be getting a bit much. I can't look at people anymore without seeing them as potential victims. I feel like I've been dragged into my very own horror film, one that is lasting a lot longer than ninety minutes.

Pulling up outside my house, I kill the engine and reach for a can of Special Brew I bought at a service station a few minutes earlier. I crack it open and empty the contents in two gulps. Warm fuzziness quickly envelops my brain. I can do this, I decide.

I let myself into the house and find it's very quiet. I walk into the living room. The parents-in-law are sitting on the sofa, both with red eyes and snotty noses. The kids are on the carpet, playing quietly. 'Hi,' I say to the room.

Ben gets up off the floor and runs to me, grabbing a leg. 'Where's Mummy?' he asks.

'Have you said anything?' I ask, addressing the adults in the room.

Arthur shakes a head. 'Not yet. They might have over-head something though.'

'We'll talk about Mummy later,' I tell Ben. 'She's not with me right now.'

'We'll stay tonight,' Gloria announces. 'We can stay a few days if you'd like.'

I nod my agreement.

'Can I have a word with you in the kitchen?' Arthur says, standing up. Gloria looks at me with disdain.

'You stay with your sister for a little while,' I say to Ben, prising his hands from my leg. I'll be back in a second.'

'What the hell happened today?' Arthur asks when we've changed rooms. 'Lucy would never kill herself. It's just not in her nature. No matter how dreadful things were, she'd never leave her kids.' The man is shaking and he swallows uncomfortably. I can smell whisky on his breath.

I open my mouth to reply, but he isn't finished. 'What were you two talking about this morning? Lucy wasn't herself when we saw her earlier.'

An opportunity presents itself. Now is the time to 'reveal' some sort of horrible truth. It has to be truly horrible, but also a lie that can't be found out at a later date. I have about two seconds to think of something.

'I'm not sure I should share this with you,' I begin. 'Today's been horrible enough without telling you about this.'

'Nothing can make today any worse than it already is,' Arthur replies. 'Out with it.'

I sigh deeply. 'Lucy ... Lucy has been struggling with a realisation that has made her very unhappy recently ...'

'What? What's she been struggling with?'

'She ... she recently came to the conclusion that she is attracted to people of the same sex. That she's a lesbian.'

'What?' Arthur face is screwed up with incredulity.

'I know. I couldn't really believe it myself, but she insists – insisted. Obviously it was putting a huge strain on our marriage, but also making Lucy feel very guilty. We're both of the opinion that homosexuality is considered wrong by God. I know many in the Church feel differently, but that's always how we've always felt. So Lucy felt she was not only in a relationship with someone she didn't feel comfortable with, but that if she followed her heart or inclinations she'd be committing a sin. An awful bind for anyone to deal with ...'

'Did she share this with anyone else?'

I shake my ahead. 'No. She could barely admit it to her-self.'

'My God. And to think I woke up this morning think-ing it would be just another day. You mustn't say anything about this to Gloria. I think it could lead to *her* doing away with herself ...'

'I'm happy not to say anything to her directly, but can't promise she won't find out eventually. I'm going to have to tell the police about this if they need any more information.'

Arthur exhales deeply. 'If you must ...'

We return to the living room and I sit in an armchair, looking at the kids. Gloria leaves the room as soon as I enter, mumbling something about preparing food. As I gaze at Ben and Chloe I can appreciate quite clearly that in murdering their mother I've done something that, if not wrong – I don't really get 'wrong' – is not ideal. I wouldn't go so far as to say that I feel sympathy for them – again, I don't really understand what that means – but I feel close to understanding what sympathy might be like. Ben picks up a yellow Tonka truck and holds it up for me to see, smiling. I smile back. I consider my kids in the way that a gardener might consider prized plants. I don't love them, but I would like them to reach maturity and thrive. I might need their help in later life; they could be a source of pride. Taking the plant analogy further, in getting rid of Lucy I've done the equivalent of a gardener loping off the tops of his seedlings. They may survive, but I certainly haven't done them a favour. I resolve to provide both kids with extra academic coaching as soon as they get to an age to be able to benefit from it. It'll be something to spend my cash on, and the very least I can do.

Later we eat a meal of soup and toast. The kids and myself eat well, but the grandparents are evidently not hungry.

'Do you think we should say something?' Arthur asks while we're at the table.

'What do you need to say?' Ben asks. He's no fool.

I look at Ben and Chloe. 'You're probably right,' I say. 'Kids, I have something I need to tell you ...'

\* \* \*

'She what ...?'

It's the day after, and I've finally gotten around to ringing Courtney. 'Yep. Just threw herself off the cliff. Died straight away apparently ...'

'Holy Shit. How you bearing up? And the kids?'

'I think I'm still in shock,' I lie. 'Don't think it's really sunk in yet. Same with the kids.'

'Well, man, I'm really sorry to hear about this. I don't blame you not phoning me yesterday. I'm sorry I called you.'

'You weren't to know.'

'Have you told Joey?'

'Not yet. Was going to ring him after I spoke to you.'

'I can talk to him if you want.'

'No, no it's fine. Life has to go on. Was going to ask you what Joey wants us to do, actually. Figure it might be good for me to stay busy at the moment.' *And I can keep an eye on you, you devious fucker.*

'Just another whore pick-up. Wants us to collect tomorrow and deliver to some Turks in Hornsey.'

'I'll come along,' I tell Courtney.

I wander the house aimlessly for a while after talking to Courtney. Everyone's home, and there's a funereal atmosphere permeating the house. Gloria still won't look me in the eye, and isn't saying much to me either. The kids are subdued but not visibly upset. I went and bought them some toys earlier, and these seem to be helping to distract them. I don't really know if they get death. They haven't had any pets that have died. Ditto relatives, though that may not be the case for much longer judging by how their grandparents are taking Lucy's death. I don't think they really understand. They probably think it's like going bust in a game of Monopoly. There's always a new game to be played the following week.

As I move about the house I keep feeling the difference between myself as an independent entity and other objects and people is blurring. My son runs towards me, and I feel like I'm running at myself. I see unwashed dishes in the sink and want to brush myself down as if my clothes are covered with gravy. I've heard of depersonalisation syndrome, and wonder if that's what I'm experiencing. Maybe I'm just going mad, plain and simple. I've got to be a good candidate for madness, given what I've been up to over the last year – last forty years you could say. Maybe I've always been mad. I take a piss, and wonder what happened to the piss in Lucy's body when she died. Does it just stay in her body, or trickle out? Thinking of Lucy makes me think of the funeral arrangements I'm meant to be making. I can't really be bothered. I think maybe I'll delegate this to the parents. I walk back into the kitchen. There's a bottle of port in one of the cupboards, with a broken, discoloured cork in the top. I pull the cork out and gulp down a few fingers of the stuff. It's far too sweet for my taste, but after about a minute I can feel that nice fuzziness again.

Courtney picks me up at ten the next morning. He's got a lit joint in his mouth and he passes it to me as we pull off. The end of the joint that's been in Courtney's mouth is soggy, but I take a big puff anyway and pass it back. 'Thought you might need something to mellow you out,' my companion explains. 'Sorry again about what happened.'

'Saves me divorcing her,' I say, immediately regretting I've been so candid.

Courtney grunts.

'I'm thinking of getting ordained into some church,' Courtney announces after a period of silence.

'You what?'

'Yeah, I'm feeling a bit left out. You guys got your church thing, I want mine.'

'But it's just a coincidence that we're members of the Church,' I say. 'We're the last people they should ever have let in.'

'Yeah, but we're the Three Musketeers, like. It ain't right that I'm not a priest. Plus being churchmen helps you. No-one suspects churchmen of crime.'

'Well, apart from child molestation and buggery,' I say. 'Anyway, you can't just become a priest overnight. I spent three years at theological college.'

'I'm gonna look into Rastafarian priesthood. It's gotta be quicker than three years. They probably give me credits for all the spliffs I've smoked ...'

'Whatever ...' I say, wondering if Courtney hasn't been overdoing it with the spliffs.

We arrive at the nunnery. 'How many are we picking up today?' I ask. Courtney's car is big, but it isn't a van. We probably couldn't carry more than three girls unless we start using the boot.

'Just two. You want to go and get them? You look more like a priest than me, and they've met you before.'

Out of the car, smooth down shirt, walk to main door, press doorbell. A big wait before the door is opened. Nun looks like a dyke. She gives me an unwelcoming look before saying, 'Can I help?'

'I work with Father LaMotta. I'm here to collect a couple of the women you've been kindly providing accommodation to.'

'Come in,' she says, with an unspoken 'if you must'.

I'm led to the same room I've waited in before, and left alone with a, 'We shouldn't be too long.'

Five minutes pass. Then another five. Then yet another five. I'm beginning to wonder if I've been forgotten, and text Courtney to tell him I'm still waiting. When ten minutes later I've still seen no sign of the nuns I get up and walk towards the door. As I reach it the Mother Superior appears in front of me, followed by two women.

'Ah,' I say. 'Thought you'd forgotten about me ...'

'No, no. It just took a little while for the girls to get their things together.'

Looking at the women I see that they're both trailing wheeled suitcases.

'Well thanks again for helping these young ladies,' I say.

'Our pleasure. The only thing I would say is that we seem to lose all touch with the women after they move on. We've often thought it would be nice to hear how they're getting on with their new lives.'

'Um ... I'll have a word with Father LaMotta,' I reply. 'He's the administrator, keeping phone numbers and things like that. I'll ask him to give you a ring.'

'That would be greatly appreciated.' I'm gifted with a beaming smile.

The four of us make our way to the front door, and after an exchange of kisses and a cheery wave from the Mother Superior, the two girls and myself walk towards the car.

Courtney gets out of the car and loads the suitcases into the boot while I try and gauge how much English the girls have. 'I'm Adam,' I say to them. 'Have you enjoyed your stay here?' This is the first time I've taken a proper look at the women, and I'm immediately struck by the shorter of the two. She looks Indian, not European, and has a beauty that I find mesmerising. There's more to my reaction than just an appreciation of her appearance, however; she's *me* I feel, as strange as that sounds. It feels like I've always known her, or at the very least always known that I *would* know her.

The other woman replies to my question, but I don't hear what she's saying. I'm transfixed.

We drive away. Courtney tries to engage me in conversation, but I'm too busy looking in the rear view mirror at the angel sitting behind me to be able to respond coherently. Is this love at first sight? I wonder. Probably not, because I don't do love, but it's got to be something similar. Infatuation at first sight, maybe. My mind starts spinning. I can't handle the thought that this woman is going to be imprisoned in some hovel of a massage parlour shortly, taking dick from any ugly, sweaty bastard who happens to have sixty pounds spare. Then it all falls into place. No Lucy, kids need someone to cook for them, me thinking about getting a live-in nanny.

'Courtney, how much ... er ... money has been promised for the cargo we're currently transporting?' I don't want to give the game away to our passengers.

Courtney glances at me before saying, 'Five each.'

'Is that all?'

'We paid two each, so not that bad ...'

'I'm going to take one of them,' I announce.

'You what?'

'Just what I said. One on the left. She's mine. I'll pay the money.'

'But you can't do that. The guy we're on the way to is expecting two girls. He'll hit the roof.'

'We'll just have to make something up,' I say. 'Tell him there's another one coming.'

Courtney shakes his head. 'What the hell do you want this Babylon woman for? You gonna put her to work?'

'Not like that. Remember Lucy's gone now. I'm going to need some help at home.'

'Well you better call Joey and tell him about this. And tell him I told you you was crazy.'

I ring Joey. I think he might be in bed with someone, as he sounds out of breath and distracted. Probably not the best time to put my proposition to him. 'You wanna do what?' he says, clearly confused and irritated.

'I want to take one of the pieces of merchandise. That's right. I'll pay whatever the other guy was due to pay.'

'You can't man. The guy you're dropping off to is a good customer. If we start messing him around we'll lose him.'

'Lucy's dead.'

'*What??*'

'Committed suicide a couple of days ago. This isn't a good time to say "no" to me Joey ...'

There's a long pause, before Joey says, 'Are you kidding me?'

'No, I'm not.'

'Why didn't you tell me?'

'I just have.'

'Jesus man ... Okay, take the broad. She's on the house. But what are you going to do with her? Get her working?'

'No, I'm going to take her home with me. Get her to help look after the kids.'

'Well you'd better get Courtney to drop you off first. Tell him to tell the guy we'll have number two for him within a few days.'

'Okay, will do.'

'You take it easy buddy. Sorry to hear about Lucy. I'll come over to see you tomorrow or the day after ...'

'He's cool about it,' I tell Courtney after ending the call.

'Pull up here, so I can explain what's happening to my lady.'

Courtney does as I ask, and I turn around to face the Indian. 'Sorry I don't know your name?' I say.

'My name is Chanda,' she replies, with a trace of a smile.

'Hi Chanda. Well this is going to sound a little strange, but it turns out I need someone to help me at home – I lost my wife recently – and I was just wondering if you'd be interested in doing that? You'd get your own room, and I'd pay you as much as you'd have earned in the ... hospitality business. Are you good with kids?'

Chanda looks at her companion. 'Just me?'

'Yes, just you.'

'I suppose so. But I would need to meet your children first. To make sure that they like me ...'

'That's fine. We could even say, give it a try for a couple of weeks. If you're happy you stay, if you're not you can do the hospitality work.'

Chanda nods her consent.

'Okay, we'll go to my place now.' I look at Courtney, who starts the car.

The next challenge is going to be explaining my new servant to Lucy's parents. They're still staying, and showing no signs of being in a hurry to leave. We pull up outside my house, and Chanda, Courtney and myself disembark. Courtney gets Chanda's suitcase from the boot, then gets back into the car with a 'good luck!' by way of farewell.

'Well here we are,' I say. 'My wife killed herself two days ago, and her parents are staying with us at the moment. They won't be expecting you, and they may seem a bit jumpy, but we'll get over that. I have two children – Ben who is five, and Chloe who is six. I think they'll like you, and I hope you like them.'

Chanda says, 'I understand. I'm sorry about your wife.'

I open the front door, and standing before me in the hallway is Gloria. She's obviously been crying, and holds a crumpled tissue in one hand. 'Hi there,' I say, stiffening up. 'I'd like you to meet Chanda ...'

'Who is *this*?' Gloria says with menace.

'This is Chanda. She's going to be helping out around the house.'

'Arthur!' Gloria shouts. 'Arthur, come here now!'

Arthur emerges from the living room and looks at Chanda and myself for a few seconds before saying, 'Yes, dear?'

'Adam has brought this ... this person home. Tell her she must go.'

'What are you up to Adam?' Arthur says. 'Is this the time to be bringing strangers home?'

'Chanda has been introduced to me by the nuns at a convent my church has a relationship with. With Lucy gone I'm going to need an extra pair of hands around here, and I think Chanda could be very helpful.'

'But that's what we're here for!' Gloria shrieks. 'Have you been carrying on with this ... this *thing* behind Lucy's back?'

'Gloria ...' Arthur says in an admonishing tone.

'Well it's all a bit odd ...'

'I think what you're forgetting is that this is *my* home,' I counter. 'As much as I appreciate your help, it is I who decides who does or doesn't stay here. Chanda *will* be staying.'

'Well if she's staying, I'm going,' Gloria says, before breaking into a sob.

'So be it.'

The kids come down the stairs at this point to see what's causing the commotion. 'What's going on?' Ben asks.

'Ask your father,' Gloria says. 'I'm going to pack.' With that the woman barges past the children and starts making her way up the stairs.

'I think your timing is unfortunate,' Arthur says. 'No disrespect to your ... friend, but we're still all in a state of shock here.'

Chanda steps forward and kneels in front of Chloe. 'My name is Chanda,' she says softly. 'And you are Chloe?'

'Yes,' Chloe says with a smile. 'And this is my brother Ben, and he stinks.'

By the following morning Arthur and Gloria have left. Arthur maintained a fatherly neutrality throughout his last hours under my roof, but Gloria alternated between hysteria and rage. With the kids at school, I finally have some time alone with Chanda. She spent most of the previous evening in her room, unpacking and keeping out of Gloria's way.

'So you think you'll be okay here?' I ask. We're sitting in the kitchen, sipping tea.

'I like it here,' Chanda replies. 'You have two beautiful children. Much better than working as a prostitute.'

I come very close to spitting out a mouthful of tea.

Chanda smiles at me. 'You think I didn't know what a "hospitality" job involves?'

'Then why did you agree to travel from India?'

'I knew my fate awaited me here. As my guru says, "if your heart is pure, circumstances can't harm you". My body is just flesh. It will melt away one day.'

'So you were willing to work as a prostitute if you had to?'

'I was confident that fate would intervene before that happened – as has happened. But yes, I would have worked in this way. In India we have sacred prostitutes – devadasi – I would have approached my work with this attitude.'

'I've heard about these sacred prostitutes,' I say. 'But that involves both participants having a respectful and spiritual attitude towards the sex act. If you were working over here that wouldn't be the case. You'd be sleeping with sweaty men whose idea of spirituality is getting drunk on whiskey.'

'The lingam is the lingam, whoever it belongs to ...'

'And what do you think of me then?' I ask. 'A priest that would lure you into prostitution?'

'I don't have an opinion. Life must have some important lessons for you in this incarnation.'

I feel like I could sit here talking to Chanda for hours, but just then the doorbell rings. Opening up, I see Joey and Courtney standing before me. Joey steps forward and gives me a hug. 'How you holding up buddy?' he asks.

'Not too bad,' I say. I suddenly feel protective of Chanda, not wanting her to be contaminated by the presence of these other two. 'Place is a bit of a mess,' I say. 'Want to grab some lunch at Entwhistles?'

The two men nod. 'Give me two secs,' I say. I walk back into the kitchen and say to Chanda: 'Popping out for an hour or two. Relax. Don't worry about tidying up or anything.'

Chanda nods, and I return to my companions.

At Entwhistles, famous for its seafood and a waitress who supplements her income by turning tricks, Joey pumps me for information about Lucy's demise. I answer his questions with an economy of words and information. I think he soon realises I'm not going to talk at length about my wife's death, and the subject changes.

We talk crap for some time, before, on the spur of the moment, I decide to see how good an actor Courtney is. Looking directly at Joey I say, 'You know that guy I've mentioned who has it in for me?'

Before he can reply I switch my gaze to Courtney. The expression on his face is serene. He's either very stoned, a great actor, or it wasn't him I saw at Jake's place recently.

'Yeah.' Joey says. 'What's happened?'

'No, it's just it might have been my imagination, but I could have sworn I saw him a couple of times when we were in Vigo. Plus, he's been causing me some trouble with the Church. If it carries on I think I'm going to have to step in. Might need your guys' help with that.'

'Step in have a word or step in break his neck?' Joey wants to know.

I glance at Courtney again. Still nothing. 'I think maybe break his neck. I'm worried he might try something stupid. Hurt the kids or go for me.'

'Let me know if you want to some help,' Joey says. 'That's no problem.'

'You be able to lend a hand?' I ask Courtney.

This time I catch a glimmer, just a glimmer, of something – embarrassment? shame? – before he answers: 'Yeah, sure. Always happy to help. I already hit him once, I guess.'

Lucy's funeral takes place on the Saturday following her death, conducted by Joey at St. Joseph's. The choice of a Catholic church for her farewell service no doubt causes some mutterings amongst the many members of my congregation that attend, but their misgivings aren't a concern of mine. Arthur and Gloria are quite direct in their opposition to my chosen venue, to the extent that I'm quite surprised they turn up. Chanda looks after the kids. I'm not opposed to them attending, but I throw a crust to Gloria in having them stay at home; she's adamant that the experience would be too upsetting for them. According to Gloria a death by natural causes would have permitted their attendance, but not death by suicide. I wonder what Gloria's stance would have been had she known that Lucy passed at my hands.

Joey seems a bit rusty as he leads the service. I know for a fact that he'd been up half the previous night with his latest squeeze, which I'm sure isn't helping matters. He keeps clearing his throat and his delivery is stilted. I have Courtney sitting to my right in a front pew. To my left is Arthur, and to his left is Gloria, splendidly decked out in black and with a box of tissues on her lap.

Lucy's sister Emma shares her memory of my wife with the congregation. They spent a year travelling the world when they were in the early twenties, and I cannot believe my ears when the woman recounts their experiences in New Zealand, where the duo spent a month 'walking, white-water rafting and bungee-jumping'. Bungee-jumping! Is the woman mad? The mention of this activity sets Gloria off. I struggle to keep a straight face.

I say my piece. I keep it short, hoping to make my words

poignant and precise. I try to set my face with an expression that reveals sorrow tinged with promise. Refreshments are provided afterwards in the church hall. Joey gets one of his more motherly bitches to take care of the catering, and I have to say she does a good job. It's with relief that the event draws to a close.

When I get back home I go into the kitchen in search of a sip of something alcoholic and experience one of those moments of incongruity as I see the evidence of a break-in. There's shattered glass on one of the kitchen worktops, and I stupidly think someone must have broken a glass before I look up and see that a window has been broken. The broken window has enabled a window latch to be turned, in turn enabling the intruder's access.

I head straight for the living room, expecting to see a missing TV and a hole in my CD collection. Instead, everything looks as it should. I rush upstairs and check my bedroom. None of Lucy's jewellery is missing. Confused, I go to my study. This, it seems, was the intruder's main focus. There are papers strewn all over the floor, the drawers of the desk are open and have obviously been rifled and my PC is on. I know it had been switched off before I left that morning.

I realise quickly it must have been Jake. The expensive Swiss watch my father left me remains in the top drawer of the desk. Whoever has been in the house was after information, not valuables. I try to think of anything incriminating that could have been found in the house. I don't keep a diary of my criminal and immoral activities. There's the clip I took of Joey and company discussing cocaine importation in Spain on my computer, but I doubt Jake or anyone else would know to look for it. There *are* five coloured snooker balls on my desk; leaving them on display is sloppy, I have to admit. Whoever broke in must have known about Lucy's funeral. Chanda has taken the kids out for the day, so the intruder's timing was perfect.

# Chapter Fourteen

A week later I'm back in the kitchen, talking to Chanda. Over the previous days I've gotten to know the woman much better. I've tasted her cooking (good), observed her interaction with my kids (firm but kindly) and come to appreciate her sense of humour. There is definitely something unearthly about her. Sometimes when I'm looking at her, her face seems to pixelate, as if she's trying to turn into someone else; other times when I look at her I seem to be looking at all of Womankind, both good and bad. This doesn't faze me, however, simply increasing my curiosity.

'Did I tell you I spent time in India when I was younger?' I ask Chanda.

'No. Were you on holiday?'

'Yes, an extended holiday. I went there to meditate and find myself.'

'And did you find yourself?'

'I don't think I did ... though I did have some interesting experiences.'

'Maybe that's why I'm in England,' Chanda says wistfully. 'To find myself.'

'You think so?'

'Not really. I found myself when I realised there was no-one to find.'

'And how did you realise that?'

'I didn't seek the realisation. It came to me unbidden.'

'Sometimes I don't really have a clue what you're talking about,' I admit.

'Words have their limitations,' Chanda says. 'Maybe there's a picture I could paint that would enable me to express myself better.'

I feel like telling Chanda all about my murderous exploits. I stop to analyse why this might be. It's not as if it would be a means of unburdening myself, because I don't feel bad about what I've done. Except about Lucy, and only because of the impact her death might have on my kids, and only because that in turn might have an effect on me. No, I think it's curiosity more than anything – an interest in what she would say if she knew.

'I still can't quite understand how you allowed yourself to be trafficked to England,' I say. 'If you knew what you were letting yourself in for, surely it would have been much simpler just to say "no"?'

'My guru taught me to grasp any opportunities that arise …'

'Would you have lain on a railway track if your guru had recommended it?'

'Probably. The train could only damage my body.'

'Were you not tempted to tell the other girls at the convent what lay in store for them? They probably won't have your philosophical attitude towards prostitution.'

'One I did tell, and she ran away. The others I judged could handle what awaited them. Either that or they would flee once they realised the truth.'

'Not as easy as that. Passports confiscated, threats of violence …'

'These women aren't really left without a choice. They just need to put their head out the window and start screaming … it wouldn't be long before they were rescued. Or they could bite the penises of the men that come to them, and be discharged that way.'

'That or have a gun discharged at them …'

We lapse into silence for a while, before I say, 'Are you not curious as to what a Minister of Religion is doing being involved in prostitution? Do you not wonder what else I might be up to?'

'My life has been full of strange happenings and peoples, so I have learned to accept that surprises are not very surprising.'

'You sound like Yoda a lot of the time,' I say, grinning.

'Yoda?'

'You haven't seen Star Wars?'

Chanda shakes her head.

'Now that *is* seriously strange ... It's a famous science fiction film. One of the characters is a shrivelled up little character with strange syntax and a knack for talking shit that sounds deeply philosophical.'

'No, I haven't heard of this character.'

'Well, you remind me of him anyway.' I look at the fingernails on my right hand as if I've never seen them before for a few moments, before fixing my eyes on Chanda. Again, I experience a sense of a loss of individuality or 'Iness' and a merging with my surroundings, and in particular Chanda. For a brief moment I see myself as if looking at my body with Chanda's eyes. The sensation is disorientating and scary, and I shake my head as if trying to break a spell. This seems to work, and now I'm being fed with images from my own eyeballs. I feel like crying. What the fuck is going on with me?

'Are you alright?' Chanda asks.

'I feel a bit strange,' I admit.

'I sense that. The illusion might be slipping.'

'Which illusion?'

'This that one.'

'What?'

Just then I hear the letterbox flap slap with its spring recoil. I get up to investigate. Lying on the hallway floor by the front door is a large A4 envelope. I pick it up and walk back to the kitchen. The envelope doesn't have an address or stamp on it. I open it, and pull out a single sheet of white paper, which has a red, blue, yellow, pink, brown, green and black dot on it. For a second I think about rushing to the door to see if I can spot Jake fleeing, but decide not to; I know full well who the deliverer is, that's obvious. I hold up the sheet of paper for Chanda to see.

'Who would that be from?' she asks.

'I have a hunch who the sender might be,' I say, but don't provide any more information. Jake's definitely onto me. In the preceding week I've spent a couple of mornings staking out his house in the hope of seeing if Courtney would make a return visit. He didn't turn up on either day. I've reached the conclusion that I might have to get rid of the pair of them.

Later that day I get a phone call from Sussex police. They explain that there will be an inquest into Lucy's death, date to be confirmed, but in the meantime there are a few more questions they have for me, and would I be available if they visited the following day? I can't really say 'no'. We agree to meet at ten the following morning.

It's one of the officers that attended at Beachy Head and another policeman I've not met before who turn up the next day.

'This is just a formality,' the officer who introduces himself as Detective Ringer explains after we're seated in the living room. 'We really just wanted to follow up on a couple of things.'

I nod.

Ringer continues: 'You mentioned on the phone the other day that your wife had been upset on the day of her death, that there'd been some sort of argument. Can I ask what the argument was about?'

'Someone I knew many years ago messed up on drugs and ended up working as a prostitute,' I say. 'Since entering the Church I've made a point of trying to help woman who sell their bodies, and this has caused ... caused some tension between us. Someone was anonymously trying to suggest that I had a more ... sordid interest in prostitutes.'

Ringer: 'Was anyone else aware of these tensions?'

'My parents-in-law know that we'd had a bit of a row the morning of the day of her death …'

'So your wife suspected you of using prostitutes?' Ringer asks.

'I don't think she *really* thought I had used them,' I reply. 'But you know what women can be like. If they're feeling a little bit insecure it doesn't take much to set them off.'

'There's something else,' the other officer, says. 'When the body of your wife was recovered we found something in her pocket.'

'And what was that?'

'It was a letter. A letter from someone called Jake. Do you know this person?'

I'm aware that I am now faced with a critical moment in my life, and how I answer this question is going to have a huge bearing on the rest of my life. The problem is that the correct answer is dependent on information I don't have – and asking for said information might be as harmful as answering incorrectly. In particular what I want to ask is, 'What does the letter say?' and 'Do you know the sender of the letter's full name?'

I clear my throat and say, 'Jake? I probably know a few Jakes. Jake who?'

'That we don't know.' My heart lifts. 'But he seems to know you and seems to think you may have committed some murders.' My heart drops.

'What?' I say. I have so many questions. 'That's preposterous! Who am I meant to have killed? Why wasn't this mentioned before?'

'The note was missed on our first search of your wife's clothes, plain and simple. It was addressed to your wife, but unopened. I'm sure she'd have said something if she had read it.' It's Ringer talking. 'I can't give you any more information about the contents of the letter, for operational reasons. That doesn't mean that we necessarily suspect that the letter's allegations are true; it's just how we have to handle matters. What I would like from you, by tomorrow, is an email with a list of all the Jakes you know or have known.'

'Do you realise what I do for a living?' I say. 'That I'm a vicar?'

'I do realise that, and as I said, in asking you for this information I'm just following procedure. If you want my honest opinion, I don't think you've ever killed anyone. Unfortunately, given the circumstances, my opinion isn't enough.'

'Fair enough,' I say.

Ringer hands me a business card. 'Email address is at the bottom. I appreciate this. We'll try and get this resolved as quickly as possible.'

We all stand up. When we get to the door Ringer says: 'Just one more thing. If, as you say, the letter is rubbish, you need to ask yourself who might have sent it, and why. If you have any thoughts on this, please include them in the email.'

My hand is shaking as I close the door on the cops. I go straight into the kitchen and help myself to a huge glass of port, then head upstairs to my study. Seated, I take a large gulp of the liquid and stare out the window that overlooks my desk, taking in the large oak tree at the bottom of the rear garden, behind it the backs of the houses that line the road that runs parallel to mine. I curse myself for being so taken by Chanda over the last week. I've taken my eye off the ball and forgotten about the real threat facing me – Jake. What *has* that fucker been up to? It sounds like he has been following me for weeks – probably *was* in Vigo during my stay there. I'm certain now that it was he that broke into the house.

I'm pleased that the cops don't know which Jake wrote the letter. The next question is, could they work out who the author of the note is? Jake's prison sentence is a matter of record, but as I was never charged in connection with the murder he was convicted of, I can't see how a link between the two of us could easily be established. Jake is going to have to die, however, and when his murder hits the papers there's a chance the spotlight might fall on me.

That leaves the question of Courtney. I still don't know what, if any, relationship there is between him and Jake. I wonder whether I should go to Joey and get his advice. What if Courtney's an informer? Joey seems sure he's kosher, but how can anyone really tell for sure?

Courtney, Courtney ... On the spur of the moment I pick up my mobile and dial his number. Four rings – a good, average number of rings – before he answers. 'Courtney! What are you up to?'

Thirty minutes later I'm sitting in Courtney's living room. I've only been to the man's place once before, and have forgotten what a strange approach to interior design he has. The kitchen, where I spend a couple of minutes while Courtney pours drinks, is all chrome and white, with sleek appliances and a tiled floor so clean you'd swear the builders had just given it a final buff after laying it. The hallway seems to be trying to indicate rustic charm, with autumnal colours, real wood flooring and prints of English rural idylls on the walls. The living room is a hallucinogenic jungle nightmare. Walls painted three different shades of green in a kind of tiger-stripe pattern, slate floor tiles and a profusion of tropical pot plants, many doing their best to punch holes in the ceiling. Despite the weather being quite mild the radiators in this room seem to be on full blast. The moisture escaping from the plants means the room isn't just hot, but also humid. On one wall, in a prominent central position, is an oil painting of Haile Selassie.

Courtney rolls a big spliff and lights it up. After taking a couple of deep puffs he passes it to me, then starts playing with the remote for his huge stereo system. Halfway through my first puff on the joint the music comes on at what can't be far off full volume, making me jump. Even I recognise the track as Parliament's 'Mothership Connection'. How apt, I think. For though he doesn't know it, Courtney is soon going to be flying on the Mothership, care of a drug called Burundanga – Devil's Breath – scientific name scopolamine. Produced from a tree native to Colombia, I have a small capsule of it in my pocket. A website called The Silk Road, where anonymous sellers sell to anonymous buyers, with the help of an untraceable electronic currency called Bitcoins, has enabled me to acquire some. I bought the scopolamine a few months ago, as it's commonly used as a date rape drug, but the package it arrived in has remained unopened until today. Administering it to Courtney should quickly render him pliable and zombie-like, with no subsequent memory of the next twelve hours. I'll soon find out what he's been up to with Jake. Slight drawback: if I give him too high a dosage, he dies. Or is that such a bad drawback?

We talk for a while as I consider how to get the drug into Courtney's drink. The music and marijuana seem to get Courtney onto his favourite topic after women and drugs: 'This music, man, it's just awesome,' he says, shaking his head. 'Soul music, funk music, reggae. It's the Holy Trinity. Have you noticed how the music just soaks into you? It's like you're gettin' marinated in sound.'

'Yeah, I guess.'

'Take soul music,' he continues. 'Some people think it's too sweet – too much harmonizing, and oohing and aah- ing and men singing in high voices. But sometimes sweet is good. Sometimes you wanna sit in a big tub of cotton wool and have you balls tickled. Sweet soul music is a bit like those Krispy Kreme donuts. You know you shouldn't but you so want to, and that crap tastes better than just 'bout anything you can get in a fancy French restaurant. If you went to a fancy French restaurant and they gave you cubes of Krispy Kreme donut – except they call it something dif- ferent – and they dribble some little sauce on it – the restau- rant critics, they would go crazy!'

'You got a point there,' I say. 'There was some conspiracy theory going around a while ago that claimed they put some sort of chemical in those donuts to get people hooked.'

'Yeah, they do put something addictive in them,' Courtney says. 'It's called sugar.'

I pass the joint back to Courtney who drags contentedly.

'You still trying to become a Rasta priest?' I ask.

'Yeah, I'm goin' to a branch meetin' next week. I talked about it with some brothers. You can pretty much be a priest just by saying you are. I and I don't have long trainings to be a priest.'

'Why do you say I and I?'

'Not meant to use the word "we". We're – I mean "I and I" are all "One". Everything is "One", everything is "I".'

He's starting to talk like Chanda, I think to myself. 'Aren't you Rastas meant to think black people are superior to whites?' I ask.

'That's the theory,' Courtney admits. 'But each man can interpret things as he want. For example, black men *do* make better athletes than whites. Fact. So in that respect it's true.'

'That's true,' I say. 'No denying that.'

I look at Courtney's glass of whiskey. He's only taken a couple of sips so far, but that doesn't mean he won't gulp the rest in one go in a second. I need to get him out of the room. I have an idea. 'Argh!' I cry, grabbing the calf of my left leg. 'Fuck that hurts!'

'What's up?'

'Fuck, fuck, fuck,' I say, grimacing. 'I get these fucking cramps. Come out of nowhere and hang around until I take my medication ...'

'You got it with you?'

'No. Shit. It's in my car. Problem is I can't walk there.'

'I'll get it if you want,' Courtney offers.

'You mind?' I pull my car keys out of my pocket with one hand, whilst continuing to massage my calf with the other.

'Glove compartment. Little white bottle with a "Spasmo-dex" label.' I throw my keys.

After I hear the front door open I quickly remove the gelatine capsule from a compartment of my wallet. I also pull out a handkerchief. I approach Courtney's drink, and using the handkerchief to protect my hands, pull the two ends of the capsule apart. Apparently just a sniff of this stuff or a bit on your skin can get you. I shake the powder into Courtney's drink, suspending breathing as I do so. I step back and drop the capsule bits behind a sofa. Looking around I see a pen on a coffee table. I use this to stir the powder into the drink. It's meant to be odourless and tasteless, so as long as he doesn't see bits of powder he shouldn't suspect a thing. The front door slams shut, and I quickly sit back down.

'Couldn't find it,' Courtney announces. He's still got the spliff in his mouth.

'It's okay. Cramp seems to have eased. Thanks for checking.' I think about toasting something to get the rest of Courtney's drink down his throat, but decide this might be too obvious. Instead I take a sip of my drink, then say, 'A lovely drop this. What did you say it is?'

'It's a Lugavalin. Single malt – obviously.' Courtney's hand reaches for his drink. I watch intently as glass meets lips. He drinks.

Courtney stubs the butt of the spliff. 'Want another one?' he asks.

'Why not ...' I'm still looking at Courtney closely. This Devil's Breath stuff isn't meant to make the imbiber go apeshit. They're meant to just do everything you ask of them without question. In Colombia it's apparently mainly used by criminals who want victims that will help them empty their prey's houses. There's no staggering or frothing at the mouth; you only know someone's had too much when they drop dead. I'll wait until Courtney's emptied his glass, then ask him if he's ever sucked cock. If he doesn't try and attack me I'll know the drug's kicked in.

Another joint is rolled, puffed on and passed to me. I take a drag, then make a big show of sipping my drink, using exaggerated movements and smacking my lips loudly after the liquid has slipped down my throat. Courtney takes a slug from his glass. There isn't much left of his drink now. It can't be long before his ass is mine.

'You okay with this music?' Courtney asks. 'Want me to put something else on?'

'No this is good. Still Parliament, yeah?'

'Sure is. You know I saw them in Chicago a while back, at The House of Blues. The main guy, George Clinton – he must be about sixty now – anyway, he came on stage wearing nothing but a diaper. Big fat belly, and wearing nothing but a diaper!'

I wonder if this is the proof I need that the drug is taking effect.

Courtney continues: 'Me, I think the music I like is part of a cosmic plan to save the planet. Like I say, the Holy Trinity. Funk is the Father – the spark, the male oomph – reggae is the Son – lots of jumping and jigging and its home in a young nation like Jamaica where we gets lots of sun – and soul is the Holy Spirit.'

'Tell me Courtney, have you ever sucked a big fat cock?'

'Yeah, once. When I was in prison when I was about twenty. It was either that or get beat up.'

Bingo. 'And how did you find the experience? Enjoyable?'

'Not really. But not as bad as getting beat up. You could say it was the lesser of two evils.'

'And you've never taken it up the arse?'

'No. Never up the arse.'

The time is now. Courtney is primed and ready. I drain the last drops from my glass, clear my throat, and say, 'Courtney, I'd like to know what you were doing at a guy called Jake's house a while back. He's someone I have a beef with, as you know, and it concerns me that you two are friends or acquaintances.'

'Oh, Jake, sure. He got in touch with me a month ago or so. Knew I knew you, somehow. He knows we're up to bad things. Wants me to help him get some big dirt on you so he can have you sent to jail. If I don't he'll get me in trouble.'

'What does he know about what we've been up to?'

'He knows about the whores. Trafficking them. He's got photos of you driving them away from the convent and dropping them off to buyers. He has an idea about the coke we're starting to shift. He thinks you've killed a bunch of people as well. He also gave me a copy of some camera footage showing you and Joey talking drugs in Spain. Joey went crazy when he saw that.'

'So he knows about Joey?' I ask.

'Yeah.'

'Has he spoken to him?'

'No, but I have.'

'What did he say?'

'He's thinking about it. Says we might have to hit this guy, but he's worried that that might not be enough. Jake says he has left a letter and a memory stick with his lawyer guy which tell everything.'

'What does Jake say about me killing people? What does he know?'

'He's always following you. He was bangin' on about snooker balls. This killer guy has been leaving snooker balls in people's mouths, and he knows it gotta be you. There's some other stuff he knows about you killing but he wouldn't tell me what it was.'

'Do you think he's right about me killing?' I ask, before reaching for a cigarette from an open pack on a coffee table.

'I don't know. You say this is the guy you said you were having trouble with, yeah?'

I blow smoke. 'Yeah. Tell me, why haven't you or Joey spoken to me about this?'

'We ain't made our mind up about what to do. No point

tipping you off in case this problem is gonna get solved with a bullet.'

'If you did sell me out, don't you think I would grass you guys up?'

'Yeah, we've thought about that. That's what makes it all pretty complicated. Joey said we could threaten to kill your kids if you open your mouth, or we could get rid of you.'

'Of course,' I say.

Thank God for scopolamine, that's all I can say. I start to get worried about how long the drug is going to work for. I've heard twelve hours or so, but lack the confidence of someone who has used it many times. I think I would probably kill the man straight away, but I've recently phoned his mobile from my landline. It would be too immediate a connection. What is sure is that blood is going to be spilt over the next few days. Maybe quite a bit of blood. Murder has been a hobby up to now. It's soon going to be a necessity.

I think I've heard enough. It's time to get away and plan my next move. 'Hey Courtney,' I say. 'I'm just going to go and empty a bunch of spirit bottles down the sink, then scatter them around the living room so that when you come to in a day or so you think you've been on an enormous bender. Okay?'

'No problem.'

'In fact, do you mind drinking a bottle of whiskey so you have a real hangover?'

'Sure, man.'

'Okay – just stay there for a bit.'

I go into the kitchen, and open cabinet doors. I pull out a half-full bottle of Bacardi, an unopened bottle of Jack Daniels and an almost full bottle of Gordon's gin. I empty the gin and rum down the sink, running the cold water tap for a bit to flush the drink. After opening the Jack Daniels bottle I walk into the lounge with all three bottles.

'Here we go,' I say, topping up Courtney's glass to the brim with JD. 'Get that down the hatch.' Courtney obliges.

I fill the glass up again and say, 'And again.' Courtney doesn't let me down. Good man.

I unscrew the lids from the two empty bottles, and chuck bottles and tops on the carpet. I then place the bottle of JD at the foot of Courtney's seat.

'How you feeling?' I ask Courtney. 'Feel that booze?'

'A bit I think,' he replies. His eyes have reddened, that much is obvious.

'Right, well get the rest down your throat. Just drink from the bottle – it'll be quicker.'

Courtney does as I instruct. Within a couple of minutes there's a third empty bottle in the room.

'Okay, Courtney, I'm off. When you came to you're not going to remember anything of what we spoke about. You'll just remember me having a quick drink with you. What you did after I left your head will tell you all about. We clear?'

'Sounds good to me.'

'Good,' I say. 'I'll probably be over to kill you in a couple of days.'

'Okay then ...'

I leave the house, and head straight home.

* * *

Shortly after we last met the asteroid Albert, it collided with an asteroid we'll call Alfred. Albert and Alfred, both composed of similar materials, and with a similar size (roughly half a mile long and about two hundred yards wide) begat a third asteroid we'll call Aldous. The impact of its parents not only created Aldous, but sent it on a trajectory that would take it out of the Asteroid Belt, and towards a small planet that contains water and has an atmosphere.

# Chapter Fifteen

On the drive home my mind is turning at about the same speed as the wheels of my car. I fear I'm facing the End Game. Within a week, I accept, I will probably be dead or in prison. If I'm not, several others will be dead. I wonder how Courtney will react when he comes to. Even if his memory of our time together post-drug is completely wiped, he'll still recall me as the last person he saw before he woke up in a mess, so I can expect questions from him at the very least. I run through my options. I could kill Jake, Joey and Courtney. Difficult to hit three people in a matter of hours, however, and it wouldn't guarantee that evidence won't remain that survives the death of its originator; the letter with a solicitor Courtney referred to, for example. I could do a runner. I have more ready cash now than a year ago – I could just take off to South America. Start all over again. I could also go to Joey and tell him that I know what he knows. Join forces with him to get rid of Jake. *Mind blowing decisions causes head on collisions …*

Suddenly I realise I want to talk to Chanda about my predicament. Her unflappability, the way she's able to retain perspective – I'm going to tell her everything.

When I pull up at home Chanda's outside, watering the front garden. She's wearing jeans with a heavily embroidered Indian-style blouse and her feet are bare. As I walk up to the house I admire the poise with which she moves, as if each step she takes is a meditation.

'Hey,' I say. 'How you doing?'

'I am fine.'

'Can I have a word with you inside?'

'Certainly.'

Seated a few moments later, I say, 'Chanda, I want to ask you for your advice. I don't know why I'm coming to you like this. I've just got a gut feeling it won't make things any worse – maybe couldn't make things any worse.'

Chanda look at me expectantly. 'Please tell me.'

'Well … I happen to be a very bad person – a murderer in fact.' I look closely at Chanda, waiting for her to throw her hands up in shock, or flee screaming. She just nods. 'I've killed people for no reason other than that I wanted to,' I continue. 'I like the thought that there are bodies buried because of my actions. I've done plenty of other bad things, and now it looks like all of this stuff is coming back to haunt me. I fear I'll soon be dead myself, in prison, or with even more blood on my hands.'

I fall silent, waiting for the reaction. Chanda is silent for what seems like at least two full minutes, before reaching over and taking my hand. 'Don't worry about the killing, except in the way that it interferes with your life and children. You are killing the body, but you don't kill the soul. The soul doesn't need the body, but the body needs the soul.'

'You don't think it's wrong to kill?'

'It's better not to, of course,' Chanda replies. 'But people worry too much about their bodies, when they should be thinking more about that which survives death. When you are killing you are just killing yourself, so your punishment is immediate.'

'Well,' I say. 'If I have a soul I'm sure it's in a bit of trouble right now, but I'm worrying more about what happens to this body over the next few days.' I go on to explain about my predicament with Jake, the police, Courtney and Joey.

'What do you think is the best course of action?' Chanda asks.

'I really don't know. I know I can't do jail. I'd rather kill myself than go there. I've got so much blood on my hands I don't see how a little bit more's going to make much of a difference. But I think I am getting tired of killing. Funny. Now's the first time I've felt this way. Up until now I couldn't seem to get enough of murdering.'

'How quickly do you need to make a decision?' Chanda asks. 'How long have you got before people start making decisions for you?'

'Let's go for a walk,' I say, suddenly feeling claustrophobic in the house. 'Let's walk and talk.' I stand up.

There's been a shower of rain since I got home, and the pavement and road glisten with moisture. The sun is weak but unobscured, and there's a light wind.

'Have you seen the local park?' I ask.

'No,' Chanda says.

'I'll show it to you.'

I take Chanda's hand as we walk. I expect her to pull away, but she doesn't. As we head down my road, I see a number of people walking in our direction, spaced at intervals of ten yards or so. As I near the first pedestrian I get a shock, as I'm convinced it has to be the twin sister of my first victim. Or did I not actually kill her? Is she still alive? No sooner have I had this thought than I pass the next walker, and discover she is the spitting image of my second victim. The woman looks at me as we pass, and though I might be imagining it she seems to have a smirk on her face. *Thought you got rid of me?*

'I keep passing people who look like my victims,' I tell Chanda. 'Look at this guy here. He looks just like someone I killed. So have all the others we've passed.'

Chanda squeezes my hand. 'Ignore them. They're not real. Nothing is real apart from Divine Oneness.'

I deliberately avoid looking at anyone else I pass before reaching the park. It's a typical suburban park. Children's play area at one side, near a small café; large grassy expanse with a border of trees; low iron fence. The only thing that sets it apart from thousands of other urban parks is the huge oak tree that grows smack in its middle. It looks as if it has to be at least four hundred years old, with a thick, twisted trunk and lower branches that have the same girth as many trees' trunks.

The oak tree's position and size invites attention, and I stand looking at it for some time. Suddenly I am the tree, looking back at myself standing a hundred yards away. I feel myself occupy the branches of the tree in the same way that as a human I'm used to having the sense of a body inhabited. Unlike the way in which human consciousness seems to be centred in the head, as a tree consciousness seems dispersed between all the thousands of leaves the tree has. I wonder what will happen after autumn. Do I sleep until the spring? I try to wave at myself by moving a large branch. I can't move the branch myself, but seconds after 'I' have this thought a gust of wind shakes the branch I had in mind. *I'm over here. Look at me!* From the distance the human me stands from myself I can't see if I am aware of the arboreal greeting I'm giving.

I stay in tree-consciousness for what seems like quite a long time. I can feel the weight of water droplets on my leaves, the swaying motion that bends me to my heart wood, the extent of my root network that extends almost to where Chanda and myself stand. I like being a tree. The sense of groundedness – it sounds corny, but I feel so secure rooted as I quite literally am in the ground. I feel a sense of timelessness, of nothing needing to be done apart from being, of nowhere to go and nothing to want for.

I snap back to my human body and feel a wrench that has to be comparable to that felt by a newborn baby. 'Fuck,' I say. I become aware that I'm squeezing Chanda's hand. 'I just had the most amazing experience. Just out of this world. See that tree over there? I was *it*!'

'Of course you are it,' Chanda says. 'You are everything you see.'

'What do you mean?'

'Well, when you look at a tree – or anything – where is that image being created?'

'In my mind – my brain.'

'That's right. You're creating the image of the tree. That tree is part of you. You can never know a tree or anything else apart from through the agency of your mind.'

'I guess, but why did I 'become' the tree just now? That isn't normal.'

'You're breaking through, I think,' Chanda replies. 'To murder is to do perform one of the most extreme acts a human can perform. You have committed several murders. I think these deeds are breaking the veil for you, allowing you to see the truth of reality. When you became a tree that is just a facet of reality – in reality you are the tree. You are the tree, and the wind, and the books you read, and the victims you kill. That is why murderers are punished straight away, because in killing another they kill themselves. Everything is One.'

'I don't want to kill anymore.'

'Good - why would you? Who wants to kill themselves?'

The enormity of the consequences of my behaviour over the last year – over the course of my life – hits me. I feel like I've just been trampled by an elephant. It's hard to distinguish between the cocktail of emotions I'm feeling, but in amongst them is something that feels like I imagine remorse must feel. I think I actually feel sorry for what I've been up to.

'This makes things simpler and more complicated.' I say. We've started to walk the path that encircles the park. 'I don't want to kill, but that leaves me with options like flight, surrender or my own death. I don't really want any of them, either.'

'In a year's time everything will be resolved,' Chanda says. 'You'll be resigned to whatever has happened.'

'Do you think I should hand myself in?'

'I trust you to make the right decision, whatever that may be.'

After a couple of circuits we start walking home. I still feel strange, my consciousness seeming to flit from where it is normally centred to random locations and objects. Despite the difficulty of the choices facing me I feel a peace that I've never really known before.

When we get back Chanda leads me up to the bedroom and we make love. It seems the most natural and obvious thing to do. Our movements synchronise wonderfully, the tempo is perfect, and we both have deep and satisfying climaxes. I fall asleep, waking after an hour or so. When I open my eyes I see Chanda. She's lying on her side looking at me, her head supported by a hand. I smile, and say, 'I'm hungry.'

'So am I,' Chanda says, moving her body onto mine.

Later that day I pick the kids up from school. I spend some time playing with them after they've changed out of their school clothes. I feel like I've returned from a long, difficult journey. They seem to pick up on the change in me. At one point Chloe says, 'Are you alright Daddy?'

'I'm just fine,' I reassure her.

Later, when the kids are in bed, I say to Chanda: 'I was always convinced I was a psychopath. From my reading of the literature, there isn't really a cure for this condition. You can maybe learn to control your urges, but the urges and essential pathology remain. Have I been cured, I wonder? What do you think?'

'I don't know about this psychopath thing. All I know is that labels cause as much problem as they solve. You are just you. If you now feel peace, then leave it there.'

I imagine going straight over to Courtney's house now and shooting him. Could I do it? A moment's self-analysis reveals that I *could*, but also that I certainly don't want to.

The next morning I get a phone call from Courtney. 'Fu ... fucking ... I ... sh ...' he mumbles.

'Courtney, are you alright?' I say.

Before he can answer my landline starts to ring. 'Courtney, I'll call you back,' I tell him. I pick up the home phone. 'Hello?'

It's Ringer ringing, wanting to know why I haven't emailed him as promised. 'On its way,' I promise him.

Seconds after putting the phone down the doorbell rings. Opening the door I'm greeted with the sight of an angry looking Joey. He barges past me, saying, 'Where is that fuckin' moron? I've been trying to ring him for hours and no-one's answering at home.'

I follow Joey into the living room. 'Who?' I say to his back. 'Courtney?'

'Who fuckin' else? He's meant to be picking up some more bitches.'

'I was around there yesterday,' I say. 'The spirits and dope were coming out. He's probably caned. He rang me just now so he's still alive.'

'Forget caned, he's gonna get canned if I don't hear from him soon. Let's go over and break his door down.'

I hesitate. Chanda appears in the doorway. Fuck it, I think. 'Okay,' I say. 'Let's go.'

On the drive over I'm tempted to think of possible responses to what we'll find when we get to Courtney's; what I'll say, how I'll react. In the end I decide not to bother. I'll just go with the flow.

Arriving at our absent colleague's house, Joey gets straight down to hammering on the door. 'Courtney!' he shouts. 'Get your fucking ass to the door!'

There's no reply, and Joey tries the gate that leads to the path that connects front garden with rear. It's locked, and he gives the gate a kick. Joey returns to the front door and resumes hammering, pausing occasionally to kick the door. He looks on the verge of conceding defeat, when the door opens. Courtney stands in the doorway, looking like death.

'What the fuck have you been up to?' Joey demands to

know. 'You're meant to be fifty miles away picking some girls up.'

Courtney looks at me suspiciously. 'I don't know what happen. I was having a drink with him. Next thing I know I'm like this ...'

'You were okay when I left you,' I lie. 'Don't blame me if you decide to party the night away on your own.'

'You look like shit,' Joey says. 'Can you drive?'

'I can try.'

'Will you go with him?' Joey asks me. 'I've gotta meet a big coke customer.'

'Okay,' I say.

I take the wheel for the outward leg. Courtney sits beside me sipping coke and looking like he's about to vomit. There's an atmosphere in the car, and I wonder how long it will be before Courtney mentions our recent time together.

It's about ten minutes later that the subject is broached. 'Did you spike my drink or somethin' when you were over?' Courtney asks.

My hands tighten on the steering wheel. 'No. Why do you ask?' I deliberately keep my eyes on the road.

'Something ain't right. I don't really like huge amounts of booze, but there's lots of empty bottles in my house. Plus I can just about remember some stuff that just ain't right.'

'Like what?'

'That's the whole point. I can't remember it. Yet.'

'Why would I want to spike your drink? You're not my type ...'

My remark doesn't elicit a response.

We drive on for another mile or so before Courtney says, 'Pull over here.'

The hair on the back of my neck stands up. 'Why?' I ask.

'Just do it.'

I pull over, making sure it's directly outside a busy green-grocer's. No point making it easy for him.

'Get out,' he says.

'Why? Why should I?'

'Get out, or I'll throw you out. You lucky I don't have a weapon on me.'

I open my mouth to protest, and Courtney punches me hard in the left temple. I open the door, causing a car coming from behind to swerve right. I get out of the car and watch as Courtney shifts into the driver's seat. The door closes and he takes off with the squeal of tires.

Fuck, fuck, fuck. I stand on the pavement watching the rear of Courtney's car moving away while massaging my head. What has he remembered? What's he going to do next? I have a clear vision of him dialling Joey from his car. No, no, no. Not while there's breath in my lungs. I pull my mobile out to ring Chanda, but discover to my alarm that it's dead. There follows a frantic search for a phone box. I find one after about fifteen minutes, but then realise I don't have any coins. Another ten minutes wasted as I break a note to get change. Finally I'm able to call Chanda; she picks up after about ten rings, saying, 'Hello?'

'Chanda, it's me,' I say. 'Listen, things are moving a bit faster than I expected. I need you to get the kids together and get out of the house. Just take what you can easily carry. Go to that Italian restaurant at the end of the road – Bepe's or whatever it's called. Get a table and get something to eat. Don't leave until I get there.'

'What's happened? Are you okay?'

'I'm fine at the moment, but it isn't safe for you to stay at home. Have you got money?'

'Um ...'

'There's a couple of hundred pounds in the top drawer of the desk in my study. Take that. Take your phone with you. You got it?'

'Yes.'

'Okay, I'll be with you in about an hour. Try and be out of the house in the next five minutes.'

'I will.'

I get money out of a cashpoint machine, and then walk along the High Street I'm on until I find a mini cab office. A couple of minutes later I'm in the back of a late model Toyota that smells of tobacco, heading towards Chanda and the kids. I know what I'm going to do first – pick up Chanda and offspring – it's what I do after that that I'm not too sure about. I have to assume that Courtney won't be a threat for a couple of hours – it'll take him a while to do the pick up and drop-off. I also have to assume that he will speak to Joey or Jake – maybe both – and that he'll be saying something along the lines of 'he's on to us'. Exactly what Courtney recalls from his scopolamine session I can't be sure, but if he has a vague memory of spilling the beans about Jake he'll probably assume he's said more rather than less. If he knows I know that he and Joey are debating getting rid of me he'll assume I'm either going to squeal to the police or try to eliminate my colleagues. Whichever course of action they think I'm more likely to take, they'll want to get to me first.

I tell the cab driver to wait after we pull up outside Bepe's. I make a quick scan of the road, then get out of the car. On entering the restaurant I discover Chanda and the kids halfway through a meal. 'Sorry guys, we're going to have to move,' I say. 'Come on, forks down, on your feet.' The kids look at me, puzzled. I wave a waiter over. 'Sixty cover this?' I say, throwing some cash on the table. Without waiting for his response I begin shepherding my charges out of the building. As we're leaving the restaurant I see a car that looks like Joey's parked about fifty yards away, but I tell myself it can't be him. He'd been so anxious earlier to meet his coke customer. When we're all in the taxi I say to the driver: 'The Holiday Inn by Preston Park.'

We check in to the hotel. Two rooms – one for the kids and myself and one for Chanda. The four of us gather in Chanda's room and I start fielding questions from the kids. Why are we here? When can we go home?

'Some builders need to do some repairs to our house,' I explain. 'We'll only be here for a couple of days.'

Chanda opens the single travel bag she packed and pulls out some toys and books, distributing them to the kids. They shift their attention to paper and plastic, and I use this opportunity to beckon Chanda into the bathroom. I leave the door open but keep my voice low: 'That guy Courtney I was telling you about knows that I know that they're thinking of getting rid of me. I think, anyway. That means they'll probably want to get to me before I can do any damage. No way we can go back to the house until this blows over.'

'How will it blow over?' Chanda quite reasonably wants to know.

'That's what I need thinking time to figure out,' I say. 'We'll be here for a while. No outside excursions at the moment. I'm going to try and sneak back to the house at four am or something – pick up a few essentials. I'll go in if I'm sure the coast is clear.'

Chanda nods. 'This is for the best. You need resolution to these issues.'

'I know. I just didn't expect us to get to this stage so quickly.'

I go down to reception to borrow a phone recharger. After returning to the room we spend the following hours talking, reading to the kids and half-watching the crap being pumped out by the television. At about seven we order some room service; sandwiches for Chanda and myself and sausage and mash for the kids. Against my better judgement I order up a couple of beers. My mobile has been on for a couple of hours but the only call I've taken is from one of my church deacons, enquiring about the replacement organist we're having to organise for the following Sunday. Not a peep from Courtney or Joey. At about eight o'clock I decide we should all get some sleep. It's past the kids' bedtime, and I want to get my head down in anticipation of an early rise. Chanda volunteers to share her room with the kids and I decide not to argue.

My iPhone alarm rouses me at three in the morning. Fighting the desire to ignore the gadget and go back to sleep I swing my legs out of bed and rub my eyes. I dress, check I've got phone, wallet and keys, then leave the room.

I curse as I leave the hotel. It's raining, and not realising this I didn't get the hotel to book me a cab. I've got a walk of a mile or more to my house. I trudge in the direction of home. Cars pass me infrequently, their tyres swishing as they displace water. As I get to within a couple of hundred yards of the house I start scanning for Joey or Courtney's cars. Courtney currently drives a banged up old Land Rover, which would be hard to miss, but Joey's wheels are a silver Japanese model, and I'm not sure I'd recognise it if it ran over my foot.

I don't see anything with four wheels that looks familiar as I close in on the house. Now I'm paying attention to every parked vehicle I pass, looking to see if they contain passengers. A few cars; no-one visible inside. A thought occurs to me: even if I can't see anyone lying in wait for me, that's not to stop Courtney or Joey breaking into the house and waiting for me there. The alarm wouldn't have been set, and I'm sure either of them could gain access in less than ten seconds. I look around for a makeshift weapon, but can't see anything more offensive than twigs.

I'm now standing in front of the house. Lights off: no surprise there. My car's still in the driveway: that's good news. I advance cautiously, examining the front door and the ground floor windows at the front, looking for signs of a break-in. There's nothing to suggest this. I creep over to the gate that guards the path to the rear garden and gingerly depress the lever that opens it, proceeding to the back of the house. I give the rear door of the house and rear ground floor windows the same inspection I gave those at the front of the house – again, no signs of someone forcing entry.

It's now or never. I go back to the front door and let myself in. As soon as I've swung the door open by about thirty degrees I pause and adjust my head to give my ears the best chance of hearing any sounds from within the house. Nothing. I open the door fully and walk into the house. I think about slinking from room to room until I've covered the whole dwelling, but decide instead to start switching lights on and making my arrival very obvious. What the heck, if there's someone waiting for me creeping around will only extend my lifespan by about three minutes.

To my relief, I discover the house is empty. After using the bathroom I go straight to the kitchen, helping myself to a half pint of port. I down it in two gulps. After that I go up to my study and pocket the revolver hidden at the bottom of my toolbox. I retrieve three passports from a filing cabinet, then go into Chanda's room and grab hers from a chest-of-drawers. Anything else I might need? I decide to pick up my laptop. I go back down to the kitchen, take another slug of port, then leave the house.

I drive back to the hotel. I nod at the sleepy member of staff manning the reception desk and make my way to the lift. Third floor, ping, and I'm out on my landing, destination room 213. I'm about to swipe myself in when I notice that the room the kids and Chanda are in, 215, is open a crack. Puzzled, I push the door fully open. The lights are on, but there's no-one in their beds. I check the toilet, just in case they've decided to have a communal bath; the bathroom is empty.

'What the fuck?' I say. I pull my mobile out of my pocket and dial Chanda's number. The call goes straight through to voicemail. I check my room just in case they're there. They're not, and in a panic I run towards the lift. Reception seems to be my only chance of finding out what's happened.

The guy on reception doing the graveyard shift looks up at me guiltily when I approach the desk. Probably been looking at porn, I think to myself. 'Did a woman and two young children leave just now?' I ask.

'Yes, they left about ten minutes ago,' he replies. 'They were with a man.'

'Fuck! What did the man look like?'

'A big guy. Black, with dreads.'

'Jesus Christ.'

'No, he definitely wasn't Jesus Christ,' the receptionist says.

I glare at him. 'I think this guy might have been abducting them. Did they look scared?'

'Not really … Abducted? Do you want me to call the police?'

'That's okay. I need to be sure about this before ringing them. Thanks anyway.'

I go back up the Chanda's room and take a closer look. There's no sign of a struggle, though that isn't altogether surprising, as I wouldn't have struggled against Courtney either. How the fuck did he figure out where we are? I wonder. And why take them away? He could have just stayed in the room and waited for me to turn up. As they know where I'm staying should I check out? I figure there's no need to, as they presumably want the kids more than me. I suppose I could just go home. I pick up the phone to try and ring Courtney, then think better of it and throw it onto the bed. They'll call me when they're ready, and I might even be able to strengthen my hand my not appearing to be perturbed at my kids' abduction.

I decide to pay Jake a visit. It's been long overdue. I don't know what I'm going to do or say when I get there; I just know it's time to see him. I re-pack the bag Chanda brought, check I haven't left anything in my room, then leave the hotel.

I feel a sense of calm as I drive the seven or so miles to Jake's house. The roads are quiet; the wind that had been gusting while it was raining has now abated.

Despite the ungodly hour, Jake answers the door shortly after I ring the bell.

'Hello, Jake,' I say. 'It's been a long time.'

'It has been,' Jake says. Looking at my former friend I can see the passage of years evident in his appearance. His hair has flecks of gray, the skin puckered around the eyes. It's still him though, still the Jake I used to run with.

'Can we talk?' I ask.

'The gun in your pocket suggests I don't have much choice in the matter,' Jake replies, opening the door fully and standing back to let me enter.

Jake leads me into the living room and we both take a seat. 'So,' I say, 'Congratulations on your efforts so far. I can't say I blame you ...'

Jake rubs his nose. It's a small, pert nose that I always used to think would look better on a woman's face. 'I don't blame myself, either,' he says. 'So what, have you come to shoot me now?'

I pull the gun out of my pocket and drop it on the floor. 'No,' I reply. 'I'm done with killing. I came to ask you if you know what's happened to my kids and housekeeper.'

'No. Why would I?'

'They've been abducted by your new pal.'

'Courtney?'

'The one and only.'

'I'd have thought he'd be more interested in you than them.'

'So would I. They obviously want to get to me through them. Tell me, why didn't you just go to the police? Why contact Courtney?'

'Why?' Jake chuckles. 'Because I wanted to fuck with you. I know enough to put you in prison any time I like. I thought I'd have a bit of fun with you first. I've had a lot of years to think about revenge – it's something I've wanted to savour. Don't think picking up that gun and shooting me will make any difference, either. There's a letter lodged with my solicitor. The day a doctor signs my death certificate is day the letter's opened and its contents communicated to the police.'

'Fair enough,' I say. 'It's what I deserve. I'm not really bothered about what happens to me. I just want my kids back safely.'

'How did Courtney find out that you knew I'd been in contact with him?' Jake asks. 'He said he and your other friend were going to need a while to figure out how to use the information that I gave them.'

'I've been watching your house, buddy. You were next on my list. Was staking out your place to see what your comings and goings were when that big git turned up. Couldn't fucking believe it. Thought it might have been coincidence at first. That you were bum chums or something. In the end I drugged Courtney and got the truth out of him that way. Stuff I used is meant to wipe your memory, but I guess I didn't give him enough or something. He spilled the beans, but must have remembered talking.'

'And now they know you know what they know they think you're going to kill them or something.'

'More likely they think you're going to squeal to the police yourself, and when I'm nicked I'll open my mouth. I don't know, I give up.' I stretch languorously. 'For what it's worth I'm sorry about what I did to you. If I stay alive long enough I'll tell the police that I left that johnny in the bed.'

'It doesn't change the fact that I killed someone.' A pause. 'So you've finally seen the light? The scales fallen from your eyes?'

'Maybe.'

We fall into silence for a while, before I ask, 'How many murders do you know I committed?'

'Including or excluding your wife?'

'Whichever ...'

'The only one I know about for a fact is Kim Catcheside, because I followed you there and photographed you creeping around her property. I did some research on unsolved murders in the area, and noticed a lot of them seemed to happen pretty close to where you live. One involved a friend of a member of your congregation. The clincher was that you've been dubbed the 'Snooker Ball Killer.'

'Congrats. Maybe if you hadn't been locked up you could have been gainfully employed locking other people up. Tell me, did you follow me to Vigo?'

'To where?'

'To Vigo, in Spain.'

'Never been there in my life. Why do you think I have?'

'I was sure I saw you a couple of times when I was there recently.'

'Probably your guilty conscience ...'

I stare down at the gun lying on the carpet. 'Well look, if you don't want to shoot me – and I'd understand if you did – I think I'm going to go and ponder my next step.'

'I'd love to shoot you, mate. Problem is, I know what it's like to spend time inside, and I'm never going back there ... I think your day of reckoning is coming without me having to put a piece of lead in you.'

'You're probably right,' I say. 'I've been a fucking cunt for most of my life, but something's happened recently ... I don't really understand it, but I feel different. It doesn't really make sense, but I feel as if instead of becoming a better person I've become a different person. If you're still intent on getting revenge on me it's too late; I'm not that person anymore.'

As I walk the hallway to Jake's front door my conscious-ness seems to split into three. It's not just that I seem to be seeing three doors in front of me, but that with each view of the door I have a different mind accompanying it. With one I feel relieved, with the second I have a mild headache and with the third I'm remembering a house I used to live in that had been painted a similar colour as that of the hallway walls, a light peach. It's a disconcerting sensation. As I reach out to turn the door handle I see three hands extending to grasp three handles. They all connect at the same time, and three doors open to three black nights. I shake my head and suddenly I'm down to two consciousness tracks, then there's a flashing sensation on the periphery of my vision, and suddenly I seem to be confronted with an infinite number of sensory inputs and associated thoughts. It's sensory overload and I'm forced to close my eyes for a few seconds. There's no way I can drive in this state. I grope my way to my car, feeling for the door handle, and somehow get myself into the vehicle. I sit in the car, looking out through the front windscreen. There's an infinite amount of information being fed into my brain. I see a tarmacked road, a tarmacked road with a pot-hole about ten yards ahead, I see instead of a tarmacked road a rough dirt track; but that's just the beginning, there's a countless number of variations on this theme, overlaid one on top of the other, staring back at me, each associated with a unique mood, thought, smell, memory and age. I feel like I have about ten seconds before the fuses of my mind are blown and I succumb to a madness for which there'll never be a cure. I climb onto the backseat and close my eyes. Although the visual input disappears I can still feel a billion minds intermingling and chattering concurrently. The Billion Mes become deafening; it feels as if my skull can't possibly contain the pressure building within it. Just when I feel my head is sure to explode I lose consciousness.

When I come to, dawn has broken. I seem to have a unitary consciousness, which relieves me to the verge of tears, but I feel its presence is shaky; like a muscle that was cramping and has now relaxed but is quivering, on the verge of contracting again. I think about knocking on Jake's door again and asking to sit with him for a while, but instead decide to go home. I climb into the driver's seat and start the engine.

I'm still feeling shaky and on the verge of another collapse into multi-consciousness as I open the front door of my house. I don't care if there's someone waiting for me inside the property; a gun-totting Courtney holds no terror for me after the madness of the last few hours. I walk into the living room and flop into an armchair. I wonder if maybe I'm just having some sort of mental breakdown. Could I have developed schizophrenia? I wonder. If smoking too much dope can bring it on, then surely smoking five or six people has to be in with a chance of being a causal factor. Maybe my nerves are just shot.

I go into the kitchen and grab the bottle of port that has been comforting me over the last week. There isn't much left so I drink from the bottle, draining it in three gulps. I find another unopened bottle of the same grog and pop its cork. I carry this with me back to the living room. I retake my seat, closing my eyes and breathing deeply. I open my eyes after a few minutes and see three of Ben's green plastic army men standing guard on the arm of the sofa. *Keep 'em locked and loaded, boys.*

My mobile rings. As soon as my fingers contact it in my pocket my consciousness splits into two. Two hands pull two phones out of two pockets and lift them up to eye level. In one reality channel the display says 'Courtney', whilst in the other it says 'Number Withheld'. Both phones are answered simultaneously, with the same "Hello" and then the replies come back. From Courtney: 'we need to meet'; from Detective Ringer: 'this is Detective Ringer, wanting to speak to Mr Cuthbert.'

Courtney Track (Me): 'What have you done with the kids and Chanda?'

Ringer Track (Me): 'Yes, speaking.'

Courtney Track: 'That's what I'm ringing about. We need to meet, sort this all out.'

Ringer Track: 'I haven't received that email you promised me. You were going to let me know about the Jakes you know or have known.'

Courtney Track (Me): 'What the fuck have you done with them? If any of them are hurt you're going to fucking die.'

Ringer Track (Me): 'Sorry, no I haven't sent it yet. You'll get it in the next couple of hours.'

Courtney Track: 'They're fine. They're doing well. Can we meet tomorrow? We need to talk about this little misunderstanding. Smooth things over.'

Ringer Track: 'If you could do that, I would appreciate it. We may need to pop over for another chat in the next few days. I take it you wouldn't be adverse to that?'

Courtney Track (Me): 'You want to meet up so you can put a bullet in my head? Yeah, I'll meet you. There's a police station off City Road. Meet me in the reception area tomorrow at ten am. Make sure you've got one of the kids with you. You'll need to hand a kid over as a sign of good faith.'

Ringer Track (Me): 'That's not a problem. Just let me know.'

Courtney Track: 'I'll need to call you back about the meet. Keep your phone on.'

Ringer Track: 'Okay, I'll be in touch. Bye.'

Courtney Track (Me): 'Okay.'

Ringer Track (Me): 'Bye.'

Two hands kill two phone calls. I feel dizzy, despite being seated. Two Adams stand up and take in two superimposed views of the room. With one I'm looking off to the right; with the other I'm gazing leftwards. I don't know what to do. I wonder whether I should ring 999/go for a walk and try and get some fresh air. Both Adams remember that they haven't showered in a couple of days, and we both walk upstairs to the bathroom. That's when things start to get really freaky. We both undress, but then one of us – I don't know if it's Courtney Track or Ringer Track – starts to run a bath, while the other one turns the shower on and gets into the cubicle. Have you ever leaned over a bath, testing for temperature, while at the same time soaping yourself up under a warm spray? Once the bath is run we both close our eyes. One of the mes climbs into the bath while the other continues to stand under the shower in blackness. We know this split will probably fade, that unitary consciousness is going to come back pretty soon, but the longer it lasts the more scared we feel.

We get out of the bath/shower at the same time. We're intermingled, sharing the same space as we dry off. One of us is using the towel I customarily use, the other a pink towel Lucy favours. After drying off we both dress in the same clothes – a second pair seems to clone itself with ease. We both walk downstairs and knock back the whole of the newly opened bottle of port in one. There's a ten second delay before we both feel well pissed. After the disorientation of the last half hour being pissed doesn't feel as out of control as it would normally – in fact there's something comfortingly familiar about the sensation.

We split up at this point. One Adam decides it isn't safe to stay in the house. He goes upstairs, grabs a sleeping bag, then gets into the car and drives to a pub about two miles away. It has a car park at the rear that tends to be half empty, which he parks in. He buys two bottles of cheap red from an off licence opposite the pub – bottles with screw tops – then goes and sits in the car. He starts drinking, figuring another bottle will lead him to pass out, guaranteeing at least some respite from the fear his current state is generating.

The other Adam goes upstairs and gets into bed. He switches on the radio that's on his bedside table and starts listening to the BBC World Service, hoping the feature on agriculture in Kazakhstan will distract him. It's quite an interesting report, but he's simultaneously aware of holding a wine bottle to his lips and then getting annoyed when he spills some liquid down his shirt. Both Adams start to cry. In due course car-park-Adam drinks himself into oblivion. Home-in-bed-Adam doesn't get respite when this happens, however, as instead of getting the feed from the car he gets a dream feed. And the dream feed is a bad one; nightmares of a huge Courtney stamping across the city, looking for him with a gun. In the dream Courtney is so big the roofs of houses come up to his ankles. His feet crush any buildings they land on as if they were made of cardboard.

The Adam that isn't asleep closes his eyes tight and starts to shake. Finally, sleep rescues him.

I wake up in unitary consciousness in the car. I'm relieved, so relieved to be just me – or just one me. Then I start panicking. Do I have another body that's lying untended in my bed? Did Courtney bust in and shoot me in bed? I rub my eyes before starting the car. It's dark. My watch says it's six in the morning, but I don't know if several hours or several days have gone by since I passed out. My head hurts. It can't have been several days.

I tear out of the car park, tyres screeching, and drive as fast as I dare back to the house. I don't so much park the car when I reach my destination as execute a controlled crash. The front bumper of the vehicle smacks the garage door with enough force to dent it. I open the door and jump out. Fumbling with my keys I let myself in and run up to my bedroom. Throwing myself through the doorway I'm both alarmed and relieved to see there isn't anyone in my bed. Oddly, the bed doesn't look as if it's been slept in.

A thought occurs to me that makes my throat tighten. What if another 'me' is at this moment standing in the car park I've just come from, wondering where 'I' am. Which 'me' is the real one?

Does unitary consciousness mean the other track has disappeared, or are we both alive simultaneously but no longer aware of each other? Oh, fuck. My only consolation is the relief of just having to put up with the one feed of awareness. Why does my consciousness keep spitting and then returning to normal? I would go and see my doctor straight away, but I'm sure he would arrange to have me sectioned, and I can't have that with Chanda and the kids in the predicament they're in.

Thinking of Chanda makes me realise how much I miss her. If she were here right now she'd say something to make me feel better. It probably wouldn't make any sense, but it would definitely make me feel better …

I remember the email I promised Ringer, and go to my study and start up my computer. I log on to my email account then pull out my wallet and retrieve the police officer's business card. Before typing the email to Ringer I check recently received emails. Top of the list is one from Arthur and I decide to read that later. The second one in my in-box is actually from Ringer and I open it. To my astonishment I discover it's a reply to an email I supposedly sent the man the previous day, one in which I confess to only knowing one Jake – the son of a member of my congregation. Ringer thanks me for letting him know and informs me that he'll be in touch if he has any further questions.

What the fuck? Does this mean I'm now on a reality track that doesn't contain the recent history of having taken a call from Ringer? Did that phone call happen or not? Am I still in bed in some other reality, one that doesn't involve having gone and slept in a car park? If so, are both realities equally valid? If I get Chanda and the kids back, will there be another reality in which they're actually killed? I feel sick. I switch the computer off and go downstairs. I decide to go and sit in the rear garden. I shiver as I step outside. I sit on a white plastic garden chair and look eastwards at the huge sun that's hanging at about forty-five degrees. It's a cloudless but misty morning. Although chilly I can feel the sun warm me as its rays hit.

After soaking up some sun for half an hour I go back inside and make some breakfast. I can't remember when I last ate; it has to have been over a day ago. As I crunch toast my pleasure at eating is somewhat spoilt by wondering when my next split-mind episode is going to occur. So worried by this am I that after eating and having half a cup of tea I walk to the local off licence and buy a couple of bottles of cheap whiskey. I'll get blind drunk when this mental aberration next occurs.

The rest of the morning is spent in a state of listlessness. In theory I have a sermon to deliver in two days, but I know already that isn't going to happen. I have just enough energy to ring one of the Church Elders and give him some crap about needing to get a Sunday replacement. I give him the name and number of a recently retired vicar who I know would be more than happy to dust off his dog collar for the occasion.

Around lunchtime Joey rings me. 'Hey, Adam,' he says. 'This thing has gone way too far. We need to have a sit down and talk about this.'

'I know,' I say. 'I've already suggested a venue to Courtney.'

'Come on, you know that ain't gonna happen. Meet in a police station my ass.'

'So what do you suggest? A midnight rendezvous in the forest?'

'Look, whya breaking my balls like this? We had a misunderstanding, a misunderstanding caused by that little prick who hates your guts. Now we just need to sort this out like men. We've all got too much to lose by doing anything else.'

'Tell me how Chanda and the kids are doing,' I demand. 'If anyone lays a finger on any of them there'll be hell to pay.'

'They're fine. They're fine. That wasn't even my idea. Courtney was really pissed about you doing whatever you did to him. What *did* you do to him? He says he lost a day or something.'

'Another time,' I reply.

'So are we meeting or what?'

'I need a bit longer to think things through,' I say. 'You're right that if we fall out over this shit no-one's going to win.

You can kill my kids and me, but I'll make sure I leave a trail behind that leads straight to you. You've seen the video clip. I wanted to get rid of Jake, but it's the same story. I kill him, and his solicitor opens a letter that drops me – and you – in it. There's no point me threatening you with talking to the cops, because if I do I'll never see the kids again. Not that you're going to want to look after them for the rest of your life, or would get away with it if you harmed them. Stalemate. Match drawn. I don't even know why we're talking about meeting. Just drop the kids off and we'll forget any of this ever happened. We'll go our separate ways.'

'It ain't that simple,' Joey counters, 'And I'll tell you why. This is why we need to meet. That cocksucker you pissed off is going to bring you down, if it's the last thing he does. We can call a truce, but he's going to introduce you to the cops all the same. Soon as they slap charges on you that mean big jail time you're going to have a big incentive to talk about your other activities – activities involving me and Courtney.'

'Jake could probably get me sent down for the whole of my natural life,' I say. 'What sort of a bargain am I going to strike? A slightly bigger cell in exchange for information about you guys?'

'That's why we need to talk. Hatch a plan. Maybe there's some way of getting some leverage over this Jake guy. Get him to get rid of any letter he's left as insurance. Discredit whatever the letter might say.'

'Give me an hour,' I say. 'I'll call you back.'

\* \* \*

Asteroid Aldous, meanwhile, is bearing down on its destination. It's now on a terminal trajectory that means it will soon be Meteorite Aldous. It has travelled two and half million miles from the Asteroid Belt in just under a year, and is now just hours from hitting the Earth's atmosphere. No-one at any of the monitoring stations whose respons- ibility it is to look out for such extra-terrestrial intruders has picked up on its proximity.

* * *

What to do? I pace the house, wondering how to resolve my dilemma. A thought occurs to me: why don't I just kill myself? Apart from the weariness I feel at the drama of the last months, and the fear I have of spending a lifetime in incarceration, it might guarantee the safe release of Chanda and the kids. Chanda's an illegal – she could never be Chloe and Ben's guardian – but Arthur and Gloria might have enough years left in them to bring my children up. In the end cowardice stops me from proceeding with this idea.

Less than an hour has elapsed since speaking to Joey before I ring him. 'Okay, we meet. We meet at the restaurant in the big BHS on Oxford Street. And you bring Chanda. I want Chanda released as a sign of good will.'

There's a pause, before Joey says, 'Okay. When?'

'This afternoon? Three o'clock?'

'See you then.'

I get to the restaurant early and after paying for a dish of what is purported to be Chicken Korma I take a seat that gives me a good view of the entrance to the eatery. Joey and Chanda turn up ten minutes late. When I see them walk into the food-serving area I stand up and wave. They walk straight over.

'Yo! Look who it is!' Joey says, as if releasing hostages is something he does every other day.

'Joey ... How are you Chanda?'

Chanda just nods. We all sit down.

'I'm glad we could meet,' Joey says. 'As I've already said, this thing has just got out of hand ...'

'Not through any fault of mine,' I say defensively.

'Well no, not directly. Our problem is Jack or Jake, or whatever his goddam name is. Question is, what are we going to do about him?'

'He's after me, not you. Forget about him.'

'It ain't that simple. He's got that video footage Courtney showed me. Of us negotiating with Jose. Why the fuck did you take that video? What kind of stupid shit was that?'

'I was worried. I thought if things got bad between us, I might need it. It was just a bit of insurance.'

'I can believe that, Adam. But you can see how it's all backfired. Now we have to figure out how to solve this situation.'

'Well that's the fucking problem,' I say. 'I can tell you I've got rid of the video, but I can't prove a negative – I can't prove I don't have it. Even if I can prove to you that I don't have the video or that I'm not going to use it, that doesn't solve the Jake problem – the fact that he's got a copy of it. To be honest, I think there are only two solutions. I can kill myself – not ideal but there are some days when I can think of worse outcomes. Alternatively, I can hand myself into the police and confess to my killings, making sure not to mention anything about our other activities. That might be enough to get Jake off our backs.'

'That's it in a nutshell,' Joey says. 'So which option are you going to go for?'

'Can I have the afternoon to think about it?'

Joey sighs. 'Time is something we don't have a lot of, Adam. We don't know when this Jake is going to move from threatening to acting.'

'Give me a few hours.'

Another sigh from the American. 'Okay. You'll ring me this evening?'

'Yep.'

'I just can't believe you're a murderer,' Joey says. 'I always knew you was a bit crazy, but serial killer? Jesus Christ.'

'Sometimes I can't believe it myself,' I say.

We look at each other intently for a few moments, before I ask: 'How are the kids?'

'They're fine. Being well looked after. I don't want them on my hands any longer than they need to be – another reason to sort this out.'

'How did you guys know we were in that hotel?' I ask.

'Courtney rang me as soon as he kicked you out of his car. I went straight over to your place and watched Chanda here leave for the restaurant, and then followed you all from the restaurant to the hotel. Simple.'

'I see …'

Joey stands up. 'I'll leave Chanda in your safe hands. Be sure to ring me as promised.' With that he leaves.

'Cup of tea?' I say to Chanda.

'That would be nice.'

'I'll get it,' I say.

Ten minutes later I return bearing a tray. After pouring tea for both of us I say, 'I'm really sorry you've had to get involved in all of this.'

'It's okay. We weren't mistreated.'

'Where were they holding you?'

'I don't know, because they made me wear a cloth over my eyes on the way there and coming here now. It takes an hour in the car. A big house. The black man brought us food and kept guard.'

'The kids must be wondering what the hell is going on,' I comment. 'Were they upset?'

Chanda puts the cup she has just taken a sip from down before saying, 'No, they were okay. I told them we were going on an adventure, and they seem to accept that.'

'Yes, but now you're not there …'

'I know, but they won't be on their own for long. You will agree something with Mr Joey.'

'Don't remind me. I really don't know what to suggest. This last couple of days have been really strange, Chanda. I think I might be losing my mind …'

'Why do you say this?'

'My mind keeps splitting. Sometimes into two, sometimes into three ... on one occasion it seemed to split into an infinite number of minds. Each mind or consciousness witnesses events independently of the others – different things are experienced by each. Last night I slept in a car park and in my bed at the same time.'

'Oh, that's nothing – like the froth on a cup of coffee. Bubbles of nothing. I told you, everything you see is just mindstuff. Your mind is just playing the trickster.'

'It doesn't feel that way,' I protest. 'I'd like you to have gone through what I did last night and say it is all "mindstuff".'

'Last night I was prisoner in a strange house,' Chanda comes back with, a smile on her face.

'How can you say that everything I experience is just some sort of illusion?' I ask. 'I can sort of understand all this talk of ultimate Oneness and everything, but illusion ... ?'

'Have you not noticed how reality seem to come up in pairs of opposites? We have night and day, cats and dogs, good and evil – it goes on forever.'

'Yes, but what's that go to do with reality being an illusion? If the tide didn't go out after coming in, there'd be no dry land. If we didn't have day following night we'd live in perpetual darkness and we wouldn't be able to grow food.'

'Okay, what is the opposite of plus one?'

'Minus one?'

'That's right. And what do you get if you add the two together?'

'Zero. Nothing. So?'

'If reality as we perceive it is made up of pairs of opposites, and all these pairs exist at the same time, then if you sum over all these pairs you get nothing. But in the nothing is everything, or the nothing is everything. So don't worry about your split minds. You have a billion minds and no mind, you're just getting a glimpse of this. What appears to us as time is what enables the illusion of this world. Time separates night from day. Without what we understand as time night and day would be happening at the same time.'

'Who the fuck *are* you Chanda?' I ask. 'You sound like some sort of sage. Why aren't you still in India, welcoming pilgrims to your ashram?'

A laugh from the woman. 'That would bore me. I'm happier looking after your children.'

'Well, all I can say is that you're quite a remarkable woman.'

'I wouldn't worry about what you think of me, think instead about what you're going to do about your situation.'

'If everything's an illusion, what's the point?'

'Ah, but just because you are a party to the truth, that doesn't give you the right to retire from the world. Remember what the Buddhists say: "Before enlightenment, carry water chop wood. After enlightenment, carry water chop wood". When you play a game like Monopoly you know you aren't really buying houses or collecting real money as rent, but you play anyway, and you play to win. It is the same thing with your current situation.'

'So what do you think I should do? Hand myself into the police?'

'The fact that you've said what you've just said makes me think that that is what *you* think you should do.'

My mind wanders back to the night at the hotel, and I ask, 'What did you think when Courtney came and got you? Did he pull a gun out?'

'He handled it quite well,' Chanda replies. 'He knock on the door and say "Room Serving".'

'Room service.'

'Yes. Then when I open the door he show me a gun in his coat pocket. He said, "Do what I ask you and I won't wave this around". So the kids never saw a gun.'

'He must have known I'd left the hotel,' I say. 'Interesting. Anyway, yes, you're probably right. I think going to the police is the right thing to do. I'm done killing – myself – and killing wouldn't do any good anyway. The truth is out there and secured in locked buildings by people I don't know. The police are on to me and are going to get me sooner or later. And I'm tired. In prison I'll have time for my own thoughts. You will visit me, won't you? Bring the kids?'

'Yes.'

'What about your status as an illegal?'

'That isn't today's worry.'

'Let's get married.'

'Let's talk about that another time.'

'Okay. Shall we go home? I'll call Joey from home.'

When we get home I ring Joey and tell him what I plan to do. 'You serious?' he says. 'You willing to go away for the rest of your life?'

'I am. I'd get caught eventually – at least this way I don't have to spend the next year waiting for a knock at the door. It's better this way. It takes the heat off you, gives Jake the satisfaction of knowing I'm in the same place he spent twenty years … just better all round. All I ask is that you drop the kids off. I want to spend a weekend with them, then I'll do the necessary.'

Joey is silent for a few moments. I can tell he's trying to figure out whether I'm being honest with him. 'Joey … I'm not joking about this. Just do what I ask, and I'll make your problem go away.'

More silence, then, 'Okay. I'll get Courtney to drop them off this evening. You gonna be in tomorrow?'

'Where else?'

'I'll come over and see you around lunchtime. And ring that Jake guy and tell him what you're going to do.'

Courtney rings the doorbell at ten to six. 'Hey,' I say after opening the door. We both do our best to avoid eye contact; it's not a comfortable moment. 'Hey, kids,' I say, bending down to greet Ben and Chloe. 'You two have had quite an adventure, haven't you? Come in.'

Chanda greets my children warmly as they rush into the house. They run to her and grab a leg each. She puts a hand on each back and rubs. I'm amazed at how quickly the three have bonded. I actually feel a little jealous.

Courtney doesn't come in; I wave him off with a simple, 'Bye!'.

The four of us spend the next few hours together, eating, playing Snakes and Ladders and watching some TV. I feel sad that this is likely to be the last time I'll ever see my kids or Chanda outside the confines of prison. I think of all the time I wasted whilst devoting myself to a life of illicit sex and criminality. My kids are happy to be in my company right now, but how will they feel when they're a bit older and realise that I deprived them of a mother? I feel guilty just being in their presence.

Bedtime for the kids arrives and I tuck them into bed. Half an hour later Chanda and I are in bed. I plan to hand myself in at the local police station the next morning.

The next morning I realise that the chaos of the last few days has led me to ignore the important bits of housekeeping I need to do before relinquishing my liberty. I need to pack a bag – I'm sure I'll be detained at the cop shop before a Magistrate's Court appearance and remand. I need to pay a few bills and give Chanda a bankcard and pin number so she can survive until she's deported. That reminds me – I need to tell her that if she can claim persecution back in India there's a slim chance she might be able to claim asylum and remain in the U.K.. I must also write a note for Arthur and Gloria, availing on them for help in the event that Chanda can't look after the kids. I get to work.

We all eat lunch together – sausage and baked beans for the kids and a salad and fruit for Chanda and myself. After we've finished eating I clear my throat and address the kids: 'Daddy's got something to tell you,' I say. Ben and Chloe look at me expectantly. 'Daddy's going to be going away for a while. Not far away, and you'll be able to visit me every week if you like, but I need you to be good for Chanda and your grandparents.'

'Where are you going?' Ben asks.

'I'm going to be going to a ... special hotel. I'll be quite safe there. All my meals are provided, and I'll have my own room with a TV.'

'Why are you going there?' Chloe wants to know. 'Why can't you stay here with us?'

'It's a long story. One I'll explain to you when you're a bit older. I know it's going to be tough, especially as mummy's not with us anymore, but like I said, we'll be able to see each other quite often.'

At just after two o'clock I call a cab. I've briefed Chanda. She's been given a bank card. When the doorbell rings, I give hugs in this order: Ben, Chloe, Chanda. Chanda and Chloe have tears in her eyes – Chanda based on the facts she has, Chloe through an intuitive sensing of what's happening.

I pick up my bag and walk to the front door. The moment my hand touches the door handle it happens again; consciousness splits, this time into three. I curse thrice. In two realities I open the door and step outside, whilst in the third I drop my bag and run upstairs.

Upstairs I dash into my bedroom and dive under the bed covers, cowering like a feverish prison escapee. In this reality I opt out of making any more decisions. I'm not going to go anywhere or do anything. Things can happen to me. I'm going to spend as much time as I can with the kids and Chanda, and if the police or Joey or Jake want me, they can bloody well knock the door down and lift me out of bed.

Meanwhile both of the other Adams are getting into the cab I called. One of the Adams is giving the driver the address of the nearest police station, whist the other one is asking for Heathrow airport – yes, I know I didn't book a cab to the airport, I tell the driver – change of plans. The me that's going to the police station is pretty pissed off. It's overcast outside with the occasional spot of rain, and the weather is reflecting my mood precisely. The me that's heading to the airport is excited. This me is also looking out of the window at heavy cloud cover, and its cold enough for condensation to be forming on the car's windows, but I'm contrasting this with the sunshine I'm expecting to be basking in in a few hours. This Adam is going to buy a ticket shortly to Cyprus. Hopefully Nicosia in Northern Cyprus, which doesn't have an extradition treaty with the U.K., but if need be Southern Cyprus, which will only be an expensive cab fare from safety in the North. South or North, I'll be in a T-shirt soon.

Stay-in-bed-Adam, meanwhile, has fallen asleep. Or has this reality just faded out? It's hard to tell. The Adam that's on the way to the airport hopes so; the one that's going to the cop shop doesn't really care.

Cop Shop Adam arrives at his destination. He glances longingly at Cyprus Adam. Lucky fucker. He'd give anything to switch places with him. Cop Shop Adam walks into the police station, ready with his spiel about wanting to hand himself in over the murder of seven people. He feels deflated when he sees there are several people before him in an ill-formed queue for an officer's attention. There should be a priority queue for murderers wanting to hand themselves in, this Adam thinks. The person talking to the officer is some dipshit moaning on about being mugged for his iPhone. The officer looks thoroughly disinterested as he takes the guy's details.

Heathrow Adam is buzzing. His car's on the M4 now, and making good progress. This Adam thinks of anything that could go wrong and realises there really isn't. Despite any suspicions the police might have, they haven't charged him with anything, so immigration at Heathrow won't have been instructed to deny him boarding rights. He doesn't know for sure how many flights there will be left to Cyprus that day, but it's not late and Heathrow is a bloody busy airport – he's bound to get a flight if he doesn't mind paying top dollar for it. Even if there aren't any seats on a Cyprus flight, he'll fly to Israel or Greece, somewhere that isn't England and is nearer his ultimate destination. He's got plenty of credit cards on him. He's used some of the cash he's been accumulating recently to overpay some of the cards, so that with two Visa cards and a Mastercard he's actually carrying a big positive balance. He could survive comfortably for a year or more. If Joey rings and asks him what's going on he'll tell him to check with the cops – I think you'll find I'm handing myself in as we speak, he'll say. If you're not happy with that, go over to my place and take the me that's asleep. He won't put up much of a fight.

After waiting for about half an hour, Cop Shop Adam is finally ready to proffer his wrists to a copper for cuffing. 'Can I help?' PC Somethingorother asks Adam. 'Yes,' Adam replies. 'I've killed quite a few people over the last year and thought you might like to arrest me.' The copper looks at him with an expression that says 'nutter', and asks, 'So who exactly have you killed?' 'My first victim was a girl who I followed from a cashpoint machine,' Adam says. 'Her name was reported in the paper, but I can't remember it off the top of my head ... Next up was ... er actually who was number two? Look, why don't you just arrest me and then I can at least be seated while I give you my confession. It's going to take a long time ...'

Joey meanwhile, decides to ring. He rings all three Adams. The sleeping Adam doesn't hear the phone and it's the same story with the Adam that's in the police station. The Adam on his way to Heathrow does hear the phone but decides not to answer it. Joey curses and rings Adam's landline. Chanda picks up the phone and says, 'Yes?'

'Joey here, where's Adam?'

'Oh, hi Joey, Adam's grinkulmsisnro.'

'What?'

'He's grinkulmsisnro.'

'What the fuck are you talking about you crazy bitch?'

You see, the first bit of Chanda's reply came out okay, but when she came to actually saying where I was some kind of physics thing stopped her from being intelligible. What do you get when you combine 'asleep', 'on the way to the police station' and 'on the way to the airport'? That's right, you get 'grinkulmsisnro'.

'Has he gone to the police?' Joey asks.

'Nes,' Chanda says.

'No or yes?'

'Yo,' Chanda says.

'Listen you grubby little whacko whore, tell me where Adam is, or I'm going to come over and stick the barrel of a gun up your cunt.'

Chanda laughs gaily and puts the phone down. Joey tucks a gun into his belt and goes out to his car.

Joey gets stuck in traffic and it takes him about twenty minutes to get to Adam's place. By this time Cop Shop Adam is making some progress in convincing the cops that he's a murderer. He's mentioned enough specifics about his murders to have been placed under arrest, and is waiting in a cell. He's been promised a murder detective will be along within a couple of hours to question him. Heathrow Adam by this time has arrived at Heathrow, and is talking to a woman at the Cyprus Airways desk. He's established there's a flight to Limassol in two hours time, though a single will set him back £289.

Joey barges past Chanda after the latter answers the door and storms into the house. After failing to find Adam in any of the ground floor rooms he runs up the stairs and finds him asleep in bed. He pulls out his gun and aims it at Adam's head.

Heathrow Adam punches his pin number into the POS

machine and after a six second wait the machine spits out a receipt. His ticket to Limassol is paid for.

Detective Connor opens Cop Shop Adam's cell door and steps inside. 'So Adam, you claim to have killed several people recently?' he asks.

Seconds before Joey pulls the trigger a streak of white like a chalk mark smears the sky, as Meteorite Aldous burns through the Earth's atmosphere. At the tip of the streak is a glowing ball of fire. The noise is deafening as it closes in on East London, breaking the sound barrier. At the moment Joey pulls the trigger it impacts at the corner of Connell and Wilshire streets, creating a deafening sound that can be heard up to fifty miles away. The police station that Adam has recently walked into is obliterated, along with approximately two hundred buildings in the surrounding area. The noise is so loud it drowns out the sound of Joey's gun's report. The house shakes as Adam takes a fatal shot to the head.

Heathrow Adam hears and feels the meteorite strike. At the moment it hits he's lifting a glass of lager to his lips, and the tremor almost causes him to spill some beer.